DETROIT PUBLIC LIBRARY

P9-DDM-242

# FINDING *home*
## by
## Stacy Hawkins Adams

Chase Branch Library
17731 W. Seven Mile Rd.
Detroit, MI 48235

JAN 17

Copyright© 2016 by Stacy Hawkins Adams

Published by Spring Rock Publishing, a division of
Claywork Enterprises, LLC
P.O. Box 25985, Richmond, VA 23260


All rights reserved. No part of this publication may be reproduced,
stored in a retrieval system, or transmitted in any form or by any
means—for example, electronic, photocopy, recording—without
the prior written permission of the publisher. The only exception is
brief quotations in printed reviews.

*To women everywhere who are seeking to thrive through life-altering seasons, and to my sister Pat – forever in my heart.*

*But he said to me,*

*"My grace is sufficient for you,*

*for My power is made perfect in weakness."*

2 Corinthians 12:9a

# *one*

Jessica Wilson Arnold decided her plan was ridiculous seconds after she conceived it. Grown women with great lives had no reason to resort to lies.

The more she tried to talk herself out of it, however, the more the scheme took shape. If she could squeeze two or three solid months out of this fantastical fabrication, a life that was already amazing would morph into grand, and she and Keith could do whatever they wanted.

It would be risky, but she had already come up with an explanation that would leave few people asking questions or making demands; and with time, this situation eventually would be forgotten. That meant for now, she *was* pregnant, kind of... with goals and dreams that might not ever be birthed if she faced another setback.

Jessica made peace with that reasoning while wrapping up lunch with Sage Bennett at a salad bar in downtown Indianapolis, where they had stopped after their meeting with the Bravo TV executives to celebrate Jessica's coup. Not many people got one shot - let alone two – at hosting a talk show on a national TV network. Both women agreed it was a big deal.

But right now, so was the "news" Jessica had just shared with Sage, to explain her recent weight gain. She might be moving on to Bravo, but in the meantime she had to keep Sage's viewers at a local news station happy.

"Now it all makes sense!" Sage said, beaming. "You've been hosting weekly segments on WNVX for three years – looking as toned and fabulous as ever. I should have known when I saw you growing puffy that you and Keith had decided to start a family. Congratulations, Jess!"

Jessica forced a smile. She no longer had an appetite, but she reached for the last slice of bread resting on the plate in the center of the table and slid a piece of it between her lips, hoping she could change the subject without having to create more details on the spot. She would if she had to, though, because Sage's reaction confirmed why the lie had been necessary: local TV viewers were noticing the twenty pounds she had packed on, and since Jessica's five-minute segments focused on how to stay in shape in order to succeed in all areas of life, they clearly expected her to look the part.

She swallowed the morsel of bread and took a sip of her strawberry-infused water before pursuing the answer she simultaneously wanted and dreaded.

"So you've been hearing from viewers...about me? Guess my black slacks and dresses aren't doing the trick, huh?"

Jessica sat back in her chair, oblivious to the noisy lunchtime crowd around them and willed herself to stay calm.

Sage shrugged.

"Not a lot, but yes...viewers have been occasionally leaving comments when we post links to your weekly segments on the station's website. Nothing derogatory, or we'd remove it. But you know how fickle people are..."

Sage's voice trailed off, and Jessica recalled the recent reactions she'd been receiving from local residents who saw her on air every Thursday, then found her motivational speaking website or met her at an event. They weren't rude, but they weren't kind either. The comments were sure to be more prevalent when she took her TV segments onto the national stage in a few months and morphed the programming into an hour-long weekly talk show. Viewers of the pilot episodes for Bravo TV were going to be ruthless, and maybe even the network executives, too. That meant for now, the only way around the devastating truth was to tell an equally devastating lie.

Sage polished off the last of her grilled chicken Caesar salad and grinned.

"Well, tell me more! How long have you known, and when are you due? What did Keith say?"

Before Jessica could respond, Sage's eyes grew wide, and more questions tumbled forth. "Oooh, when are you going to tell the Bravo execs?? Why didn't you tell them today, when you discussed terms of the deal?

"I mean, it's one thing for us to announce the news on our channel; you're on once a week as a community professional. It's another to launch a brand new cable show with a different look than you had when they hired you – just keeping it real. But you know what? A baby is always good news. They'll understand and find a way to film your segments before you deliver."

Jessica nodded and feigned calm, even as her heart pounded. She was thirty-four years old, but the foolishness she had just created made her feel like a teenager trying to wiggle out of punishment for missing curfew. The more she said, the deeper a hole she dug. But she couldn't stop now; Sage was right – her career hinged on how she handled this, and the truth would do nothing but cause one or both of her opportunities to implode.

She quickly estimated when a baby would arrive if she were about six weeks along.

"The doctor says I'm due around October."

Sage nodded, and Jessica recognized the glow in the producer's eyes. An idea was brewing.

"You know what…. Why don't you let me help you tell our viewers and also your new Bravo TV producers? We'll send one of the station's anchors to your house to interview you, maybe in the room that will be your nursery? Then we can show your ultrasound on air…and the countdown for Baby Arnold can be woven into your weekly segments on staying in shape and taking good emotional care, especially when you're pregnant. What do you think?"

Jessica parted her lips to dismiss the idea, but her brief hesitation gave Sage room to keep going.

"Better yet, maybe we should just send a cameraman over and let you decide on the flow of the story. Maybe you can interview your OB/GYN about preparing for and enjoying pregnancy...."

Jessica raised her hand, both to quell the panic rising in her spirit and to quiet Sage.

"Can't do all of that, just yet. Keith and I haven't told our families, or closest friends," she lied, already worrying how she was going to explain all of this to her husband.

Still, she couldn't talk Sage out of filming a segment in her home, which would include Jessica revealing her pregnancy to viewers by showing the first ultrasound of the baby.

"This is going to be exciting for viewers," Sage said and sat back in her chair, nodding to herself.

It was clear to Jessica that her boss and friend was already calculating ratings, and there would be no way to get around the plan she was pulling together. "Former University of Indiana basketball star about to become a dad with superstar motivational speaker wife. Great stuff."

Jessica's thoughts raced. It seemed impossible to wiggle her way out of moving forward with Sage's plan, but executing it would be an impossible feat, too. Where on earth was she going to get an ultrasound? How was she going to get Keith to go along with this lie, and ultimately, how could she make this fake pregnancy go away, without causing a stir and adding to her mounting deceit?

# *two*

By the time they polished off lunch, Sage had confirmed a plan for filming the news segment in Jessica's home, and had convinced Jessica to schedule a phone meeting with the Bravo execs tomorrow morning, to share her baby news and details about the WNVX story in the works.

"Just reassure them that you can handle pregnancy and motherhood along with the new show," Sage said. "If we spin this the right way, they'll see it as a win-win. I can follow up with a call of my own, or join you on the conference call if you'd like. Since they want to film your pilot segments in WNVX's studio, they'll play nice with me."

Jessica appreciated Sage's support. This deal was in her hands – too close to throw away for reasons she couldn't control. She wasn't going to lose a second chance to take life to the next level.

She hugged Sage goodbye, and the two women strolled in opposite directions. With her shoulders rounded and her head bowed in an effort to block the chilly March wind, Jessica carefully sidestepped the small mounds of snow that peppered the path to her dark blue SUV, and simultaneously tried to ignore the terror rising in her spirit. What had she just done? How was she going to pull this off?

In the brief time it took her to settle behind the driver's

seat and buckle in, however, she had convinced herself that this unfolding farce had to happen, because the truth would bring everything to a screeching halt.

The meeting this morning with the cable network execs had been exciting, and she was ready. Her gut told her that Bravo TV could turn her talk show into a hit. This was her time, which meant she had no choice but to keep some things to herself, and shade the truth about others. She needed help to pull it off, though, and her friend Evangeline was her only hope.

Jessica tucked a flyaway piece of her flowing black tresses behind her ear, then pulled her cellphone from an interior pocket of her leather shoulder bag. She checked her texts and recent calls. No message from Keith yet, which meant he hadn't listened to the voicemail she'd left him an hour ago, squealing the news that her weekly healthy lifestyle show on WNVX was going to the big-time this summer.

This was probably for the best, she mused, because if he called right now, he'd hear the fear and stress in her voice. She would be tempted to confess it all, and before the ink dried on her Bravo contract, network producers would be ripping it up and moving on.

She pushed away the twinge of guilt that washed over her for feeling desperate enough to go this route, and for also keeping her husband in the dark about the medical condition she'd been officially diagnosed as having. He wouldn't be able to handle that, for sure. Or, was the issue that she knew he'd handle it in a way that limited her?

Jessica avoided answering herself by tapping Evangeline's picture to automatically dial her number.

"Indianapolis Physicians for Women, may I help you?"

"Hi, can you forward my call to Dr. Atkins' private line? This is Jessica Arnold."

The request was met with silence, and Jessica envisioned the receptionist on the other end of the phone reassuring herself that if Jessica knew about Evangeline's direct number, she must have been given access to it.

"Certainly, Ms. Arnold; putting you through now."

Jessica launched into her request seconds after sitting through Evangeline's brief, poised voicemail greeting.

"E- it's me, Jess. I need to see you today. Call or text and let me know what time I can come in. I'll explain everything when I get there."

Jessica ended the call, laid the cell phone on the passenger seat and rubbed the knuckles of each aching hand.

*Can I really do this?*

She squeezed her eyes shut and willed away the threatening surge of tears. She could not, would not resort to feeling sorry for herself right now, nor focus on the dread attempting to spread through her spirit like poison ivy.

That declaration made, she opened her eyes and refocused on the world around her. An elderly man was curiously peering at her as he strolled by her SUV, on the way to the bus stop on the corner. Jessica acknowledged him with a nod before sliding on her sunglasses and pulling out of the parking spot.

The digital clock on her dashboard read 2:00. If Evangeline could see her right away, Jessica should be able to grab what she needed and follow up with Sage before the end of the business day.

She missed Keith, but for the first time since he left for the weeklong business trip, she was glad to have the house to herself, to think things through. Keith would return from Phoenix in three days, and not only did she need to have her story for the local news station checked off her list, she also needed an explanation compelling enough to convince her husband to go along with the ruse. Keith wasn't going to be happy; but he had lived through her disappointment three years ago, when her previous national TV opportunity fell through, and if all went well this time around, she would not only be able to fulfill her dreams, but also help execute some of his.

The traffic light shifted to green and Jessica cruised onto the busy interstate toward Evangeline's suburban medical office, so she'd be close enough to zoom over whenever E. responded. She turned off the radio and navigated the lanes of traffic in a contemplative silence, willing her heart to stop racing, even if her mind couldn't.

The pros and cons of what she was planning seesawed through her conscience. Simply put, this was wrong, and she knew better. But if she succeeded, it would make a difference on so many levels. Keith wouldn't try to keep her from traveling for the work she loved. Her local viewers wouldn't continue ridiculing her changing appearance, nor would she risk losing her chance for prominence and influence beyond Indianapolis and the professional speaking circuit. This wasn't about the money, although that would give her the freedom to do whatever she pleased; this was about proving to herself that she could start and finish well, rather than be kept down by something beyond her control.

If one thing went wrong, however, everything might go wrong. Jessica shook her head, as if physically doing what she was thinking would shake loose the potential negative consequences. This had to work, so it would.

# three

Less than two hours after Jessica crafted her scheme, her friend shut it down. Jessica sat across the desk from her gorgeous, bespectacled OB/GYN and former college roommate, withering beneath Evangeline's frown. This whole idea had been idiotic, and she should have known Evangeline would call her on it.

"What you're asking me to do, Jess, could cost me my medical license. Nevermind the fact that you want me to compromise my integrity. What's gotten into you? What's so wrong that you're trying to falsify a pregnancy? Are you planning to lie to Keith, too?"

The heat of shame crept up Jessica's cheeks. She lowered her eyes and focused on a quadrant of the diamond-patterned carpet to buy some time. Her response had to satisfy Evangeline's logical concerns, yet also tug at her friend's heart, because she needed this plan to work. But no reason worth uttering came to mind, and Jessica sagged into the sofa. In giving Evangeline some justification for this crazy request, she was going to have to acknowledge the scary reality she was facing; and saying the words out loud would be painful.

Evangeline rolled her leather chair away from the glass-topped wooden desk before rising and smoothing invisible wrinkles from a white medical jacket embroidered with her name. She walked around the desk and eased onto the C-shaped sofa next to Jessica.

"You know you can tell me anything, Jess, like always. I won't lie for you, but I also won't lie to you. What's going on?"

Jessica exhaled for what felt like the first time that day, and the dam she'd been holding at bay broke. Her friend and gynecologist leaned toward her desk and grabbed several tissues. She extended the soft, peachy mass to Jessica, who pinched her eyes shut in an effort to staunch the flow of tears. After a few minutes, Jessica composed herself enough to reply.

"In the two months since we last got together I've gained twenty pounds, E., and it's not because I'm pregnant. But that's what I'm planning to tell everyone, and that's why I need an ultrasound photo taken by a pregnant woman. I thought maybe you could make a copy of one you gave to one of your newly pregnant patients this morning."

Jessica recognized the confusion clouding Evangeline's caring green eyes, and she was certain it mirrored the expression she must have worn two days earlier, when her primary care physician shattered her world with a slate of test results.

"I have rheumatoid arthritis, E. I got the results from Dr. Vanessa Raymond on Tuesday."

There. She managed to share the news without releasing the angry screams swirling within, or fretting aloud about ending up bitter and lonely like her maternal grandmother, whose arthritis had crippled her.

Evangeline scooted closer and hugged her.

"I'm so sorry, Jess. Is Dr. Raymond sure?"

Jessica used one of the tissues to dab beneath both eyes again and nodded.

"She ran exhaustive tests, and she says she's sure, but she welcomes me getting a second opinion," Jessica said. "I've been on some pretty heavy meds for the past few months to help me deal with stiffness and joint pain, but Dr. Raymond initially thought I had gout, and even when her intuition led her to test for other things, I held out hope. I've seen the damage arthritis can do. Gout would be a gift.

"Plus, this couldn't have come at a worse time, E. You know how hard I took it when my talk show for Oprah's network fell through a couple of years ago. Well, right after Dr. Raymond gave me her diagnosis, I got the news that another production company is interested in elevating the topics I report on each week for WNVX. I've landed a deal with Bravo to shoot four pilot episodes of a talk show. This is the real deal – again – and I have to be on point. I can't tell these people my health is deteriorating before they've formally hired me. On top of that, look at me already!"

Jessica's eyes canvassed her own body, stopping at her pudgy belly, which strained against the black slacks she wore with a coral silk blouse.

"Dr. Raymond agreed to wait until I get a second opinion, but she wants to up my dosage of steroids, to get the inflammation under control, and I know how that medicine makes you swell. Not subtly – suddenly. What am I going to look like in eight or ten weeks, when it's time to film? I needed a quick solution, E, and this was what came to mind. They'll accept a pregnant woman, but not a sickly one."

Evangeline leaned forward and pulled Jessica toward her, and gripped her in another hug. Jessica clung to her friend for a while, before realizing that Evangeline had closed her eyes and was praying. The gesture both touched and annoyed Jessica. She knew Evangeline likely wouldn't do this with a routine patient, but still. When had it become acceptable to mix medical care with prayer?

Jessica's upbringing as a preacher's daughter hadn't been for naught, though. She still had a reverence for prayer, wherever it took place, so she closed her eyes, and waited for Evangeline to finish and loosen her hold. When Evangeline raised her head, Jessica gave her a thumbs up; but the smile she tried to muster failed, and soon she was in tears again.

"I know," Jessica said, in response to the sorrow she read in her friend's eyes. "I'm stunned, too. And I'm scared. Does this mean I'm going to eventually walk with a cane? Or have curved fingers and toes, before I reach forty? The weight gain has been the most horrible part of it all. I look puffy and fat already, even though I've tried to continue exercising between bouts of pain and achiness.

"At this point, I just need a quick and easy way to explain to everybody what's going on with me. I get up in front of people every day, and go on TV regularly, advising people how to achieve their goals, but I'm not well known enough like Oprah – or her sidekick Gayle - for people to understand my condition and cut me some slack. I'm just starting out, and I need to secure my spot. But look at me: I'm turning into Miss Piggy. The network and producers will start to question whether I have the discipline and focus to take care of myself, let alone advise their viewers. And you know that TV always adds ten pounds. "

Evangeline rubbed the back of Jessica's hands, but didn't interrupt. When Jessica fell silent again, Evangeline zeroed in on what she obviously viewed as most important right now. "You were planning to lie to Keith, too?"

Jessica noted the past tense verb Evangeline inserted in the question – "were" – as if Jessica had changed her mind about her desperate request. She responded to the query with what she knew her friend wanted to hear.

"No, E, I guess not," she said. "I just hadn't figured out how I would tell him. Keith knows me so well that he'd sense I was hiding something. This whole idea of getting a fake ultrasound is a fail, I guess.  When he gets home from his out-of-town conference I'll talk to him about the arthritis. This is going to crush him, because he actually does want a baby, and this stupid medical crisis is going to keep us from trying for a while."

Talking about Keith's long-time desire to be a dad made Jessica even more ashamed of herself. Even though she was nowhere near ready to start a family, her plan to fake a pregnancy and pretend she was happy about it, just to land a business deal, was trite and selfish.

*Am I really that desperate?*

The fact that she was sitting here now, with Evangeline, seemed answer enough. She was pitiful.

Evangeline squeezed Jessica's hands, reminding Jessica that she knew her well, and had probably guessed what she was thinking right now.

"Don't beat yourself up. You've had a rough few days. Keith is out of town and you couldn't process all of this with him, as you typically do. You've always been Miss Fix It, so that's what you've been trying to do."

Evangeline paused, as if to give her assessment of Jessica's actions time to marinate.

"But I'm so sorry, Jess. You aren't going to be able to find a quick solution for this. And lying to your business colleagues and the TV network isn't going to solve anything. How were you going to handle the fact that no baby would eventually be born?"

Jessica sighed.

"I figured I would tell them I had a miscarriage."

Evangeline leaned toward Jessica, forcing her to make eye contact.

"Do you know how hurtful that would be to the dozens of women I see every year who experience miscarriages, or who are struggling with infertility? You don't want to play like that, Jess. Some of those people are your potential viewing audience, and they live with a level of heartbreak you wouldn't wish on anyone. Think about this, too: God blesses you with a great opportunity, and you honor it by launching into it with a lie? That's not the Jessica I know. That's not the Jessica you are. And as far as Keith is concerned, that man loves you."

Jessica nodded.

"I know he does, E., but I'm still scared. This arthritis...it's going to change our lives. And on top of that, I could lose my career."

Evangeline lowered her voice to a near whisper.

"Jess, why can't you just tell everyone the truth? Normally I don't advise my patients to put their business in the street; but in your case, you're a professional speaker who uses personal stories to help others be their best. Why can't you just share that you're managing a chronic health condition? I still don't understand the need to make up some fantastic story, all for the sake of a job opportunity. I think I've already made it clear: I'm not giving you an ultrasound image of a fetus that doesn't belong to you. As your OB/GYN and your friend, my prescription is to practice what you preach: trust Keith, and everyone else who matters, with the truth. And trust that you're going to be fine. Will you be getting treatment from a rheumatologist you feel comfortable with?"

Jessica shrugged. "I haven't gotten that far yet, but Dr.

Raymond recommended two people who are affiliated with the IU Health System. She said Dr. Kent is one of the best.

Evangeline nodded. "I've had no reason to work with him directly, but I've heard of him. He's highly respected, so I think you'll be in good hands. And I know Vanessa is going to do a good job of managing your care, too. I'm so sorry for the diagnosis, but you are going to be fine, Jess."

Evangeline's eyes swiveled from the door to the Fitbit watch on her wrist, and Jessica remembered that E. had a waiting room full of patients.

"I'm sorry to burden you with this, E, and I apologize for stepping out of line with my request," Jessica said. "I would never want you to jeopardize your career to save mine. I just don't know what I'm going to do, and I didn't know where to turn."

Jessica rose from her chair and Evangeline stood and hugged her.

"Remember what our Bible study leader in our freshman dorm used to say?" Evangeline asked.

Honestly, Jessica didn't recall, because attending Bible study hadn't been on her list of priorities back then. Even in those days, E. had brought the Good News into their space.

"She used to always tell us 'Fear is just what it spells: false evidence appearing real,'" Evangeline said and smiled. "You are going to be okay, and everything is going to work out as it should regarding the TV show. I know that's not what you want to hear, but you have to just trust that everything will be fine - without you trying to fix it in ways that are not the best."

She paused and tapped Jessica's chest with her forefinger.

"The Jess I know, the Jess whose heart I love, is still in there. She won't change for the worse because of an unexpected curveball in life. Wake her up, and let that Jess guide you. And let Keith in. He and I both will be here for you."

Jessica produced a meager smile before following Evangeline out of the office and down a narrow hallway. Evangeline paused before a patient room and knocked on the door. She winked at Jessica on her way inside. Jessica watched her disappear, before exiting to the lobby and leaving the building.

Evangeline was unequivocally right - she should have never thought about lying in the first place. What would her ever-righteous parents think? Or her friends and colleagues? How would Keith have handled being collateral damage in her deliberate deceit?

Jessica circled back to the same questions again and again as she pulled out of the parking deck and finally headed home. They weighed on her. But so did the knowledge of what was at stake: This was probably her last big chance to get *Boundless* on the air. She wouldn't be able to live with herself if she didn't give it a try.

And she would tell Keith the truth. But how? And when? Evangeline meant well, but she alone had to walk this path.

# *four*

Jessica's shame shifted to anger on the half-hour drive home.

Here she was, on the verge of becoming more successful than anyone in her family, and this had to happen? Shiloh, one of her two older sisters, always said God had a sense of humor. This was indeed laughable, but Jessica didn't appreciate being the punch line.

She was leaving Evangeline's office, but her primary care doctor's face and pronouncement ricocheted through her mind as she weaved in and out of late afternoon traffic: "According to the test results, you have early onset rheumatoid arthritis."

With just eleven words, her world had stopped turning.

Words and phrases like therapy, more prednisone, stiff and swollen joints, chronic pain management, and no cure swirled through Jessica's mind, just as they had two days ago when Dr. Raymond uttered them. And just like on Tuesday, she let them slip and slide through her brain, refusing to latch onto any of them.

Jessica alternated between wanting to weep and scream. She gripped the steering wheel and tried to calm herself enough to drive the speed limit.

*Why God? Why now?*

She recalled the countless speeches she'd given over the past eight years, urging her audiences to stand up to life's challenges. On numerous occasions she'd shared her journey of being diagnosed with dyslexia in third grade, struggling with her weight, and later, struggling to qualify for the track team in college, and having to rely on determination and focused persistence to eventually land a prime spot her junior year. She told those stories often, to inspire the college students and other young adults she worked with to keep pushing. But this... this was a different giant; something she couldn't conquer with positive thinking, platitudes, or probably even prayer, which she knew Shiloh, her parents and in-laws, and even Keith would recommend the second they found out. How did you tell someone to go on, when going on might be a never-ending journey of pitfalls and pain?

For the first time in her speaking career, Jessica wondered if her messages had ever left some of her audience members resentful, because her recommendations were too cookie-cutter perfect, or because the audience members assumed she didn't really understand. If any of them had felt the depths of despair invading her spirit now, she realized she'd been offering candy-coated cures to people whose mountains might need miracles, and she was deeply sorry.

# *five*

If Jessica's virtual assistant, Tari, hadn't texted to remind her of today's mid-morning conference call with a new client, Jessica would have overslept and been none the wiser. She texted Tari a quick reply.

Completely forgot! Not up to the call today. Please ask if we can reschedule?

While she waited for Tari's response, Jessica peeled back the covers and extended her arms and legs for a good stretch. Unsure of what to expect, as had been the case just about every morning since the beginning of the year, she exhaled when she felt minimal pain and stiffness. Today might be a good one.

She carefully swung her legs to the side of the bed and slid her feet into her Crocs, preparing to cautiously navigate the staircase. Within minutes she was in the kitchen, chasing down the handful of pills Dr. Raymond had given her to take each day with a full glass of water. Then she turned to brewing coffee, the task Keith usually handled when he was home. Downing at least one cup before doing anything else was mandatory. It would help clear her mental cobwebs, in case the speaking engagement call couldn't be postponed; but with everything else going on right now, she had no interest in discussing the message this small university in Louisiana wanted her to deliver in six weeks. It would be best to wait.

Tari's reply pinged her phone just as she leaned against the counter, adding sugar and cream to her favorite mug.

No problem, TV Star in the making! I'll contact Ms. Anderson & move the phone meeting to next week - any day except Fri, since you'll be driving to Illinois for your cousin's wedding. Get some rest & feel better!

Since Tari was three hours away, in Chicago, Jessica's excuse of being under the weather was easy to pull off, and Tari never seemed to question Jessica's increasingly frequent reports of "allergy headaches" or "gout." They were among the explanations doctors had given her in recent months as the cause of her severe achiness and fatigue, and now that she formally had a grimmer diagnosis, she longed for either of the suspected conditions to be her truth.

Jessica smiled at Tari's reference in her text to the looming talk show pilot with Bravo TV. Tari had been with her through thick and thin, including the disappointment of OWN producers deciding not to move forward with a show, and Jessica was happy that Tari was as excited as she was about where this new opportunity could lead. She just wished Tari's "feel better" message could make everything all right.

For a split second she thought about returning to bed and snuggling under her silk sheets for a little while longer. Then she remembered she still had a To Do list to address, including keeping her promise to Dr. Raymond and securing a second opinion. Because what if it *were* gout? Or something else easily treatable that was simply mimicking arthritis? She sipped her second cup of coffee and pondered this possibility.

*Please, God?*

Posing the rhetorical question didn't make her feel better, especially since she couldn't recall God ever answering; so after a few more minutes of ruminating, she shifted her attention to something more constructive – namely, the big problem she had to fix today - how to get out of filming news of her fake pregnancy or find a way to make it look authentic. Now that her conference call had been rescheduled, she had no obligations and could figure this whole thing out. She would also make an appointment with a rheumatologist for a second opinion, then push those concerns from her mind, at least temporarily, so she could prepare a romantic welcome home for Keith in two days.

Jessica swigged the last sip of coffee and placed her mug in the sink before easing into a seat at the small table in her breakfast nook. The sun streamed through the massive bay window, turning it into a mirror that reflected her cocoa brown complexion and wild hair. Keith had called right as she was settling down for the evening last night, and she wound up crawling into bed while they chatted and celebrated her talk show opportunity, without first wrapping the shoulder length mass. Now it stood on end in some places, and framed her heart-shaped face in odd configurations in others. If WNVX was coming to film tomorrow, she needed a hair appointment pronto.

Jessica pulled up her stylist's number and texted a request for an appointment this afternoon, just in case Sage wouldn't budge.
Yep, I was just there two days ago, but need a quick fix for an important reason! ☺

After hitting send, she scrolled through emails on her phone and read a portion of WNVX's and the local newspaper's online stories, before heading upstairs to comb through her closet and find something comfortable to wear to the salon, praying that that pain would stay away, so she could do everything she needed to prep for the TV station to interview her tomorrow about her so-called pregnancy. Thank goodness Sage had agreed to hold off on airing the segment for a week. That bought her time to summon the courage she needed to tell Keith what she had done, and gave him time to release his anger before the story aired.

Just as she reached the landing at the top of the stairs and turned toward her bedroom, Jessica's cell phone pinged again. She paused and smiled at the message that greeted her. Thinking about her babe must have put her on his mind, too. In addition to the I love you he had sent every morning since being away, he texted a flirty message this morning that made her smile, and quickly reply.
Done, babe. Can't wait for you to get home now; can you? Let the countdown begin.

In the same second of time that she sent this heartfelt message, guilt coursed through her. Keith had been gone less than a week and here she was turning into a soap opera wife, manipulating and hiding the truth from the person she loved most, and from others who trusted her. Could she really do this, knowing that weeks later her friends, colleagues and extended family, and maybe even her viewing public, would be grieving with and for her, over a child that never existed? Keith would know the truth from the start, but what if he thought less of her for doing this?

Jessica slid into the master suite and plopped herself on the cushioned bench at the foot of her king-sized bed. She closed her eyes and reminded herself of why she had come up with this scheme in the first place. At thirty-four, she was at the prime of her career for this opportunity. And what if she and Keith really did start a family in a few years? Babies would take precedence over broadcast, at least in her husband's view.

And then there were these crazy health issues. *What if she had to take the steroids forever, and the weight never melted away? What if...*

Jessica's cell phone rang and startled her, mid-rumination. Sage's name graced the screen, and she reluctantly picked up on the second ring.

"Decided not to do the segment after all? No worries? We can make an announcement much later, like nine months from now."

Sage chuckled. "Ha ha. Just calling to double check what time we can arrive tomorrow. Hayden wants to film the segment before 3 p.m., if you don't mind. That will give her time to get back to the station before she goes on air at 6. You game?"

Jessica sighed and squeezed her eyes shut. No one was forcing her to do this. She was a grown woman and she could say no. She had every right to say no.

*But...*

"You there, Jess? Are we good?"

*Was this really worth all it was going to cost her? Worst case scenario she would still be hosting her weekly show in Indianapolis...*

"Hello? Jess, you there?"

"I'm here, Sage," Jessica finally answered. "Just wondering if I really want to do this. I mean, Keith is out of town; this strips me of my privacy... I'm just not sure I want to handle it this way."

This time Sage fell silent.

"*You* still there?" Jessica queried after a few minutes.

"There's no nice way to say this, Jessica, but please take it in the loving spirit I mean it, okay?" Sage uttered the earnest plea in a soft whisper.

Jessica's light brown eyes morphed into saucers. "Okay... go on."

Sage hesitated, then dove in. "If we don't formally announce your pregnancy in an on-air story, I think we need to explain your weight gain in some way for viewers, especially as it increases. Some will surmise that you're expecting and just not talking about it, but come on – the segment you host each week is about being fabulously fit in all aspects of life. You have to bring viewers along for this health ride, just like you've done when you've hosted shows on physical fitness, emotional and mental fitness, and even professional fitness. This will affect your brand with WNVX viewers, and truthfully, Bravo TV may want to hold off until after you have the baby. Have you called them yet?"

"I'm calling later this morning," said Jessica, admitting to herself that all Sage outlined was true. If she wasn't going to really come clean just yet and tell the viewers about the arthritis diagnosis, she had to tell them something; and she couldn't discuss the arthritis without jeopardizing the Bravo project.

As she and Keith had chatted about last night on their call, not only would the nationally televised show give her a larger platform from which to share her message with people from all walks of life and elevate her reach as a motivational speaker, it also would increase their incomes to a level that would give them the financial freedom to retire early and travel the world, support the causes they believed in at a new level, and allow Keith to fund a long-held dream that would benefit youths in the region.

All good reasons, indeed; but still, was this worth the lie it would require to buy access? Would Keith still agree if he knew the steps she was taking to preserve the opportunity? And how quickly would he force her to slow down and settle down once she told him about her diagnosis? She and Keith had managed to continue treating their relationship as a gift to each other, and to work on what they called their family partnership. Her successes had always been his to enjoy, and vice versa. This would be no different, if all worked out as planned.

So he wouldn't know until he needed to know that RA, as rheumatoid arthritis was known, had invaded their marriage.

This deceit was simply a delay, not a lie. Hopefully Keith would distinguish the difference and understand.

# six

"Look, Jess," Sage finally said, interrupting Jessica's mental wrestling match. "Hayden is leaving town on Friday for a week; so if we don't film your story tomorrow, we can shoot it on Thursday. Either way, we won't air the segment for at least a week. Will the extra day give you more time to get comfortable?"

"What if we wait until I enter the second trimester?" Jessica said. "That's when most women usually share their news – not at six weeks."

Sage fell silent again, giving Jessica hope that her reasoning would yield a victory.

"I guess we could wait that long, but will you still tell the Bravo execs right away?" Sage asked. "That's the professional thing to do. And it's way less exciting to share news like this with your viewers by the time you're obviously pregnant. You should stop overthinking this and take viewers on this first-baby journey with you. Nothing's gonna go wrong; you'll gain a built-in village for Baby Arnold."

Sage's extended plea did come across as self-serving at this point.

"You've pitched this item to the top folks at WNVX, haven't you?" Jessica asked. "That's why you don't want to wait. They want to air it during sweeps next week, right?"

Sage's lack of response told her she had nailed it. Sage had been trying to prove herself since being promoted to lead producer a year ago, and this was her opportunity to increase ratings, tell a story the community would be buzzing about, and hopefully move WNVX out of second place in ratings. Plus, Jessica surmised, it would be just her luck that three months from now a fake pregnancy would be much more difficult to hide – and closer to the timeframe that she had planned on declaring a miscarriage. If she was going to fake a trimester of pregnancy, the first three months were the most logical. It also made sense to have the camera and props all over the house before Keith's homecoming, and Thursday afternoon might be cutting it close.

Jessica relented, once again.

"We're on for tomorrow at 3 o'clock. If you guys are a minute late, I have the right to change my mind."

Jessica didn't usually speak that forthrightly to Sage, but her agreeing to tape the story was clearly a win-win. They ended the call with Sage's obvious elation and a promise to tailor the report to Jessica's specifications, and with Jessica feeling fearful and antsy. Forget the health issues she had been struggling with; living a lie would exhaust her.

# *seven*

Jessica lugged the final shopping bag from her morning errands into the kitchen and plopped it on the granite island, before plopping herself on the barstool tucked beneath it.

She briefly closed her eyes and willed the achiness spreading through her feet and knees to go away. The pain was causing her to sweat, and she mopped her forehead with the back of her hand. She was worn out, but at least she had checked every task and item off her list.

When the TV news crew arrived in four hours, they would find a dining room filled with pink and blue balloons, including two with the celebratory phrases "Congrats, Dad!" and "Welcome to Parenthood;" a miniature cake decorated with pastel baby booties, and the ultrasound Sage had requested that she share. The image Jessica pulled from an acquaintance's Facebook page sat in her laptop's download file, ready to be printed.

To keep Hayden and her cameraman from handling the picture and doubting its authenticity, Jessica intended to print it on flimsy photo paper similar to the density used in doctor's offices. She would tuck it inside a small, decorative frame she had picked up in Dollar Tree, while ordering the balloons.

*I can change course any time you say, God. I'm listening.*

Even as she broached this silent dialogue with God, Jessica

admitted it was halfhearted. Mama, and her older sister Shiloh, would be quick to remind her that of course God was speaking; she just needed to be open to hearing and seeing what His plan for her life looked like, rather than looking for His endorsement of her vision.

*Yeah, yeah.*

Jessica shook herself out of that reverie and slid off the barstool. She winced and reached for her satchel purse, to retrieve two over-the-counter pain pills. As soon as the dining room was set up to her liking she was going to take a hot shower and lie down, in hopes that the achiness would fade and energize her for the interview. Worst-case scenario, she'd have to fake it, and for once there was no internal debate; she'd come too far to do otherwise.

First, though, she sorted and stored the groceries filling the bags on the island. Along with buying the supplies she needed to stage today's announcement for WNVX, she had shopped for groceries to cook Keith's favorite meal. Flank steak. Bacon-wrapped asparagus. Russet potatoes for boiling and mashing. Organic carrots to steam and glaze. Her speaking engagements and related travel schedule didn't permit her to play chef often, but when she did, Keith's happiness was palpable.

Even if every joint in her body was inflamed twenty-four hours from now, she was going to find the will to navigate their kitchen and welcome her sexy teddy bear home tomorrow, to the aromas that reminded him he was loved. After his appetite was sated, she would ease into a confession about the news interview and prepare him for next week's airing of the pregnancy announcement. When she would tell him about the arthritis, she still didn't know....

Thirty minutes later, she stepped out of the shower feeling refreshed and ready to be "on" when the WNVX team arrived. She eased into her purple silk robe and knotted the belt at the waist, then splayed her body across her bed, on top of the comforter.

Jessica closed her eyes and inhaled and exhaled several times, slowly and deeply, to center herself. For someone who prided herself on being a genuine reflection of the messages she shared with audiences worldwide, the steps she was about to take felt akin to committing murder. And maybe that was the case: In following through with this plan, she'd be killing a part of her soul, as well as some aspect of self-respect – not to mention altering Keith's perception of her, once she told him what she had done.

Within a few minutes, however, she managed to alter her frantic thoughts into a stress-free run-through of her plan.

Maybe, just maybe, she needed to reframe this experience as an opportunity to remove some of the pressure to be perky, pretty and most importantly, thin without fail. Pregnant women were cut some slack, but society and the professional world in which she operated wasn't as kind to everyone else, even if you were dealing with a health condition you couldn't control. Her brothers and sisters in the black community often celebrated thicker women as fabulous (hello, Jill Scott); but even in black culture, there was a difference between being fit and thick, and pudgy and puffy; and right now, due to her medication, Jessica was racing toward the latter. And secondly, she assured herself, maybe this faux gestation period could be a trial run for the real deal. Someday she and Keith would be celebrating an actual pregnancy, with an official ultrasound to hold onto and cherish.

In the light of day, her reasoning seemed flimsy; but she kept returning to the fact that the Bravo show had landed in her lap out of nowhere. It seemed meant to be. Plus, while they were comfortable now, she couldn't ignore the fact that living her dream at a new level would take them both to new heights of opportunity and experiences.

As 3 p.m. drew closer, however, so did a new surge of jitters. Jessica touched up her makeup and ran a comb through her hair once again, while noting that she couldn't recall the last time she prayed with regularity, since leaving Daddy's church in Atchity, Alabama for Stanford all those years ago. But this afternoon, she found herself mentally reciting the few verses from the 23rd Psalm that she could remember, along with Philippians 4:13, the scripture Mama had insisted that she and her two sisters memorize on their respective first day of middle school, to guide them through adolescence.

Did she truly believe the Lord was her shepherd, leaving her without want? Or that she could do all things through Christ, rather than in her own strength?  The unsettling diagnosis she'd received this week made her doubtful that such verses applied to her, because *couldn't God have fixed this?*

Despite that latent resentment, an urge to feel at peace with the Creator before she took this big step mushroomed in her spirit. She had no idea why, other than her desperation to pull this off and come out unscathed; and by all accounts, God was the grantor of mercy and favor. Yet, how hypocritical. Who sought out the Man Upstairs when you were frustrated with him, and especially as you prepared to orchestrate a Jurassic-sized lie?

If God did still speak, she clearly wasn't on his preferred frequency. Jessica decided to take his silence literally- as a sign to stay on course, with Plan A. In less than an hour, there'd be no turning back.

# eight

By the time the TV crew arrived with their lights and camera, Jessica had transformed into the positive, energetic ball of womanhood that viewers were used to seeing in her weekly TV segments, and that keynote audiences found themselves mesmerized by when watching her on stage.

Since they were filming in her home and the interview was more personal, she opted for dressy casual, and greeted Hayden and her cameraman, Jim, in jeans, stilettos and a striking royal blue silk blouse, with three-quarter length sleeves.

Hayden grasped her in a gentle hug before stepping inside the foyer and taking in the fifteen-foot ceiling, soft peach walls, and general ambience of the space.

"What a lovely home, Jessica! How long have you lived here? Seems like a great neighborhood."

Hayden had been WNVX's evening news anchor for five years, just before Jessica began delivering her special segments for the station each Thursday, and while they'd always been friendly, they had never grown close enough to hang out as friends. But the green-eyed, auburn-haired beauty was as warm and gracious as they came, and her friendly demeanor this afternoon quickly put Jessica at ease.

"Thanks, Hayden," Jessica responded. "Keith and I built this house about four years ago, and we love it here. There are a ton of families of all sizes, with kids of all ages."

Jessica greeted Jim with a hug, too, and ushered them into the dining room, to show them the display she had created. The balloons were at the far end of the room, positioned just behind an upholstered dining chair at the head of the massive square, rosewood table. The burnished gold 4x6 frame featuring the ultrasound sat in the middle of the table, next to the small round decorated cake.

"Awesome," Jim said and nodded. Hayden's thirty-something, laid-back sidekick had always been quiet, but talented at producing memorable video packages. Jessica watched him canvass the room with his eyes, calculating how much artificial light he needed to add, where they should start and end the interview segments, and what parts should be filmed when.

The doorbell rang and Jessica left him and Hayden discussing options while she went to welcome Rob and Paula Tennyson, the owners of a local production company in the area who had been hired by Bravo to serve as her network liaison and also shoot her pilot episodes. They, too, were casually dressed, and Rob even wore a pair of shades on his Hershey-bar brown, bald head.

"I really appreciated your call yesterday," he said and shook her hand, with Paula following suit. "And thanks for inviting us to be here today. I called Mark, the lead VP of the Bravo team that flew down a few days ago for your contractual meeting, and gave him an update on your condition. Right now, he thinks he'd like us to move up shooting the pilot episodes, so we can gather all of the footage before you begin to show. But we can talk about all of that later and make a final decision in the next week or so. We'll send him the interview you're filming today once it's ready to air, and that may give him and his staff some other ideas."

Jessica nodded. She loved how he got right to the point; working with him and Paula was going to be a pleasure.

"Sounds like a plan. I appreciate you taking time to be here for this."

Paula gave her a thumbs up. "We'll be a team for the next few months."

Jessica and the couple entered the dining room just as Jim finished positioning Hayden near the doorway, to give an opening spiel about why she was visiting Jessica's home.

"Now, Jessica, after Hayden opens the segment and mentions your name, she's going to invite you onto camera with her," Jim said. He pointed to a spot adjacent to Hayden. "When she smiles and looks your way, you'll stand right there and step into the camera's view, and the interview will begin. At some point, she'll pose a question about your big surprise, and you can start walking toward the far end of the room and stand near the bouquet of balloons. Have you thought about what you'll say?"

Jessica chuckled. "Ad nauseam. I figure I'll let it flow naturally; but basically I'll indicate that I'm sharing the news first on WNVX and invite viewers to tune in to my show to follow my experience."

A dose of panic raced up her spine as she thought about possibly having to do a follow-up interview to this one in a few months, announcing her miscarriage. What if that led this lie to take on a life of its own? What had she done?

# nine

Thank God it was over. The taping had gone well, and Jim and Hayden hadn't requested any retakes.

After wrapping up the formal interview segments, they asked Jessica to stand in front of the house holding the framed ultrasound for a few outtake shots. Not comfortable being seen by neighbors before having her talk with Keith, she had persuaded them to record the stand-alone shots in the backyard instead, and afterward, they called it a wrap.

Now Jim was loading his equipment into his car. Hayden had dashed off minutes earlier, to prepare for her live broadcast on the 6 p.m. news.

Jessica escorted Rob and Paula from the backyard through a gate that led to the front of the house, and walked them to their van.

They had quietly taken it all in, jotting a few notes here and there, and giving her another thumbs up an hour later, when all was said and done. The petite and plump Paula had compelled Jessica to lean down for a congratulatory hug, and when they connected, Jessica's face got lost in Paula's lush afro.

"Great interview, and great start for where you're about to go," Paula told Jessica. "Eyes haven't seen, nor ears heard what's in store for you, my dear."

Jessica raised an eyebrow, but didn't respond.

Paula appeared to be about her age, but she paraphrased scripture like Mama. Was working with her going to be less comfortable than she thought?

Paula seemed to notice Jessica's reaction, but didn't respond. She grabbed Rob by the hand and smiled up at her tall, slender husband. "As the host of a cable show we often work with says at the end of each broadcast, 'Our work here is done.'"

Rob rolled his eyes.

"There she goes..."

Paula dismissed him with a wave and laughed. She climbed into the passenger seat of the van, and with the door ajar so she could still chat with Jessica, buckled her seatbelt.

"We're heading to our daughter's first tee ball game. She's very excited, so we'll get there early to show our support. Good times like this are ahead for you, too!"

Jessica's heart clenched, but she managed to smile and wink at Paula.

When the couple had driven away and turned the corner, she remained in her driveway for a few minutes, breathing in the fresh air, appreciating the crisp cool afternoon, and meeting a feeling of dread she couldn't shake.

# ten

With her guests gone and the house all to herself, Jessica removed her makeup, changed into her favorite yoga pants and T-shirt, and prepared for a quiet, stress-free evening.

She couldn't wait until Keith came home tomorrow, but some quality alone time tonight would allow her to finish reading the novel on her nightstand, enjoy a bubble bath, and simply rest. Dinner would be light and quick, she decided, and she'd deal with cleaning up the dining room tomorrow morning, since nothing filled her calendar.

She rummaged through the fridge and pulled out a can of chilled tuna, some grapes and the condiments she'd need for tuna salad. That on a bed of crackers would hit the spot.

Jessica quickly fixed her meal, grabbed her cell phone from the counter, and took both into the family room, where she settled on the sofa to watch the news while she ate, grateful that the pain pills were working. Between bites and during a commercial break, she finally checked her phone, which she'd had to ignore most of the day.

There were texts from Keith, Tari, her neighborhood girlfriends, and even Evangeline. E's message lured her first.

Hey, just checking on u. I know you're having a rough time. I'm here for u. Call if u want to talk or get together. This is all going to work out okay. Keep your head up and know that I love ya.

Jessica hugged the phone to her chest as if it were her college roomie. She loved E., and always would. She'd give her a call sometime tomorrow, before Keith arrived.

She clicked open her hubby's text next, and frowned at the message he'd sent her, about four hours ago, around the time she was taping the news interviews.

Got a surprise for you. Hope you're gonna love it. In your arms before you know it.

Please let this man not have gone out and bought a pet or something. The last thing she needed was another species to take care of. Jessica started to speed dial him and ask for a few hints, but decided that neither a pet nor anything living could be the surprise, because he wouldn't be able to travel with an animal; and why would he be states away searching for something like that anyway? Her curiosity now piqued, she texted him back several emojis that conveyed she had questions, wanted answers, and couldn't wait.

Keith didn't respond right away, and the more she sat watching the TV, the heavier her eyes grew.

She startled awake about half an hour later, and decided the sofa wasn't the softest place for current condition. Her neck was stiff from the position in which she'd dozed off, and her knees were as well. She unfurled herself from the uncomfortable position she had assumed and grabbed the remote to turn off the TV. After returning her few dinner dishes to the kitchen, she would be on the way to a bubble bath, as planned. And other than waiting to hear from Keith, the remaining texts could be answered in the morning.

Jessica strolled down the short, dimly lit hallway toward the kitchen and frowned when she saw light spilling from the open space. It had been daylight still when she prepared the tuna, and she didn't recall turning on the light, let alone leaving it on.

She shook her head.

"Getting old, girl," she muttered. "Got to do better."

When she reached the kitchen, a tall, dark figure turned toward her and she screamed, dropping everything. For a split second, terror seized her heart.

A second later, she was fuming.

"Keith!!! What are you doing?! Do you realize you almost made me pass out?!"
Keith held up his palms in surrender and approached her, his eyes revealing both contrition and amusement. As angry as she was to have been scared out of her mind, and now to have a mess all over the floor, she fell into her husband's embrace.

"Man, you know what?"

"Surprise, babe. I came home early to celebrate your Bravo TV contract. Told you there would be something special in your arms tonight."

Still in his arms, Jessica smirked and swatted his backside. She wanted to remain furious at him, but she couldn't because she was beyond happy to see him, and he knew it. Every single time Keith walked through the door - all six feet two, caramel chocolate, goateed inch of him, Jessica remembered she was a blessed woman.

This time, she also remembered her special plans, to have dinner waiting for him when he arrived home, and her heart sank.

She stepped out of the cocoon of his arms so he could see her pouting.

"You know you ruined *my* surprise, right?"

Keith grinned and leaned toward, planting a long, soft kiss on her lips.

He twirled her around and she squealed. "What on earth are you doing?"

He put her down and kissed her again.

"I'm celebrating, babe. Nothing is spoiled. You set it up just perfect, and I am the happiest man alive."

Confusion left her speechless. She frowned at her husband, trying to grasp where he was going with this; but he didn't make her wait.

Keith cradled her face with his broad hands and smiled at her, as tears filled his deep brown eyes.

"I can't wait to be a daddy to the baby we've created, Jess. Thank you."

# eleven

Keith was still celebrating as the truth hit her in slow motion.

The balloons. The cake. The picture of the framed ultrasound. All of that in the next room, set up perfectly, as if it were just for him. *Lord, have mercy.*

Jessica felt dizzy. She needed to tell Keith the truth before he celebrated any longer. But how could she explain this away without breaking his heart, or leaving him to wonder if she possessed one? Or, without confessing that she'd set up this entire ruse to hide the fact that she was suffering from arthritis?

He would be sad, and maybe even mad, about there being no baby; especially since he'd been wanting to start a family for a few years. But if he knew she had a chronic illness, Jessica was certain that he would insist she back out of the Bravo deal and focus on her health.

Therein lay her dilemma: End this lie right now, before Keith fully embraced his so-called new status and before the news story ever hit the TV airwaves, or fight for her dream?

When she gazed at her husband and felt the same amount of enduring love that engulfed her on their wedding day nine years ago, the answer seemed obvious.

*How could she lie to this good man?*

Even if she hadn't uttered the words "We're pregnant" or

purposely set up the display to fool him, the fact that he received it that way, without correction, would be lie enough. She stood in the middle of the kitchen, waiting for him to return from a quick trip to the dining room.

He reappeared with the framed ultrasound picture in hand, and took a selfie with it.

"What do you think we're having – a boy or girl?" He said and grinned. "Doesn't matter; we made a perfect baby, either way."

Jessica forced a smile and watched him pace the floor with the picture, talking more to himself than to her about little league football games if it were a boy, or perhaps basketball or soccer for his daughter. She swallowed hard, and parted her lips, but the lump in her throat and her thudding heart choked her ability to speak. In that moment, she knew she would take the coward's way out, just as she had done during lunch with Sage, a few days ago.

It would be better at this point for Keith to believe they were pregnant and later experience a miscarriage. His heart would be broken, but at least their marriage would be intact.

She wasn't doing this to hurt him, she mused, and sooner rather than later, she was going to have to deal with her condition, especially if the second doctor she visited determined the RA diagnosis was accurate. In the meantime, she needed to hold on to the part of herself that made her special, and that was her work, and her audiences. Keith was her soul mate; but even before falling for him and marrying him, she had decided she would always take care of Jessica, so she didn't wind up like Mama, or like her sister Shiloh – living in the shadow of the man she loved, and becoming little more than a shell of who she might have been.

From her perspective, little had changed for her since childhood; to be noticed, she had to be truly seen. Rheumatoid arthritis might eventually lead her down an alternate path, like it had her maternal grandmother, Granna. But if she didn't want to wind up lonely and perpetually cranky like Granna, she owed it to herself, and to Keith, to fight with everything she had. If it meant this lie had to be part of the first round of battle, so be it.

This time the tears filled Jessica's eyes, and an inexplicable sadness invaded her heart as the weight of what she was doing settled there.  Whatever happened going forward, she could never recreate the experience of a first-baby announcement. The details of this evening would be etched in both of their memories forever.

But it was done, now. She had made this bed, and there was no turning back. Jessica hugged Keith's neck, closed her eyes, and whispered a sentiment that was muffled by his collared shirt. "Congratulations, Dad."

# twelve

Keith was attentive by nature, but the second he learned about the baby, he flipped into overdrive.

Because it was the weekend, he had more time than usual to smother Jessica with affection and anxious questions. So when he announced a few minutes ago that he was heading to the store to replenish his after-trip toiletries, she felt like helping him out of bed and walking him to his car. Last night, they had enjoyed a celebratory, intimate homecoming; this morning, guilt was making her cranky. She tried to squash it by lingering under the covers while Keith got dressed.

In his excitement, he had easily accepted her explanation about the WNVX crew coming by to film the new baby segment and share the news during a broadcast next week. His only request was that they tell his mom and sister before then, during their usual Sunday dinner.

Keith left for the store, and she buried her head beneath her pillow, wishing she could somehow shut out or erase her actions of the past few days, and also the doctor's diagnosis. If she could turn back the clock by just six months, life would feel normal again. She stayed in that position for a while, and finally stirred when her home phone on the nightstand next to her chimed. Mama was one of the few people who still used the number, and on a Saturday morning, the call had to be from her.

"You're still in the bed at 10 a.m.?"

Jessica closed her eyes and pressed her lips together to avoid delivering a curt reply. Mama still didn't know about her health issues; why wouldn't she expect Jessica to be up this time of morning?

Jessica had avoided mentioning her suffering to prevent Mama from boarding a flight from Alabama and invading her life. She certainly wouldn't be telling Mama about her faux pregnancy, and she had exhaled with relief last night when Keith agreed to keep their baby news from her out-of-state relatives until she made it into the second trimester. His mom and sister lived in the area, so it made sense to inform them before the news broadcast.

"I'm sorta up, Mama," Jessica finally responded. "Still easing into the day. How are you?"

Mama rattled off all of the errands and chores she had completed already this morning and how she had the rest of the day open to read and maybe find a new dress for a family wedding next week.

"You got Chloe's wedding gift yet? And when are you arriving in Springfield?"

Mama had so quickly changed the subject from basic chitchat to her niece's looming nuptials that Jessica realized this was the real reason she had called: to discuss the wedding of her sister Flora's youngest daughter. Jessica was planning to drive to Chloe's wedding since the state capital of Illinois was just four hours away. Mama would be flying from Atchity with Shiloh, and Jessica's eldest sister, Dayna, was traveling to the festivities from her home in central Florida.

"I can't wait to see my three girls," Mama crowed.

Jessica chuckled. Funny how they had not become Mama's "girls" until she, Shiloh and Dayna were all grown. As kids, they had been forced to play the part of prim and proper mini-adults, to suit the expectations that actual adults placed on them because their father led a congregation as prominent as Riverview Baptist.

Jessica sat up in bed, as if the physical movement would also shift her thoughts away from the resentment that surfaced every time she returned to memories of her childhood in Atchity, or recalled the relief she experienced when she went away to college in California, far from the rigid rules and routines her parents considered sacred. She was certain those requirements and customs made her the reluctant churchgoer she was today, attending two to three Sunday services a month at Keith's insistence, not because she felt connected to God or the congregation.

"Yes, Mama, your three girls will be with you at the wedding," Jessica said, and she could almost hear Mama smiling through the phone. She had to admit, Mama had grown more sentimental with age, and Jessica liked her better this way.

"I'm guessing you and Aunt Flora will sit in the corner after all the festivities are over and cackle like two hens," Jessica teased.

"Tee hee hee!" Mama's signature giggle filled the airwaves that connected them. "That's what sisters are supposed to do."

Mama could be frank sometimes, but Jessica knew she hadn't meant this as a barb. It was no secret that she wanted Jessica, Shiloh and Dayna to be closer than the mostly birthday-calling siblings they had turned out to be. Jessica couldn't help it that they were so different, with little in common beyond their blood ties. Plus, the only memories they jointly shared involved the church. There had been few fun family outings and little, if any, routine encouragement to show each other sisterly support. The church and congregational needs had always come first in their household.

In recent years, Mama seemed on a mission to turn things around. The four of them attending this wedding together had been her idea. Daddy was staying home, and so were all of the other husbands.

At least until now.

Keith snuggled up behind Jessica on the bed, startling her and almost causing her to drop the phone. When had he returned from the store? He was going to have to halt these stealthy moves.

"Is that your mom on the phone? Tell her I said hello, and I'll see her on Saturday. I'm driving you to Chloe's big event."

Jessica repositioned the phone so she could listen while Mama rattled on about the wedding details Aunt Flora had shared, and glare at her husband, both for interrupting her conversation and trying to invite himself on her trip.

"You still aren't feeling well, Jess. Plus you've got another reason to be extra careful."

"But you didn't RSVP for the reception, Keith. Crashing would be rude, and awkward."

He paused, then shrugged.

"No biggie. I'll drive you and join you at the ceremony, then I'll find something else to do during the reception."

Frustration left her momentarily speechless. This was why she hadn't wanted to get pregnant in the first place – or tell him about the arthritis diagnosis. Whatever "condition" she was in didn't mean she needed to be under his thumb, like Mama had always been with Daddy – a subordinate instead of a partner.

Keith seemed confused by her reaction; but she ignored his curious stare and turned her attention back to Mama, resuming their conversation as if he hadn't interrupted.

Her ankles, knees, feet and hands were beginning to throb, and so was her head. Maybe it was because a new fear was choking her spirit. She needed some long-term solutions for dealing with her health, and with her doting husband, or she might find herself imprisoned by her own life.

# *thirteen*

The weekend weather couldn't have been any nicer, but the hours couldn't have crawled any slower, with Jessica fixating on the future.

She and Keith spent Saturday afternoon in the Broad Ripple area of Indianapolis, taking in a movie before meeting friends for dinner at Mississippi Belle, their favorite soul food spot. This morning, they drove an hour to Muncie, to attend service at Keith's childhood church and enjoy a leisurely dinner with his mom and sister afterward.

Keith was so attentive that his mother mentioned it.

"He was gone for work only a week," Mom Carolyn said and rolled her eyes. "You two must have really missed each other – geez!"

Karis, laughed. "You and Daddy were just like that, Mom. That's where Keith gets it from!"

The mention of Daddy James made all of them smile. Eight years after he succumbed to liver cancer his presence in the family still loomed large.

Mom Carolyn nodded at her daughter's joke.

"You got that right. That's why Jessica got a good one; we taught Keith well."

Jessica chimed in with a smile and leaned against her

husband's chest. "That you did."

Despite their usual comfortable fellowship, Jessica's quest to move time forward – on to her second medical opinion and to her follow-up meeting with the Bravo executives - kept her from fully relaxing, not to mention the fact that Keith wanted to expand her lie and tell his family she was pregnant. As soon as he uttered the words, tears flowed.

Mom Carolyn's first grandchild; Karis' first niece or nephew. Another memorable moment marked by falsehood. When Jessica's tears began to flow, her in-laws didn't realize they were sorrow-filled, for the way she was betraying her family.

Mom Carolyn left the room briefly and returned with a handful of tissues and a hug.

"I'm so excited, sweetheart," she said and kissed Jessica's cheek. "I'm here for you, whatever you need. This has given me a reason to hope again."

Jessica had no response. Only silent pleas for God to forgive her.

# fourteen

The arrival of Monday morning inched Jessica one step closer to a medical second opinion and one week closer to ending her charade.

The WNVX news story about her pregnancy would air on Thursday, and she would meet via teleconference with Ron, Paula and the Bravo TV execs today to learn how they'd like to proceed, given her baby news. Ron and Paula felt confident that Bravo wouldn't cancel the contract – and couldn't for legal reasons if they were tied solely to her becoming pregnant. The goal was to keep Bravo excited about the show so they wouldn't shelve it until the contracted time to complete the pilots simply expired. Jessica intended to deliver some powerful pilot episodes, with help from Ron and Paula, to keep the executives, and viewers, longing for more.

This morning, when Keith headed out for work at a quarter to eight, she had been relieved. Working from home had always been a blessing, but today especially, she needed time and space to let down her guard, even if just for eight or nine hours. Having to pretend to be pregnant and watch what she ate or how she responded to Keith's questions and concerns was already wearing on her. How was she going to do this for five more weeks?

Jessica woke this morning with intentions of tidying up the

bedroom before going downstairs to her home office. But her hands were swollen and hot with pain, so the bed and the room would stay as they were. Her primary care doctor had informed her that flare ups like this would occur, and despite her frustration over the reality unfolding before her, she was glad Dr. Raymond had prepared her, so she wouldn't be alarmed.

Diverting to Plan B, she made her way to the dresser and retrieved four bottles of medicine she'd been stashing in the back of her lingerie drawer since Dr. Raymond prescribed them last week. Some of the pills were the same as she'd been taking all along, to treat suspected gout; but the prednisone prescription had been doubled to sixty milligrams, and she also had a stronger medicine for pain and inflammation. It took twenty minutes, and the help of a dry washcloth, to twist off the caps of the two new drugs, and by the time Jessica had accessed them and filled a glass with water from her bathroom faucet, she almost felt too weak to swallow the pills.

She downed them and glanced at the clock radio on her nightstand. In another twenty minutes Tari would be calling for their Monday morning check-in. She needed to make an appointment with the rheumatologist before then. Too worn out to get dressed and meet that deadline, Jessica decided to tackle her wardrobe after her call with Tari. That way, she could take as much time as needed to carefully dress for the Bravo meeting, which would be held downtown as it had been last week, at Ron and Paula's production company office.

For now, she slid into her robe and gathered her phone and calendar, to head to her office. She grasped the banister in the upstairs hallway and clung to it during her descent down the stairwell. The minutes it took to navigate the steps felt like an eternity. Finally, she reached the first floor landing.

Jessica was breathless by the time she reached her office, and also ticked off. It took all the strength she could muster to keep herself from shoving everything off her desktop and easing herself onto the space to curl into a fetal ball. Instead, she plopped herself awkwardly in the rolling chair in front of the desk and leaned forward, resting her forehead on her folded palms.

Lying about the pregnancy was one thing, but how was she going to hide the fact that she sometimes could barely use her hands, or walk? Jessica raised her head and peered out of the window at a blue jay perched on the tree closest to her view.

"Get it together girl," she said aloud. "Other people have dealt with worse."

Speaking the words seemed to be just the fuel she needed to halt her pity party. It wasn't going to get her anywhere. She would give herself a few minutes for the medicine to kick in, then she would get on with her day, the best she could. Scheduling an appointment for a second opinion sat atop her list, but if this morning were any indication, a second round of testing wasn't really necessary. Her body clearly was betraying her; question was, how could she not only live with this, but also thrive?

# fifteen

Jessica felt more nervous this afternoon than she had last week, when the Bravo executive team had joined her in person in Indianapolis to conduct a final interview, watch her give a mock interview on camera, and extend the talk show offer.

Today, she sat in a small conference room with a movie-sized screen, flanked on either side by Paula and Ron. She wore a fitted navy dress that cinched at the waist, and a silver choker inset with sapphires.

The first question the talk show divisional VP tossed to her centered around last week's meeting, and why she hadn't mentioned the pregnancy then.

"That's a fair question," Jessica responded, knowing that it was impossible for them to hear her pounding heart or racing pulse, but feeling self-conscious about it anyway. "I had hoped to wait until the end of the first trimester to announce this news, as most expectant parents do; but when I shared it in confidence with Sage Bennett, the WNVX producer who accompanied me last week, she thought you might want to know sooner, in case this affected your timeline for shooting the pilot episodes."

Before members of the team could chime in with a follow-up question, Jessica delivered what she considered another important piece of information for them to consider.

"I want to assure you that if you move forward with the pilot episodes, and ultimately with a season-long show, I'll continue to give 1000 percent to making it a success," Jessica said, leaning forward, to connect with the four men and two women gathered around a table at Bravo's headquarters in New York. "This is about more than just saying I have a TV show for me. I believe in the work I do every day, and this is an opportunity to inspire and educate the masses about how to live more successful lives. I don't plan to waste it."

Her answer seemed to please them, and one of the women at the table piped up.

"How would you feel about taping the three pilot episodes over the next month or two, before you begin ... showing?"

The unspoken words were the ones Sage had kindly mentioned: *before she began gaining weight.*

The timeline was tight, and Jessica would have to clear her schedule of quite a few things, but she was willing to give it a shot.

"You'll have to bear with me as I see if I can line up some star power guests that quickly," Jessica said. "I will certainly try. I'll also have to fit this in around speaking engagements that are already booked during that time frame."

Ron leaned forward and chimed in. "With some flexibility and a liberal budget, we think we can help her pull this off. But what about post-pilot plans? What are the next steps if the show is well received?"

Ron's queries reinforced to Jessica why her professional speaker colleagues were urging her to hire a talent agent. He was making requests and asking critical questions that were way out of her realm of experience, and proving to her that one didn't know what one didn't know.

The team members in New York exchanged glances, and the lead VP responded.

"Our contract indicates that if the pilot episodes receive a certain level of viewership, we'll move forward with shooting three more episodes, to round out the first season. In your case, with a baby due in late fall, your new episodes might be delayed until spring of next year, when you could resume taping; but let's play all of that by ear."

Jessica was savvy enough to translate this feedback: They weren't going to take away her opportunity, but they were going to wait and see post-baby where her interests and focus lay.

She was the only one in the meeting who knew there would be no post-baby experience. What she would be struggling to deal with instead was how to manage her steroid experience, to control her weight and prevent RA treatments from costing her everything.

# sixteen

Jessica's outing from her home office today would be a secretly scheduled appointment with a rheumatologist at Indiana University Medical Center, who just happened to have a cancellation. First, however, she needed to finish a Skype session with Tari, to prepare for the month's upcoming events.

The keynote planning call she had canceled last Friday would take place later this week. Her mid-week webinar with second-semester freshmen at a Delaware university was confirmed. Now she and Tari had to find some time for her to both plan her Bravo episodes, and shoot them.

"I'm sure we can pull this off, but I'm curious.... Why are they rushing this, all of a sudden?" Tari asked.

Jessica didn't want to lie to the person who had been her loyal and efficient assistant for so long, and Tari deserved an explanation for why they needed to pull off this feat. But how could she tell Tari what she had done, especially when Keith didn't even know the truth?

The pregnancy lie hovered on her lips, but she couldn't bring herself to utter it. Could she possibly take her assistant into her confidence?

*God, please help me know what to do, and whom to trust.*

The prayer slid from her heart to heaven before she realized she had uttered it, and for the first time in years, issuing it hadn't felt so awkward.

She turned her attention back to Tari.

"All of this is good stuff, but there's more," Tari said, and Jessica could tell she was struggling to contain her excitement. "The producers are already talking up your show, and they've arranged for you to be featured in the June issue of *Essence*. A reporter for the magazine wants to visit sometime in the next couple of days to interview you for a profile article. It's scheduled to appear the same month the TV pilot launches on Bravo."

Jessica sat up straighter at her desk. "Say that again?"

"I know!" Tari squealed. "Can you believe this is really happening? I work for someone famous. You are about to blow up!"

Jessica chuckled. Tari was usually unfazed by celebrity or things related to a high-profile lifestyle. In the three years they had worked together, Jessica had never heard or seen her so animated.

"If I blow up I guess you're blowing up, too," Jessica sang in a silly falsetto. "There's no me without you...."

Both women laughed.

"How are you feeling this morning? And how did your doctor's appointment go last week? I forgot to ask when we talked on Friday."

Tari's innocent and caring query plummeted Jessica to reality. Why had she decided to lie her way through this? How was she going to keep up the façade?

"Still waiting on some tests, believe it or not," she responded, hoping Tari couldn't hear the forced confidence in her tone. "I have a few more scheduled for tomorrow. And just snagged a last-minute appointment at 10 a.m. today."

"Okay," Tari said. "I'm sure it's all going to be fine. Do you need me to do anything for you? Are you still in a lot of pain?"

Jessica's eyes grew blurry with unanticipated tears, and she blinked them away.

"Not too much," she lied again. "I'm managing. So...how do I go about scheduling the interview with *Essence*? We're leaving on Saturday morning, instead of on Friday, for my cousin's wedding in Springfield, but we'll be home late Sunday evening."

"We?"

Jessica sighed. "Yes – we. Dear hubby has decided that his sugar mama needs some company on the road."

Tari laughed.

"What – his golf date or poker night fell through? Now I hope he knows I didn't RVSP for him when I sent in your wedding response; so he can't crash the reception."

Jessica chuckled. Tari's directness was one of the things she loved most about her.

"He's just driving 'Ms. Daisy;' he won't crash the party."

"Then don't complain!" Tari said. "Get your beauty rest on the way there and back. I'll touch base with the *Essence* reporter to see what date and time she wants for the interview, and we'll go from there. Today, I'll be following up on a handful of requests that have come in, inviting you to speak sometime over the next six months into early next year. There are also some email requests for you to write guest blog posts, mostly on career counseling websites geared to college juniors and seniors. I'll forward all of those to you a second time, so you can decide which opportunities suit you. Need me to tackle anything else for you today?"

Jessica scanned the notes scribbled on her desktop calendar to make sure nothing urgent needed to be addressed, then turned to her computer to peruse her emails. Tari routinely read them on her behalf, but she liked keeping abreast of what was coming in.

"I think we're good. Send along the blog post requests, and I'll note the deadlines and begin gathering info for those today."

The women exchanged goodbyes, and Jessica ended the call feeling ashamed that she hadn't brought Tari up to speed.

She pushed her chair back from the desk and realized that the medicines had finally begun working. Her joints and bones still throbbed, but they didn't feel on fire anymore.

Jessica calculated how much time she'd have to get herself together before taping the test run shows for Bravo. Would she be better or worse in another four to six weeks? And honestly, could she pull off an interview for a major magazine without lying her way through, or giving herself away? It had been less than a week since her defining actions, and the stakes seemed to be getting higher everyday. She had never been good at keeping a poker face, but now seemed to be a good time to hone that skill.

Her cell phone chimed, and she smiled when Keith's name appeared. She opened the text to find one of his usual reminders that he loved her, along with a picture of two smiling brown, toothless babies –a boy and a girl.

If u happen to have one of each growing inside I won't complain…

Jessica's response was swift.

Sure… but u want to carry them?

She knew her hubby was teasing her, and under different circumstances she wouldn't mind playing along. However, keeping up this ruse was the most taxing thing she'd ever done, and this was just seventy-two hours in. It struck her that this was why executive and leadership coaching were so important. Monumental tasks or feats required high-level support, and she felt like she needed some herself right about now. But whom could she trust to help her keep her secret? Jessica mentally skated through all of her girlfriends, and quickly checked off the reasons they wouldn't work.

She kept coming back to Tari. She *was* paid to help however needed; but it wasn't wise to mix personal and professional situations. Evangeline? She had already distanced herself from this risky business. Her sisters? They weren't close enough, either physically or relationship-wise, to bring them up to speed and ask for this kind of loyalty.

Then it struck her: If she were about to grow in visibility, with the talk show and accompanying media, she best not confide in others. This could be a TMZ paycheck in the making for somebody, and the end of her dream. To avoid any possibilities along those lines, she'd have to keep walking this shameful path alone.

# seventeen

Jessica should have known better: Just because miracles still happened didn't mean one awaited her.

It didn't matter that this wasn't her first time receiving this diagnosis; Dr. Ryan Kent's pronouncement this morning still cut deeply.

"According to our extensive testing and the results, you do indeed have early onset rheumatoid arthritis, Mrs. Arnold."

Was the room spinning, or was that just her mind playing tricks? When she received this same pronouncement from Dr. Raymond a week ago, she'd been able to put off accepting the diagnosis by reminding herself that medicine is practiced, not perfect, and because it's not an all-knowing science, Dr. Raymond could have made an honest mistake in her findings.

However, between Dr. Raymond's extensive monitoring of Jessica's health over the past few months, a weekend bout of more pain and more stiffness than usual, and now this medical specialist rendering the exact diagnosis as Dr. Raymond, the truth hit Jessica like a Mack truck traveling at breakneck speed. She felt like she was having an out-of-body experience.

*Rheumatoid arthritis. In the prime of her life. With devastating, life-long consequences, especially for the most severe cases.*

That's what Dr. Kent called hers - unusually severe - especially for someone her age. Jessica sagged in the cushioned chair in his office and tuned him out. A river of tears zigzagged down her cheeks, and she didn't bother to keep them from dripping when they reached her chin. She closed her eyes and concentrated on breathing.

In and out. Inhale and exhale. In and out.

She was a good person. She worked hard; she gave back to the community and helped her neighbors; she ate right and exercised regularly. She believed in God, and sometimes she prayed. What had she done – or not done - to deserve this?

If only Keith were here, to hold her, to decode what the doctor was saying, to tell her everything was going to be alright. But how could she call him now, when all he thought she had was a temporary case of gout, and his first child in her womb?

Dr. Kent shuffled through his notes more than once as he talked with her, and Jessica wondered whether he had displaced a particular note, or test result, or if he were trying to distract her, to calm her down.

"Did you hear that, Mrs. Arnold?" His gentle question lulled her back to the present, and Jessica willed herself to pay attention.

"Actually, Doctor, I have to admit that I didn't," Jessica said. "I'm sorry – I zoned out for a few minutes."

Dr. Kent waved a hand in acknowledgment.

"Completely understandable," he said, then leaned forward to make eye contact with her. He appeared to be in his late forties and owned a broad smile and dimples that reminded her of actor Eddie Cibrian, who played Nia Long's love interest in the movie *Best Man Holiday*. If she'd been meeting him under different circumstances she'd be sizing him up for a potential blind date with her single sister-in-law. Today, she noted his attributes with little more than passing interest.

"I've been a rheumatologist long enough to know how traumatic receiving a diagnosis like this can be; I'm so sorry," he said. "I'm not saying that your life has to come to a halt; but I hope you will heed the advice I'm offering about medicine, therapy and slowing down. What's going to preserve your health the most is to take extremely good care of yourself – baby yourself at times, if necessary, especially when you're experiencing a flare up.

"It will be easy at times to feel like there's nothing wrong, and like there's no need to rest or take your medicine on a particular day, or to exercise regularly. You'll feel like all this fuss was for nothing. Then the very next day you may be in severe pain, with no energy, and limited ability to move. The most important thing is to recognize that this is a chronic condition, and you have to manage it daily. Keep this in mind, even on your good days, and hopefully you'll have more good days than bad.  Dr. Raymond has started you off with a decent course of meds to follow, but given the aggressiveness of your inflammation today, I'm going to up some of the dosages."

Jessica wanted to run and hide, or cover her ears, as if doing so would prevent the gravity of this situation from invading her life. Instead, she soothed her frazzled nerves by zeroing in on Dr. Kent's melodic baritone. This information was critical and she needed to hear all of it, even though she couldn't quell her rising resentment.

It was so easy for someone else to say what you should be doing and how you should be living; Dr. Kent didn't know about the contracts, speaking gigs and other opportunities she had lined up. This was the year she was supposed to expand her reach with college students and high school seniors, and other prominent clients. Her motivational advice show on Bravo was only going to create more demand. Slowing down was penciled in for two years from now, when she'd told herself she would be established enough to consider starting the family Keith wanted.

Jessica played with the buttons on the tan linen jacket she was wearing over a white blouse, with jeans, today.

"Dr. Kent, I hear you," she said. "But I hope you understand where I am in my life and my career right now. I want to manage the stiffness and the pain; not have it manage me. You know what I mean?"

He gave her a wary look.

"Mrs. Arnold, in order to maintain your health, you're going to have to cut back on traveling and working long hours, and build in more pockets of rest and downtime – at least in the short term.

This is the reality of where you are physically right now. If you push too hard, your body is going to shut down, and you'll have no other choice but to comply."

Jessica's heart sank. "I understand."

Minutes later, after departing from Dr. Kent's office and climbing behind the wheel of her SUV, which was tucked in a quiet corner of the medical center's parking garage, she pounded the steering wheel with her fist and released her frustration in one word. "Ugh!"

What was she supposed to do with those recommendations when she had about a month to pull off the performance of her career?

An hour later, she finally cranked the engine, prepared to drive home and research some guests for her first pilot episode. But just as she was backing out, her favorite satellite R&B radio station eased into a Mary Mary tune. The sound of the gospel group's haunting song *Yesterday* enveloped her, and she shifted the Lexus back into Park, and cried harder.

# eighteen

Jessica loved Carolyn Arnold, but the last person she could handle today was her high- strung mother-in-law.

She and Keith were used to their monthly Sunday visit with Mom Carolyn and Karis, but this weekday dinner invitation had come just two days after their last get-together, and it was falling on the night that she and Keith sometimes met up with two couples in their neighborhood. Plus, she was still drained from meeting with Dr. Kent this morning. She needed to get herself together before Keith made it home.

Her tears had abated, but the despair wouldn't budge. Instead of responding to the emails Tari had forwarded throughout the day, or researching topics for the blog posts that were due soon, she stretched out on the taupe leather sofa in her family room and alternated between sleep, putting a heating pad on her aching knees and hands, staring at the ceiling, and revisiting childhood memories of Granna. At her maternal grandmother's funeral two years ago, she mused how Granna had managed to live the last three-quarters of her life in such a narrow way – focused on little else but her aching, shriveling body and all the things she hadn't been able to do since her early thirties. Seeing Granna so miserable had been one of the factors driving Jessica to embrace a glass half-full attitude, even as a teenager. Now here she was, at a place that technically put her in Granna's shoes, and for the first time, she saw why it had been tempting for Granna to give up and submit to the disease.

*Please, God, help me not do that.*

With Mom Carolyn wanting her and Keith to drive to Muncie, Jessica feared her raw emotions would be on full display. She couldn't handle critiques of her wifely, homemaking skills – or lack thereof - tonight. Not every great wife cooked every meal, cleaned her home without help, or grew her own vegetables, and Jessica wasn't up for the debate, even in jest.

She staunched the flow of mind chatter by turning on the television, and found herself engrossed in a Steve Harvey talk show segment featuring female guests who had read his latest relationship guide. The format of the segment and the manner in which he rendered advice somewhat mirrored how she was planning to keep her show entertaining, while coaching college students and recent college grads how to carve out meaningful lives that included both personal and professional success.

Jessica was still making mental notes about the show's format when Keith appeared in the doorway.

"What are you doing home so early, babe?" Instead of being annoyed by his quiet entrance this time, she was simply happy to see him.

"Maybe I missed you?"

Keith strode to the sofa and leaned over to kiss her, before lifting her feet so he could sit beside her and rest them on his lap. The swift and fluid motion was painful, but she tried not to wince.

"You must be really caught up in that show to not hear me come in," he said. "But it's cool to see you relaxing. Good job!"

He raised his hand for a fist bump, but stopped short when he noticed the electronic heating pad splayed across Jessica's hands, which were resting on her belly. Concern filled his eyes.

"Rough day?"

Jessica nodded, hoping he wouldn't probe too deeply. If she started talking, out would spill the details of today's visit with Dr. Kent, last week's diagnosis from Dr. Raymond, and maybe even the truth about the baby plan she was orchestrating. Who could sit this close to her best friend and not let him into her world? Before she could muster up yet another justification, Keith lobbed an unexpected question.

"Babe, I'm sorry you're hurting, but should that heating pad be resting on your stomach like that? Is that safe for the baby?"

"I- I don't know," Jessica stammered. She slid the heating pad to the floor beside her and turned its dial to the off position.

Keith frowned and fell silent, and she knew he was pondering a nice way to tell her to be more careful.

"Let's ask the doctor about that, okay? I know you've got to do whatever you can to reduce the pain, but don't forget that some of your remedies may have to change until the baby's born."

Jessica nodded. His advice never came across as demanding or self-important, and that was one of the things she loved about him. His easy way made it easy for others to feel good about complying, which was why he was one of the senior managers at Kline-Carter Pharmaceuticals.

"Let me move so you can get comfortable."

Keith kissed her again and shifted to the nearby loveseat, then joined Jessica in watching Steve analyze his guest's dating issues. After a few minutes, he shook his head.

"Aren't you glad you got a good one and don't need to worry about any of that?"

Jessica smirked.

"Umm hmmm. Likewise, buddy!"

Keith had produced a much-needed smile. She wanted to curl up under him and have him cuddle her worries to oblivion. Trouble was, even her husband's loving touch couldn't change her reality; especially since she had created most of the problems weighing on her.

"Your mom called and invited us to dinner, but aren't we supposed to hang out with the crew? Have you talked to Evan or Damian today?"

Keith shrugged.

"Mom went to noon Bible study, so she has the evening free, for a change. That's why she issued the invitation out of the blue," he said. "And yeah, I talked to Ev. He and Autumn can meet us as usual at Mama Carolla's. Brigit can come, but Damian has to work late. We can tell them we have other plans tonight and just meet up next week."

That meant they were going to his mom's. Great. She slowly pushed herself into a sitting position and glanced down at herself, at the faded blue jean dress she slipped into whenever she intended to relax and not leave home. It was comfortable, but not presentable for a visit with the mother-in-law.

"Okay, let me change."

Keith frowned.

"What's wrong with that dress? We're just going to Mom's. Slide on some shoes and we'll head over there in about thirty minutes."

Jessica ignored her still-throbbing right knee and rested a hand on her hip. She looked herself up and down again and gave Keith a frank stare.

"You know good and well that if I walked into Carolyn's house in this faded, flowy dress she'd have a fit," Jessica teased. "Coming up in there dressed like a slob, on the arm of her handsome baby boy? Please. I'll throw on some jeans and a cute top. Won't take me long."

When she reached the doorway she turned toward her husband and saw that he was watching her, his eyes still filled with concern.

"You're moving slow. And you don't seem like yourself. Everything okay?"

In twenty seconds flat a range of emotions raced through her mind. This was her chance to tell him the truth. To come clean. He loved her and would forgive her, and the lie of a miscarriage was so much worse. It would break his heart....

She parted her lips, then hesitated.

*Too much is at stake. Essence has called. The TV contract is signed. You're on the brink of fabulousness....*

There was that temptation again. It won.

Jessica shook her head, both to answer him and clear her mind.

"I feel alright, babe. Pregnant women can be moody, you know.

I'm just tired and a little achy."

That last part slipped out unintentionally, because she had decided to limit her complaints about the arthritis to keep from alarming Keith. But the confession moved him in a surprising way. He approached her with extended arms. She stepped forward, into his embrace, and felt an immediate rush of comfort. No place had ever felt safer, not even the hugs from her dad.

"Tell you what?" Keith said. "I'll call Mom and tell her we can't make it tonight. I'll let the fellas know, too. Let's just stay in and relax together. Deal?"

Still in his arms, Jessica squeezed him tighter in response. He had no idea how grateful she was.

"Sounds good, babe."

Keith towered over her just enough to kiss the top of her head.

"We'll get a few extra outings under our belts before the baby gets here; but we've got to get you well, first. Let me know when you go back to Evangeline for your next prenatal checkup, and to Dr. Raymond to discuss this gout. I'll go with you. We gotta make sure we're doing all the right things to help you get better, sooner rather than later."

Jessica laid her head on his chest without responding. He couldn't know that she had gone to a specialist this morning who confirmed that she was indeed an arthritis sufferer, with some serious inflammation damaging her joints at the moment; and he certainly couldn't go with her to Evangeline's office for a checkup. E. would out her in a minute.

Her heart was pitter-pattering. Looked like she might have to execute the next phase of her plan sooner than she estimated, before Keith began asking more questions or pushing more insistently to visit her doctors. After nine years of marriage, Keith knew her like no one else. If he had the slightest inkling that something was amiss, this fake pregnancy could cost her more than just a chance to become a household name.

# *nineteen*

Sage had been so excited about the Thursday news story of Jessica's pregnancy that she had insisted on coming over to watch with Jessica, and Keith had come home early from work.

The announcement was going to air on the 5 p.m. broadcast, which often served up lighter news, before seguing to Jessica's pre-recorded segment for the week. She had interviewed a local fitness coach on how to form new habits of body and mind and how to make them last. But Hayden's special piece would air first, and Jessica was curious to see if she'd get any reaction, given that many people were commuting home from work around that time.

"Between the thousands who are watching live with us, the video being posted on the station's website and Facebook page within the hour, and general word of mouth, this will be big news all over Indy by 6 p.m.," Sage said.

Keith and Jessica cuddled on their love seat so Sage could have the sofa, and he rubbed her shoulders as the 5 p.m. anchor teased the story right before a commercial break. Sage grinned at Jessica.

"Ready for your life to change?"

Truthfully, the answer right now was a resounding no. But Jessica knew this was one of those moments in life you couldn't take back. She was going to have to find her way forward, and pray that it wouldn't be littered with potholes and other dangers.

Mom Carolyn texted her and Keith simultaneously to let them know that she and Karis were live streaming the newscast on Karis' computer in Muncie; and Paula texted next, to remind Jessica that she and Ron were watching too, and were prepared to send the video link to Bravo when it was posted online.

The final commercial before break faded away, and the 5 p.m. anchor smiled broadly as the camera zoomed in on her.

"Now we have a special treat for you. Two of your favorites featured in one news story – a story that features a sweet surprise. Our lead evening anchor Hayden Greer visited recently with Jessica Arnold, WNVX's go-to source for tips on physical and emotional wellbeing and how to use both to succeed in work and life. Well, Jessica has a new opportunity to practice the messages she preaches due to a big change on her horizon, and she invited Hayden into her home, to help her share the news with all of you."

Jim had filmed the segment at the perfect angles, and Keith grinned at the opening shot of the dining room, and how Jim zoomed in on the cake and the framed ultrasound, before panning out to capture the balloons.

Hayden's voice then filled the segment, before she or Jessica were shown on screen.

"What do balloons and cake and a framed photo have to do with renowned motivational speaker and Indianapolis' favorite encourager, Jessica Arnold? Over the next few months, everything. Jessica usually offers advice to young adults, corporate professionals and others trying to reboot their personal or professional lives, but in the near future she may be adding a new category of clientele – young mothers like herself. That's right – Jessica has some big news, and it's life-changing. "

Jessica cringed when she saw her puffy face and arms on the TV, but at least her jeans helped slenderize her.

"Tell us what we're in store for," Hayden said.

Jessica smiled into the camera, looking as enthusiastic as one would expect, and said brightly, "I'm going to be a mom. You heard it here first."

The family room erupted in applause from Keith and Sage, so Jessica didn't hear Hayden's parting sentiments before ending the segment, but she sat stuck in place, reeling from watching herself boldly declare an untruth.

She felt sick to her stomach. But before she could react, her phone exploding with both calls and texts. Evangeline was calling, but so was her neighbor Brigit, while her friend and neighbor Autumn simply texted her two rows of question marks, coupled with the word "CONGRATS" in all caps.

Paula texted a smiley face, followed by a message from Ron: The Bravo execs will love it. Perfect set up for taping the pilots early then taking a break til spring.

Keith kissed her cheek, then took a call from his mom. He gave Jessica a wink as she went on and on about the segment while he listened.

"I agree, Mom," Keith finally managed to say. "It was a neat way to tell everyone, and we're excited, too. I'll let Jess know you're proud of her."

By now, Sage was on her laptop, checking the online reaction to the story, and grinning from ear to ear.

"When you get a chance, maybe later tonight, go to the Facebook page and see all of the wonderful comments your story is garnering. I told you this would be a hit!"

Jessica maintained her smile, curled up further on the sofa. Keith made his way back over and gave her a high five. Then he peered into her eyes.

"Why are you so nervous about this?"

This man knew her too well. "I'm still in the first seven weeks, babe," Jessica responded. "I just feel really exposed, and I wonder if this was the right thing to do."

He sat next to her and rubbed one of her hands.

"Most everybody who sees it is going to wish you well, and that's a kind gesture you can embrace. Anything less than that, you just block it out. This isn't about caring what the viewers think, anyway. WNVX wanted you to share this sooner rather than later, and the Bravo executives needed to know, too. You did what was right for you and for your family, and that's all that matters. Got it?"

Jessica smiled up at him and wished Sage wasn't working across the room. When their company was gone, she would show him how much she loved him. For now, she prayed that nothing about this imaginary experience she was creating would push his love away.

# twenty

If Keith hadn't insisted on driving to Illinois, Jessica might have missed her first cousin's wedding.

Not only did she awake this morning to aching hands and hips, her feet and ankles were firing on all cylinders, and she didn't know how she would have been able to press the gas pedal for the nearly four-hour drive. She leaned over and kissed his cheek every so often as he drove, to express her gratitude. Her biggest worries now were how to navigate the wedding ceremony at the church and the reception, without limping.

The drive from Indianapolis to Springfield had been sunny and pleasant, giving her and Keith time to chat about all the things uppermost on his mind these days.

"So which of the bedrooms do you think we should turn into the nursery?" he asked. "And what do you think about decorating it? Do you want to do something unisex or wait until we know whether it's a boy or girl?"

Keith focused on the road as he drove, glancing at Jessica occasionally. She kept her eyes fixed forward, on the dark blue VW right in front of them on I-74.

His eager questions filled her with guilt yet again.

"I don't know, babe," she slowly responded. "We've got time to get it all straight."

"Well, what do you think about names? Are you up for a junior?"

Jessica raised an eyebrow. "I thought you weren't a 'junior' kind of guy. Something change your mind?"

Keith shrugged and kept his eyes on the road.

"I don't know; it might be cool to have a son named after me. But I still stand by what I've been saying for years; every child needs his or her own identity; so I'm not stuck on that idea. Have you started thinking about names? Everyone at work has been asking me since they saw your story on the news."

Most mothers-to-be would be doing that, but Jessica had no idea what to say. All of the emails the WNVX news story had yielded from other expectant mothers, who contacted her to congratulate her, share pregnancy tips or share info on the best pregnancy and baby websites, had left her overwhelmed. She had no right to engage in conversations with them about an exciting time in their lives that she couldn't actually relate to, nor wanted to relate to right now. And none of this was fair to her husband.

"I really haven't started thinking about it yet, Keith, but I promise I will. We will – together. Let me get past this achiness and all that first, okay?"

Keith grew quiet, and Jessica kicked herself for making a comment that she knew would trigger a new round of worry for him.

"When do you go back to your doctors? I know you're in a lot of pain, but I really don't want you on all those medicines while you're carrying the baby, Jess. Does Evangeline have any concerns about this affecting the baby? Has she researched whether treatments for gout are harmful?"

Now it was Jessica's turn to fall silent. If she answered him, she'd be telling a whole new set of lies – ones that might be harder to clean up once he eventually learned she had arthritis. But she couldn't *not* answer him.

"You know…" she started speaking while her response was still forming in her mind, and just as she ran out of words, her cell phone chimed.

She held up a finger as a request for Keith to give her a second to answer, then picked up the call on the third ring.

"Hey, Mama, We're about an hour away. What's up?"

"I was just checking. Shiloh, Dayna and I just came up to our hotel room from breakfast and I told them I'd see how far away you are. When you get here, just call me, or text one of your sisters, and we'll come on down and jump in the car."

Since they had flown in and Jessica was driving, they had agreed that she would swoop by their hotel and get them to the ceremony.

Jessica checked the dashboard clock.

"Looks like we'll get there with plenty of time to spare, so Keith and I may come inside for a few minutes."

"Absolutely," Mama said. "We've got a suite, so Keith can take a nap on the sofa if he needs, since he's been driving."

Jessica chuckled.

"It's just about three and a half hours, Mama – maybe four with the traffic. He's not going to be that tired."

Mama sighed. "Is that so? Well, you young people think you're invincible. We'll give him a key in case he wants to come back here and rest during the reception. How about that?"

"That might work," Jessica said. "And we've talked about getting a room and staying overnight, since the reception will last a while. I'll tell him what you've offered, in case he decides he'd like to do that and drive back tonight."

Jessica ended the call and filled him in on Mama's suggestion, surprised at how excited she felt about seeing her family.

She wished she could tell them about all she was dealing with, but they'd never understand – especially Mama and Shiloh, who had a full-time minister husband that required her to serve as First Lady in the church Daddy once pastored. Dayna had everything so together in her health care administrator career and in her marriage to Warren that she'd never be able to relate to Jessica going to such extremes to hold onto her dreams. So she'd just live up to her family label today: superstar, over-achieving baby of the family. Sometimes you really did have to fake it until you made it.

# *twenty-one*

The wedding was absolutely beautiful, and Chloe was a stunning bride. At five feet three, she was the most of petite of their group of seven first cousins, and today she looked like a miniature Barbie doll, heading toward the six feet tall groom – her college sweetheart Marco.

Jessica knew Mama would cry during the ceremony, as was her practice during all nuptials; but she was surprised to feel herself getting misty-eyed. Events like this usually didn't make her mushy, but for some reason today was different. Or maybe some of her emotion was simply stress, she mused.

She had managed to climb the fifteen or so steps that led to the church's sanctuary, but she'd been sweaty by the time she reached the top, and her knees were on fire. Just as she'd learned to do for some of her speaking engagements in recent months, however, she smiled through the pain and kept moving.

Now here she sat, still achy, but glad to be here. Her family didn't get together often because they were all so busy, and unlike Mama and her siblings who had all stayed in Alabama after reaching adulthood, Jessica, her two sisters, and their cousins had scattered around the nation. This spring wedding was a positive reason for a mini-reunion.

A baby near the back of the church squealed, just as the pastor officiating the wedding asked if anyone objected to the vows, and both bride and groom nervously chuckled. Keith smiled, and leaned close to whisper in Jessica's ear.

"Seven or eight more months before we'll be dealing with that, huh?"

Jessica forced a reciprocal smile, then tuned into Chloe and Marco's vows, including their promises to treat each other with utmost respect. Their words were a reminder that she was doing the exact opposite with the man she loved with everything in her.

No one was perfect, and there was no such thing as a perfect marriage; but because of Keith's kind temperament and consistent devotion, Jessica knew what she had was rare. Sitting in this sanctuary on this sacred occasion drove home the truth like nothing else had of how selfish she was. And wrong.

Her motives hadn't changed – she wanted more than anything for her Bravo talk show to take off. But she realized as she watched the love flowing between Chloe and Marco that her pushing so desperately toward her dreams could cost her her own beautiful love story. There was only one thing to do. On Monday she'd call for an appointment with Dr. Raymond and get the wheels in motion. This miscarriage was going to have to happen sooner rather than later.

# twenty-two

Snaking through the crowd of two hundred guests to gain access to the bride and groom was a feat, but Keith and Jessica succeeded. Keith wanted to wish them well before the formal picture-taking extravaganza began.

"Come on to the reception," Chloe urged. "We had a couple of last-minute cancellations; plus, you drove all the way from Indianapolis – you can join us!"

Keith smiled. "Thanks, Chloe...but I think this is supposed to be a mother-daughter outing for Jess and her fam. I'll pass and let the Wilson ladies celebrate with you. Have fun, and congrats again."

He hugged her and Marco before leading Jessica back through the thick crowd, protected by his partial embrace. Jessica appreciated being guided through the throng of family and friends, lessening the risk of people bumping into her tender hands and knees.

The two of them waited on Mama, Dayna, and Shiloh in the foyer of the church, and when the trio eventually appeared, Keith drove all four women to the city's historic Union Station for the reception.

"You ladies enjoy your evening; I'm going to get a room and chill out with some ESPN," he said. "Just call me when you're ready to be picked up."

He peered through the rearview mirror at his backseat passengers.

"I know Jess is going to behave; the rest of you ladies don't go all crazy since you have a designated driver."

Mama, who didn't drink anything stronger than a hot toddy, and only turned to that when she had a severely stubborn cold, chuckled. "You have nothing to worry about, son. We'll behave."

Jessica appreciated his thoughtfulness, but also knew he would much rather catch up on *SportsCenter* than share a table with four cackling women. She kissed him when he hopped out of the SUV and came around to open her door. With his help, she gingerly climbed out of the front passenger seat and prepared to follow the stream of wedding guests inside. Mama and Shiloh walked ahead to catch up with one of Mama's cousins, but Dayna waited for Jessica.

When Keith was gone and they were strolling toward the venue, Dayna lightly placed an arm across Jessica's shoulders and leaned into her.

"Now why did he say he knew you were going to behave, baby sis?" she asked. "Don't you still drink socially? Got some news to share?"

*Great. She would suspect I'm pregnant.*

Jessica decided she wasn't going to expand the circle of people affected by her lies, especially since she was already timing the announcement of a miscarriage. She slowed her already snail's pace and leaned into Dayna's ear.

"I've been dealing with some minor health issues and I'm on some medication that doesn't mix well with alcohol."

Dayna paused and turned toward Jessica.

"Nothing serious, right?"

Jessica hesitated and Dayna touched her arm.

"No need to elaborate if you don't want to, Jessica; I'm not prying. I just hope you're okay."

Jessica relaxed. "It's okay – you're not prying. I brought it up because I thought you had noticed. Doctors have been testing me for a few months to determine the source of some pain in my hands and feet and occasionally other places, trying to rule out gout."

She tried to word it in a way that wasn't a blatant lie....

"Oh my, Jessica. I'm sorry! You sure it's not serious? Gout can be painful."

Dayna was the vice president of a major health care system in Florida; of course she knew about conditions like gout...and arthritis.

"I appreciate your concern, Dayna, but I'll be fine." Jessica gave her eldest sister a light hug – one that was still quite formal for siblings who had grown up in the same home, but a start nonetheless. "Will you please not say anything to Mama or Shiloh? I just want us to have a good time tonight."

Dayna nodded, but clearly was curious.

"You got it. But tell me, how long have you been dealing with this?"

Before she could respond, Mama and Shiloh appeared.

"We've been standing at the registration table for five minutes waiting for you," Mama scolded. "They have seat assignments for tables, and we didn't want to go in without you."

Dayna patted Jessica on the upper back, but didn't say more. They followed Mama inside, where a hostess led them to a table near the dance floor.

*That's a waste*, Jessica thought, then wondered if she'd ever be able to dance again, with the moves she most enjoyed.

She swiveled in her seat and caught Mama gazing at her.

"What?"

"Looks like you've put on weight, dear. Be careful. Gotta do what you did to get Keith, to keep him. Don't be letting yourself go."

Jessica's stomach turned. She tugged at her beaded dress as the heat of embarrassment flushed her face. If her own mother could get a rise out of her so quickly, how would she handle national talk show viewers, who would inevitably say or write worse?

# twenty-three

"So, Jess..." Shiloh coughed into her fist, eyes wide on Mama. "Um...I never got a chance to send you the boys' latest school pictures. Let me show you."

Ever the peacemaking middle sister, Shiloh sliced the awkward silence, and Jessica had never been so grateful to see pics of her nephews. Shiloh pulled up their images on her cell phone.

Lem, now a college sophomore, looked like he'd grown at least an inch.

Shiloh beamed at his photo. "He loves living in Louisiana and is talking about staying in that area after graduation. And can you get over my other three young men?"

Jessica gaped at images of the boys, who had all morphed into handsome teens, hoping that Mama was no longer gaping at her waistline.

"Working as a high school music teacher with both genders has taught me a lot," Shiloh said and chuckled. "Boys don't open up as much as girls. They prefer to eat, sleep, watch sports, play sports and start the routine all over, instead of 'pontificating' about their latest life drama. As long as they're fed, and have clean clothes and a comfortable place to sleep, they don't bother me much. I kind of miss when they were younger and needier."

Dayna smiled. "Sounds like my two young men. Didn't expect

this when I added 'stepmom' to my list of accolades. But Mason and Michael are good boys. Wouldn't trade them for anything. Their independence just frees up more date time for Warren and me."

Shiloh turned toward Jessica. "Guess having no little ones in the nest yet means every night is date night, huh?"

Jessica smirked. "He wishes."

Even Mama chimed in on the laughter at Jessica's soft sarcasm.

"You are a mess," Mama said. "You better keep them date nights, no matter what. Your father and I always went out on Thursday, even if we could only afford to take a picnic dinner to the park, or buy ice cream cones to pair with an evening stroll. It was important."

None of the sisters commented, and Jessica wondered if they, too, were assessing Mama's memories from their own perspectives. Her version of those parental getaways included lingering sadness over a Thursday date night when she was in third grade and scored the lead role in her elementary school play. Mama and Daddy got her there on time and sat on the front row, beaming, as she performed two songs in the opening act. Then they tipped out, to make sure they enjoyed their weekly date. Dayna, who was driving by then, had been responsible for staying until the program ended to bring her baby sister home.

Unsure why a moment so long ago could still evoke such tender emotions, Jessica shifted her focus back to the present and reached for the glass of tea on the table in front of her. Searing pain sliced through her fingers when she sought to grasp the widest portion of the goblet, so she slid them down to grab the stem, hoping no one noticed her wince. Before anyone who might have seen her struggle could ask about it, Jessica took control of the conversation, asking Shiloh about the teen girl she began mentoring in Milwaukee, before returning to Atchity several years ago.

"How is Monica these days? Is she still studying music?"

Shiloh lit up as if she were talking about her own daughter.

"Yes, indeed, and she just landed a prestigious summer

fellowship at Oxford, similar to the one I once received to study in Paris. I'm so, so proud of her. She, her grandmother and her father are doing very well. Her dad got remarried – to a member of our former church that his mother set him up with! I love that family."

"So glad to hear it," Jessica said. "You've been a blessing to all of them, from what I can gather. Hope they're coming again to enjoy Thanksgiving with our fam?"

Shiloh shrugged.

"I think we might lose the bid this year, and in the years to come, since his new wife is from Milwaukee. But I'll let them know you asked about them."

"That is just awesome," Jessica said, before turning her gaze to Mama.

"So, what's going on in Atchity these days?"

As soon as those words breezed across her lips, Jessica wanted to retrieve them. She knew better. An open-ended question like this was an invitation for Mama to launch into a never-ending saga about her favorite subject - members of Riverview Baptist. Nevermind that Daddy retired three years ago and only served as pastor emeritus now; Mama kept up on the latest happenings better than Shiloh, and even sat on the front pew with Shiloh when her husband Randy preached each Sunday. That church and its members were all Mama knew, and all she seemed to truly care about. Jessica and her sisters exchanged wary glances, but Mama, caught up in giving her update, never noticed.

"Well, nothing much, other than Sister Thomas trying to get her grandbaby out of jail for the third time. That young man just won't do right. And old Brother Fleming? He finally retired from the deacon board due to his health. Sister Waynewright's daughter just moved back to town and joined the women's choir..."

Mama chortled on until the wedding planner rapped the side of a wine glass to silence everyone and announce the entrance of the wedding party. Jessica and Dayna exchanged smiles, acknowledging their relief over the interruption.

Five lovely bridesmaids, dressed in different styles and lengths of dresses that were all the same shade of salmon, made their entrance on the arms of the groomsmen, and Jessica decided to join the other guests in rising to give the bride and groom a standing ovation when they made their entrance to Chrisette Michelle's ballad *A Couple of Forevers*. She pushed her chair back from the table, then realized she'd probably need to use it as leverage to lift herself to a standing position. Without looking her way, Dayna extended her forearm for Jessica to anchor and steady herself. A rush of love at a depth she'd never before felt for her sister engulfed her.

She rose to her full height, then leaned into Dayna to give her a light hug. Dayna responded by rubbing her back and using her eyes to tell Jessica all would be okay.

Chloe's and Marco's formal introduction as Mr. and Mrs. yielded cheers, and the couple's first dance, to Ella Fitzgerald's version of "At Last," was a tear-jerker. Everyone at Jessica's table, which included her family and two of Chloe's teaching colleagues, dabbed their moist eyes. Guests' dinner selections of swordfish, filet mignon or roasted chicken were served, followed by the guest DJ's bold invitation to fill the dance floor. When Chloe's dad, Uncle Herb, came over and asked Mama to dance with him, she feigned annoyance, but quickly complied.

"Just one song, now," she said as she rose from the table and smoothed her semi-formal emerald dress. "I can't have Pastor back home hearing that I'm out here being fast."

As she swayed and two-stepped at her own pace to Beyoncé's *Love on Top*, the three sisters snapped pictures with their cell phone cameras and goaded her to stay on the dance floor. She complied and began bopping to a second song. When it was clear that Mama was immersed in her footwork, Shiloh moved her chair closer to Jessica and peered in her eyes.

"So sis, how are you - really? Everything okay?"

Shiloh's concern caught her off guard, and Jessica sought to maintain her composure. "Why? Does something seem wrong?"

Dayna sat back in her seat and turned away from the dance floor, toward Jessica. "Talk to us, Jessica."

"I saw what a challenge it was for you to pick up the glass of tea earlier," Shiloh said, her eyes filled with compassion. "Then when we stood for Chloe's entrance with Marco, it took you a minute to get up. What's going on?"

Jessica knew both of her sisters were purposely steering clear of mentioning the weight gain, since Mama had already put her foot in her mouth. She felt tears forming and willed them away. What was she going to tell them? Plus, this was a celebration, not time for an intervention or pronouncement.

"Well, my exciting news this week is that the talk show Oprah decided to pass on is now being optioned by the Bravo network, and I'm scheduled to shoot three pilot episodes very soon. On top of that, *Essence* magazine wants to do a feature on me, to help promote the show."

Dayna and Shiloh's eyes stretched in awe.

"Look at God's favor!" Shiloh said. "See? Everything works out for good. I know you were so disappointed when the OWN project fell through; but that's life, right? That wasn't meant to work out, so this could. I'm so excited for you, Jess. Congrats."

Jessica felt like she was in fourth grade again, winning a Girl Scout badge. Who knew her sisters' pride over her accomplishments could stir such joy? For the first time in what felt like a long time – if ever - she felt their authentic support, and she appreciated it.

After explaining that shooting the pilot episodes was step one in determining the fate of the show – the step that gave viewers a taste of what to expect, to see if it would be officially picked up - they assured her that she shouldn't worry.

"Oprah knew it was a gem," Dayna said. "Business is just business, Jessica. Other projects came along that happened to have better staying power in her producers' minds at that time; but clearly your show was worthy of airing, since she originally selected it. I'm happy for you, young lady."

Jessica blushed and rolled her eyes at the same time. No matter how much she matured, she was always going to be the baby sister in their eyes. She glanced at her hands, and noticed that her knuckles were slightly swollen, and when she looked up, she saw Dayna and Shiloh gazing at them, too.

"I've been struggling with some health issues lately," she finally responded. "My doctors have been treating me for gout. It's been a challenge, but I'm working my way through it."

The rueful look on both of their faces told her they weren't buying her story, and she didn't blame them. She'd never been a convincing liar, even though she seemed to be developing a penchant for it.

Why couldn't she tell them the truth? What harm would it do to be honest with her sisters and her mother? Jessica didn't have a rational answer, other than the fact that she rarely brought her family into her personal choices or issues, so why start now? Besides, Mama had always been uncomfortable dealing with challenges any deeper than the death of a parishioner from routine causes. Throw in some controversy or some uncomfortable circumstances, or find yourself dealing with a shameful situation, fall from grace or loss of status, and she'd pretend all was well, regardless of the reality staring her in the face. Jessica knew that all too well.

If Mama didn't like the look of the extra weight on Jessica now, what would she think or do if she knew this was just the beginning of arthritis wreaking havoc with Jessica's body? How would she handle the reality that the arthritis that her mother, Granna, suffered from had now attacked her youngest daughter?

"Enough about me; I'm going to bounce back," Jessica said, with a perkiness that sounded forced to her own ears. "Anything noteworthy going on in either of your lives?"

Shiloh leaned in and shook her head. "Nope - nothing. Now, back to you..."

Jessica was surprised by Shiloh's uncharacteristic stubbornness. She wasn't going to let this go.

"We haven't had a history of being close as sisters, but I want you to know I'm here for you, Jessica. I'm so sorry you've been suffering, and managing without our prayers and support. If there's anything I can do, just call. I'm a plane ride away, and I'm willing to take it. Like I said, the boys are older and don't need as much hands-on care as in the past. You've got support, if you want and need it."

Jessica resisted a frown. Where had this olive branch come from? Whatever the source, it meant more than she would have anticipated, and she grew weepy again. She reached over and lightly squeezed Shiloh's hand.

The song ended, and as Mama made her way back to their table, Dayna leaned forward to chime in before she arrived.

"Ditto to everything Shiloh said. Running the hospital means my schedule isn't as flexible as hers, but I can be there if you need me. Just say the word. Gout is serious, Jess. It's painful and uncomfortable, especially for someone who stays on the go, like you. Lower your stress as much as you can, follow your doctor's orders, and don't worry– you are as beautiful as ever. Mama was just being Mama."

Dayna's encouragement lifted her spirits, and Jessica winked at her to acknowledge it.

Mama slid into her seat, grinning as if she'd won the sparkling ball on ABC's hit series *Dancing with the Stars*. Even at nearly seventy years old, she was slaying - maintaining her petite, shapely figure, dyeing her hair her favorite shade of dark brown, keeping her nails manicured and eyebrows waxed. Mama was the complete package, and it wasn't surprising to see older men pause whenever she made an entrance. Mama liked it that way, too, although everyone who knew her had no doubt that her heart and soul were devoted to Daddy.

Even in her senior years, Mama was a hard act to live up to, and Jessica wondered if her sisters had felt as pressured by the effort as she had, growing up. That was the past, though, and she knew she should be thankful for this great evening they were sharing now. Plus, Dayna and Shiloh had extended themselves to her in a way they'd never done before, and their gestures were a salve on Jessica's heart. Even so, she found herself fighting to squelch the persistent question invading her moment of joy: *Why hadn't these two been there all those years ago, when she'd needed them even more?*

# twenty-four

Jessica had every intention of keeping Keith company on the drive back to Indy, but when she awoke, he had driven more than two hours with satellite radio as his companion, and they were just ninety minutes from home.

"I am so sorry, babe," she said as she squirmed in her seat and slowly rotated her neck. "How did that happen?"

He smirked and shook his head.

"I don't know – you tell me. You and the other 'Golden Girls' left the reception early, and I know for a fact that you were in bed and knocked out by nine-forty-five."

Jessica laughed. "You know what my medicine does to me. Besides, I did have a big breakfast this morning. Pancakes are good comfort food. They probably helped me fall asleep once we got going."

"Um hmm," Keith said. "I had a three-stack to your double."

Jessica patted his shoulder. "Thank you for driving me, babe. Guess I couldn't have made this trip without you."

She leaned over and kissed his cheek, and kept kissing it until he blushed.

"There. Got a reaction out of you."

He shook his head again and stole a quick glance at her before returning his eyes to the road. "You are something else. Guess that's why I love your butt."

"Ditto, Mr. Arnold."

She rummaged through her carryall bag on the floor of the passenger seat and pulled out a handwritten draft of the blog post she needed to submit to a Tennessee high school tomorrow about the value in planning for success. As she searched for a pen, she made a mental note to ask Dr. Kent if the new dosages of medicine he'd prescribed were supposed to make her so tired and drowsy. If so, she'd need to switch to something that allowed her to stay awake and work during the day.

Keith, of course, attributed the lethargy to her being pregnant, and was thrilled that she was listening to her body and resting. Every so often he'd take one hand off the steering wheel and rub her slightly pudgy belly.

Against her will, Jessica succumbed to a second nap on the road, but Keith didn't tease her when she awoke this time, as he was steering the SUV into their subdivision. It was just after four p.m., and they were greeted with sidewalk waves from one of their favorite couples, Brigit and Evan Miller, who were walking their schnauzer. Keith reduced his speed and lowered the driver's side window. Jessica peered over his shoulder and waved.

"You guys just getting back from Springfield?" Evan asked as he approached the window and slapped palms with Keith. The greeting between them always made Jessica chuckle. Keith had taught his Caucasian brother-friend the soul shake well – Evan had it down to a T.

Before Keith could respond, Brigit trotted over and leaned around him. "Hey you guys. We missed you at dinner last Wednesday. Are we on this coming week? And by the way, congrats!! Too bad we had to find out on the news!"

Keith glanced at Jessica before responding. "Let's plan for it. And thank you. Jess had a deal with the news station that meant they'd share the news first."

Jessica appreciated Keith covering for her, but the gracious smile Brigit flashed let her know that Brigit's feelings were hurt. She'd have to make it up to her, and to Autumn.

"I understand," Brigit said. "Did you enjoy the wedding?"

Jessica nodded. "It was lovely. How was your weekend?"

Evan shrugged. "Pretty quiet. I stained the deck, and Brigit went into the office for a few hours yesterday. There's always paperwork to catch up on, when you're a CPA."

Jessica checked the time and made a spur of the moment decision.

"How about we get together for dinner tonight, if you guys don't have plans? I don't feel like cooking and Keith has been driving so he probably doesn't either. Want to meet at our usual spot around six-thirty or seven? We can call Autumn and Damian too, to see if they're available."

Brigit shrugged and turned toward her husband.

"I have a roast simmering in the crock pot, but we can always eat that tomorrow. Ev?"

"Works for me," he said. "I haven't talked to Damian today, but Brigit can text Autumn and see what they're up to. Usually we'll see them out walking the baby, but no sign of them today."

Jessica's heart lightened. With the fear and frustration she'd experienced in recent weeks, it felt good to be spontaneous, and even if she was a little tired, being around friends might elevate her energy, and her spirit. Once they got home, she would freshen up and put on a cute top and some makeup.

She hated for Mama's words about her maintaining her looks to keep her husband intrigued to plant a seed of doubt in her spirit, but it had. She also hated for Mama to be somewhat right; remaining attractive to Keith was important, and she would keep it a priority, at least in the ways she could control. Maybe hanging out tonight was just what she needed, to get her mind off her woes. As long her friends didn't know about the supposed pregnancy, there'd be no reason for more complicated lies. She'd be on safe ground, and able to relax – even if only for one night.

# twenty-five

Whenever Brigit made an entrance, double takes were inevitable, and Jessica still enjoyed watching her friend cause a room to fall silent.

It shouldn't have continued to happen at the neighborhood Italian restaurant they often frequented as a group, but her beauty had that effect no matter how often she came around, on men and women alike. Brigit strolled into the cozy, family-owned eatery this evening in the pair of faded blue jeans and the gold and black Purdue T-shirt she had been wearing earlier that day, with her blonde hair pulled back into a ponytail. Even with just a hint of lip gloss and some mascara, she appeared magazine ready, which was appropriate since she was an in-demand makeup artist.

"I need some pointers, girlfriend," Jessica said once Brigit and Evan were seated across the table from her and Keith. "I've got to get ready for an *Essence* magazine interview and photo shoot in the next week or so."

"Get out of here!" Brigit slapped the table, then high-fived Jessica. "For what?"

Evan looked confused. He and his wife had been fast friends with Jessica and Keith since both couples moved into houses two blocks apart on the same day four years ago. But Brigit still seemed to be teaching him some things about black culture, which she became well versed in, among others, during her childhood as an Army brat.

"Babe," she said and stroked Evan's cheek. "*Essence* is as big as *Elle* or *O* Magazine. This is a big deal."

He shrugged, and Brigit waved him away. "Never mind. Just know it's a really big deal."

She turned toward Jessica.

"You do your look every week for the WNVX segment, right? That's always flawless. But when is the photo shoot?"

Jessica took a sip of her soda and smiled at their waitress, Cat, who had placed the diet beverage in front of her without asking.

"Next week I think, but I don't know for sure. The reporter called to schedule the interview for an article that will appear in the September issue. Guess they'll be calling soon about the photos. I always get nervous, no matter how many times I've been profiled, and this is one of the bigger ones, so you know I'm flipping out. Plus, I can always use some tips from a pro like you."

"You got it," Brigit said. "I'll even do your makeup, if you want. Unless your spread is big enough that they're taking care of that, too? We'll figure everything out. Congrats, Jess! "

She stood and reached across the table to give Jessica another high five – this one firm enough to shoot a spike of pain down Jessica's wrist.

Brigit's eyes widened. "You okay?"

Before she could respond, Keith had traded beverages with her, sliding his water with lemon in her direction while raising her diet Coke to his lips, with a slight grin.

"What the–"

She stopped herself mid-question when she remembered that her husband thought she was pregnant.

Jessica gave him the side eye, then took a sip of water through the straw he had already opened and placed in the drink.

Brigit grinned. "That's what you have to do, pregnant lady. Follow Daddy's rules."

Jessica rolled her eyes, and as if on cue, Autumn and Damian Rodgers came sauntering and barreling in. If Brigit's presence and motion were gracefully breathtaking, with her husband Evan serving as her adorable sidekick, this second couple could be described as members of the Kardashian clan driving through the restaurant in a Hummer. Autumn and Damian looked like the odd couple, with his intimidating height and linebacker physique looming over her petit, curvy frame.

Damian gave Keith and Evan hearty pats on the back before taking it down a notch and taking turns with his wife to deliver sisterly hugs to Jessica and Brigit. He pulled out the empty chair near Jessica for his wife to take a seat, then assessed the bread loaves and olive oil, and beverages crowding the table as he plopped down beside her.

"Ya'll drinking baby milk," Damian boomed. "I'm thinking something a little stronger needs to come with my meal."

He laughed at his own joke and reared back in the chair.

Autumn shook her head. "Maybe some baby milk would keep you from acting so silly."

She caught Cat's eye and nodded for the waitress to bring their usual drinks – hot tea for her and a mixed drink for Damian.

"Guess I'm the designated driver tonight," Autumn said, before turning to Jessica and flashing her one-hundred-watt smile. Jessica marveled, as always, at how right down to the flawless chocolate skin and gorgeous eyebrows, this girl resembled actress Meagan Good. If she wanted a different career, she could have been the actress's body double.

"How was the wedding?" Autumn asked. "And since I haven't seen you since the news broke, congrats, mommy-to-be!"

Jessica accepted her congratulatory hug just as a waiter delivered a bubbling dish of lasagna to a diner right across from them.

"Lord, have mercy," Autumn whispered. "I'm salivating over all that gooey goodness."

Damian grinned at her. "You're always salivating, these days."

All eyes swiveled to Autumn, who poked her husband in the side. "Damian!"

He grinned and smoothed his massive hand over his bald head.

"Give it up!" Keith said and pointed from Autumn to Damian.

Autumn narrowed her eyes and poked her husband again. "Might as well tell them now."

She pinched off another piece of the roll she had half consumed.

Jessica's heart was fluttering as she smiled at her feisty friend and waited for her or Damian to utter the announcement she anticipated. Autumn clearly was irritated, but all of them, including Damian, knew she wouldn't stay mad at him for long.

Damian peered at Autumn, as if giving her time to change her mind, and Brigit sat on the edge of her chair, about to burst. When Autumn continued to cast her eyes downward and nibble on her bread, Damian finally turned his attention to the group.

"We're pregnant."

"I knew it!" Brigit said and raised her arms in a cheer. "Alright, now! Congratulations."

She scooted her chair back and trotted over to Autumn and Damian to give them both hugs.

Keith and Evan rose from their seats so they could lean across the table and slap palms with Damian.

"Congrats, man!" Evan said. "My wife has been working me out overtime, but you two must be having a ball, creating contributions to the world's population. You guys have too much time on your hands."

Brigit released Autumn from a hug and blushed. "Ev!"

He shrugged and sat back in his seat, his blue eyes twinkling.

"I'm not complaining; it's been a treat. The Rodgers' big news is our motivation to keep trying."

Jessica leaned over to hug Autumn again.

"I'm gonna get you. Why didn't you tell me?"

Autumn put a hand on her hip. "Why didn't you tell *me*? At least you didn't have to hear my news as part of a general public announcement."

Jessica raised her hands as an admission of guilt, and turned to face the group.

"You guys, I'm really sorry it happened that way. We missed our Wednesday night outing with you and the news story aired the very next day. Plus, I was nervous about how it was going to turn out. If it makes you feel any better, I still haven't told my family."

Brigit frowned.

"Say what?" Damian asked. He looked from Jessica to Keith, as if to verify he had heard her correctly.

Keith shrugged. "I told my people; they're right up the road in Muncie. But her family is in Alabama and Florida and Illinois, so she figured she could buy some time."

Autumn shook her head and folded her arms.

"Have you heard of the internet? Girl, you are wrong. And you were just with them, at the wedding."

They all sat in silence and let the curiousness of Jessica's actions settle, before Evan took the lead in moving the conversation in a less awkward direction.

"Well, however you all are handling this, just know we're happy for you guys," he said, then turned toward Autumn and Damian. "And for you guys, too."

Autumn grinned.

"Thanks, Evan. I'm scared and excited to be taking on two babies, and yeah, this kind of snuck up on us. We weren't planning to make Briana a big sister just yet, but God knows what He's doing."

"Yeah, when you're having fun, life happens, right babe?" Damian leaned in and hugged her around the waist.

"Um hmm," Autumn said, a smirk gracing her face. "I wanted to wait and tell you guys after we passed the first trimester, when the doctors say it's usually safest, but Daddy Damian here has a big mouth. And Jess, we haven't told our parents yet, either. But when he saw you on the news the other day, he said we should film our news too, and send them a video. Copycat."

Jessica chuckled. "Aw, don't be too hard on him – he's didn't meant to let it slip. And I love that idea. You should definitely record your announcement. How far along are you?"

"Nine weeks, and surprisingly no morning sickness," Autumn said.

"That's great," Jessica said. "I'm just a week or so behind you. And your news is safe with me until you're ready to tell the rest of the world."

"We got you," Evan said. "We'll keep it under wraps."

Keith nodded his concurrence and raised his glass of iced tea, which Cat had brought in to replace the water.

"Blessings on this new chapter," he said. "May you be graced with a healthy and happy baby, and with the patience to teach the rest of us everything you learn!"

The group's cheers and laughter filled the restaurant, and other diners craned their necks or turned in their seats to witness the impromptu celebration. When their food arrived a few minutes later, they settled down, and even Brigit, who carefully managed her diet, cleared her plate.

Their evening banter veered in numerous directions over the next few hours, but kept circling back to Damian and Autumn's and Jessica and Keith's life-changing news, and Jessica realized that all of them were fascinated by the journey about to unfold in their close-knit circle. For some odd reason, baby number two made Damian and Autumn seem like bona fide adults, although both were firmly in their mid-thirties and clearly had embraced adult responsibilities for a while. In a way, all three couples were getting a taste of the parenthood journey through the Rodgers' experiences. And while she was happy for them, their news reinforced Jessica's belief that she wasn't ready for the firsthand experience of raising a baby just yet.

The prospect of so much responsibility – for the rest of her life - was frightening. She knew life would never be the same after becoming a parent. When she turned her gaze toward Keith, however, he was beaming, and she could tell that their discussion was only cementing his desire to become a dad.

They made it through dessert without Jessica uttering a word, even as Autumn rattled on about the due date for her baby, potential names, and how much more tired she felt this second time around. For Jessica, desperation was setting in. All she wanted at this point was another two weeks to keep up the ruse, when she'd technically be nine or ten weeks into her pregnancy – right behind Autumn.

Right behind Autumn.

That realization made her heart catapult. Watching their

friend carry a pregnancy to full term while believing he'd lost his child was going to splinter Keith's heart even more. Tears welled in Jessica's eyes as she thought about the pain he was going to suffer, because of her.

Keith grabbed her hand under the table, and she jolted back to the present to find concern filling his eyes. She smiled to reassure him that she was okay, and squelched her tears.

A couple of hours later, on the ride home, Keith opened up.

"It's gonna be cool to go through this pregnancy with Damian and Autumn. She can give you some pointers. Are you as excited as I am?"

Jessica rubbed his cheek, as he steered through their neighborhood, onto their dark, tree-lined street.

"I'm excited, babe," she said. "Probably more nervous than anything, but excited too."

A comfortable silence filled the car for the rest of the drive, as she and Keith returned to their individual thoughts. After pulling his car into the garage and parking, he leaned toward her for a kiss.

"Don't forget to make that doctor's appointment, and give me the date so I can clear my schedule. I want to see my baby move."

Jessica nodded and felt what was becoming a familiar knot of stress fill her abdomen. She could falsify a picture of a baby on ultrasound, but how was she going to get them into an appointment for a live one? Impossible. Jessica forced a smile and asked herself a question she didn't know how she would answer: *How do I get out of this, with my sanity, and Keith's heart, intact?*

# twenty-six

Being a long-time pharmaceutical rep afforded Keith an insider's view of medical office operations, so he didn't question the delay when Jessica informed him that her regularly scheduled follow-up with Dr. Raymond was three weeks away, and they couldn't get in to see her OB/GYN friend Evangeline for an ultrasound for at least two weeks.

Jessica knew his firsthand knowledge of how busy well-regarded doctors stayed would prove she wasn't making excuses. And actually, Jessica's explanation was partially true. She did have an appointment scheduled with Dr. Raymond in three weeks – a follow-up on her second opinion visit with Dr. Kent, so she could shift the medical management of her arthritis to the rheumatologist. To avoid a visit to Evangeline's office, Jessica planned to announce a few days before the anticipated appointment that something had come up with Evangeline, and that she, along with Evangeline's other patients, would need to reschedule.

With that plan in place, Jessica had been fairly calm this week, and she was excited about her interview this morning with *Essence* reporter Londa Collins. Jessica kissed Keith on his way out of the door and got ready to put on her game face – makeup for sure, but more importantly, a smile that didn't waver even if her swollen joints made her want to scream for mercy.

Her knee resembled a large bruised apple by the time she entered the lobby of the downtown Westin, and she was grateful her outfit served as a shield.  Figuring that details about her outfit would find their way into the article, she'd worn a cobalt blue sleeveless blouse, matching slacks, and four-inch silver wedge sandals to make a statement; but now that she had to cross the marble floor of the hotel lobby with a slight limp, the attention her presence garnered turned out to be embarrassing rather than empowering.

She blushed when she passed the concierge and saw him assessing her constricted gate, and she was thankful that her mocha skin masked her flush.

"You need help, ma'am?"

Jessica gifted him with a smile and slowed her pace.  "If you can point me to Shula's that would be great."

He nodded in the direction she was strolling. "The restaurant is at the end of that hall; make a right and you can't miss it."

Jessica followed his instructions, and by the time she paused in front of the hostess station thirty seconds later, she was damp with sweat  - just the look she did not want for this interview. Plus, she was winded from the effort it had taken to walk on her swollen knee. Had she not been so nervous, she might have laughed at her predicament.  The Tylenol she swallowed before struggling to get of the car should kick in soon, she told herself; and if she was going to be effective during this interview, she needed to calm down before the reporter arrived.

"I'm here to meet someone, but I'm not sure she what she looks like," Jessica told the pretty brunette hostess who appeared to be college-age. The petite woman shook her head.

"We have a few couples here this morning, but so far no guests who are dining alone or waiting for someone. Would you like to go ahead and get a table?"

Jessica consented, and the woman led her to the center of the room.

"Actually, can we have a spot in a quiet corner?" she asked, assuming that something more discreet would give her and the reporter some privacy.

The hostess guided Jessica to a booth in an empty section

of the restaurant and waited for her to seat herself. She placed a menu in front of Jessica, and one on the opposite side of the table. By the time she returned to the hostess station near the restaurant's entrance, a striking ebony woman with a regal stance and a short, strawberry-blond afro was waiting there and scanning the dining area. Jessica recognized Londa Collins from the picture that accompanied her regular articles in *Essence* and waved her over.

She shifted in her seat to rise and greet the writer, but just as Londa reached their table, a bullet of pain shot through her knee, immobilizing her. She gasped.

"Are you okay?"

Jessica pulled herself up to her full height and prayed that she was greeting this woman with a smile rather than a grimace. She nodded and extended her hand.

"Londa? Nice to meet you. It's just an old sports injury that sometimes likes to flare."

What else could she say to a reporter who would be taking note of her every word and deed for the next two hours?

"I understand old sports injuries well – I played basketball in high school and college, so I'm a little banged up myself," Londa said.

The two women settled into the booth and ordered coffee. Once they had perused the menus and made their breakfast selections, Londa sat back and smiled at Jessica.

"I hope this doesn't offend you, but has anyone ever told you that you look like actress Malinda Williams? Your hair is longer and you're slightly taller, but you could definitely pass for sisters."

Jessica added cream to her coffee and chuckled.

"I get that all the time! She's not a well-known actress, so it's stunning how often I'm asked when I'm traveling if I'm her, or how someone will bring up the resemblance in casual conversation, just like you did. I'm a fan of her work and I think she's lovely, so hey, if I look like Bird, I'll take that as a compliment," said Jessica, referring to the character Malinda portrayed in the cable TV series *Soul Food,* which aired on Showtime in the early 2000s.

Londa retrieved a miniature digital recorder from her red

designer handbag and held it up.

"I hope you're okay with me recording our chat? It makes it easier to have a conversation, and it's much less intimidating than having me take notes."

"No problem; I appreciate your wanting to be accurate," said Jessica, who often received this request from reporters.

Londa smiled and slid the recorder across the table, positioning it close to Jessica's glass of water.

"Where should we start?" Jessica asked.

Londa whizzed through the usual foundational questions, asking about Jessica's place of birth - *Atchity, Alabama*; siblings - *two older sisters, Dayna and Shiloh*; educational background – *cum laude graduate from Stanford and star on the track team junior and senior year*; and current family status – *no pets, no children, but a handsome and loyal husband named Keith, a native of Muncie, Indiana whom she met through a friend from college.*

"How long have you been married?"

"Nine years," Jessica said, just as a waiter slid plates filled with veggie omelets in front of each of them. "And we dated for two years before that."

She knew what the next question would likely be and had her answer ready.

"Do you two want to become parents someday?"

Jessica delivered a well-honed noncommittal smile before rendering one of her two standard answers. Sometimes she indicated that she preferred to keep her private life personal. Other times, like this morning, she decided to be more candid, calculating that sharing this part of herself would make her more approachable to *Essence* readers, many of whom would probably never understand a woman who lacked the desire to be pregnant and raise children.

Obviously Londa hadn't heard about her recent TV news announcement, and since this article was coming out months from now, Jessica decided to adopt the 'Don't ask; don't tell' policy, and not mention a 'pregnancy' that would be history by that time.

"We'll see what happens," Jessica answered. "My husband has been in grad school for two years and just finished last spring; and honestly, my work has been my like my child. Every time I take the stage and pour into the college students or other young adults I get to encourage, I become invested in wanting them to succeed. My show on Bravo will give me an opportunity to do more of this, one-on-one, with my special guests, while also giving me a chance to help the millions who are watching on TV or online."

Londa took a bite of omelet and seemed to be pondering her follow-up question, but Jessica wasn't expecting the one she received.

"So you're planning to follow in Oprah's footsteps and let your work serve as your child?"

Jessica hesitated. How was she supposed to answer that on the record? First of all, had Ms. Winfrey ever publicly stated that as her choice, or was Londa about to brew a controversy at her expense? Secondly, dedicating herself to her career instead of having kids might be exactly what she had in mind, but Keith didn't need to find out in the latest issue of a national magazine. She knew she needed to mention the WNVX announcement but by the time this issue of the magazine hit news stands, she would have announced her miscarriage. Once again, she shifted into PR mode.

"Of course my husband and I want to start a family... and just a week or so ago, we announced on a local news station that we are expecting. But since I'm only about eight or so weeks along, I'd prefer not to mention the pregnancy in your article, unless you feel it's necessary."

Londa shrugged. "I'll leave that up to you. This piece won't run for another two or three months in the magazine, so you would be in the second trimester at that point. But I can understand the difference between announcing something like that nationally, in print, versus locally, with a specific set of viewers."

Jessica sighed. "Thank you so much. How about we go with this statement, in regard to your question: When the time is right for us, we'll eagerly expand our family. We'll see what life brings; in the meantime, we're continuing to enjoy our time with each other."

Londa nodded and seemed satisfied with that answer. Jessica relaxed and toyed with the grits and the remaining section of omelet on her plate. Between her aching knee, the mini lies she had uttered just twenty minutes into this interview, and her growing concern about saying the wrong thing about Oprah or anyone else, her appetite had faded. She swallowed a sip of lukewarm coffee and smiled again, mentally willing the writer to shift her queries away from her personal life to safer ground – areas where she could tell the whole truth, and nothing but.

# twenty-seven

Jessica's luck seemed to be holding; Londa stopped lobbing hot button questions and turned the conversation to general topics while they polished off breakfast.

When both of their plates were empty, she made a visible switch back to professional mode and her reason for conducting this interview: the recent announcement that Jessica's renown as a motivational speaker and college career coach had helped her land a talk show. Londa revealed that she was also interviewing two other new cable talk show hosts of color for her article – a female comedian who interlaced personal growth messages with humor, and a cancer survivor whose show would help guests facing a crisis find the strength to overcome and fulfill a dream.

"Have you met the other two hosts – Tanya Graves and Dan Brauder?"

Jessica shook her head. "I'm surprised I haven't heard of them, or crossed paths with them on the speaking circuit."

"Me too," Londa said. "All three of you are sharp, high energy and focused. You'd like each other."

Londa pulled an iPad out of her purse and flipped open the red leather case. She gently tapped the screen and scanned it until she found the document she seemed to be looking for. "Want to make sure I cover some of your background. Is it true that you landed a deal to host this very talk show on Oprah's network a few years ago?"

Jessica nudged her plate closer to the edge of the table and leaned forward on her elbows.

"That's the short and sweet version," she said and chuckled. "It was a long process, with many steps and many months of waiting, but yes, that's true. One of my mentors in the National Speakers Association read about a contest in *O* magazine in which she was seeking videos of potential talk show hosts to hire for her network. My friend sent an email to a dozen professional speaker colleagues, including me, challenging us to give this a try, with the idea that if it worked, we'd take our careers to the next level, or at the very least, we'd have some great new videos to use in securing speaking engagements.

"I realized right away that the work I do on the college speaking circuit would be wonderful for a TV audience – for high school students considering career paths, and for college students who haven't heard my live presentations or received my training, and even their parents. I talked with my husband about it and he thought I should give it a try. He even came up with the name for the show  - *Boundless* – to give it a broader focus, so that I wouldn't have to solely target college-oriented young people, and could offer help to any young adult seeking some form of success."

Londa nodded. "I like that."

"Keith used his iPhone to shoot a brief video of me sitting in our kitchen, pitching my idea to Oprah, then I worked with my professional video editor to incorporate clips from several previous speaking engagements. The friends and colleagues I shared it with loved the concept."

"I've seen your audition video – it was inspiring," Londa said. "Thank you!"

Jessica was impressed; Londa had done her homework.

"I have a sense of how the rest of this unfolded; but I'd like to hear the story in your words, so I can quote you in certain places in the article," Londa said. "What happened next?"

Jessica sat back and crossed her arms, journeying back in time, to just over two years ago.

"Well, we submitted the video through Oprah's website as required, then I put it out of my mind, and focused on the obligations I had at the time, and Keith did the same. He's a project manager for a pharmaceutical company and stays pretty busy, so neither of us was keeping tabs on where things stood. I was stunned when I received a call from a producer eight weeks later, informing me that my video had made it into the pool of the top twenty-five candidates. Then I made it to the top ten, and then the top five, which landed me a visit to Harpo Studios in Chicago and included a personal meeting with Ms. Winfrey and the president of her network. When the network called two days later to share the news that I was one of the three winners and would have an opportunity to shoot a three-episode pilot of my talk show, I nearly fainted."

Jessica chuckled at the memory and Londa laughed, too.

"Nearly? I would have passed out for sure," Londa said. "Tell me more about what it means to have the show produced as a pilot."

"Good question. All of it is exciting, but I keep reminding everyone that a pilot is just a trial run. At this stage of the game, it's simply giving viewers an opportunity to see if they like the show, and networks a chance to see if they find promise in the viewership numbers. Although things wound up not working out with OWN, I'm looking forward to seeing whether Bravo TV viewers will lend their support and spread the word. I'll have an opportunity later this summer to shoot three episodes of the talk show, featuring three different guests in need of motivation and guidance, and those three episodes will help determine if there's enough viewership to shoot an entire season."

"So it's not a done deal until that happens?"

"Correct; but whatever happens, I'm thankful to have gotten this far," Jessica said. "I'm a preacher's kid from Atchity, Alabama; who would have thought I'd be doing anything like this? I'm humbled and grateful."

"Tell me more about that?"

Jessica raised an eyebrow. "What do you mean?"

"How did you go from 'PK' to taking the stage yourself, and in some ways, motivating hundreds like your preacher dad?"

Jessica cocked her head to the side. "Hmph, I never looked at the work that my father and I do as being similar; but I guess you're right – we're both informing and encouraging the masses."

"Are you and your dad close?"

There Londa went again, traveling into personal terrain.

Jessica shrugged. "Our relationship is like that of a lot of fathers and daughters – sometimes we understand each other, most of the time we focus on respecting each other, and we continue to love each other, no matter what."

She couldn't tell this woman that she didn't know her dad well enough to be super-close to him, or that she felt like his church members could answer questions about his daily life and his preferences, way better than she. That thought pricked her heart, as it always did, especially in the two years since he'd had a mild heart attack and she feared that her family could lose him.  That scare had proven to her she loved him, no matter what, and she'd rather have a distant dad than no dad at all.

She hoped her convoluted answer satiated Londa's curiosity. Talking about her personal life always drained her, and turning the lens on her parents was all the more taxing. They did their best in raising her and her sisters, and if she had to say so herself, she thought she had turned out pretty well. She just hoped Bravo viewers would agree. Maybe then Mama and Daddy would find a way to appreciate her, too.

# twenty-eight

By the time Londa shut off the recorder and tucked away her pen, she and Jessica were trading opinions about the nation's best annual jazz festivals and about their favorite scenes from ABC's hit series, *Scandal.*

"Add me to the list of women who now want to be Kerry Washington," Jessica declared. Londa raised her hand in agreement. Jessica didn't know what this rapport would mean for the article, but she could tell Londa liked her.

"Now I have to ask: Being a preacher's daughter, you don't have a problem watching *Scandal* with all of its...scandalous scenes?"

Jessica hesitated. "What do you mean? Is that an issue in church circles?"

She realized as soon as she uttered the question that her ignorance about the pulse of the Christian community was a telltale sign that she wasn't an active part of it. Keith would have been able to answer this question better than she, since he served as an usher and Sunday school teacher at Greater View Chapel, the church he'd attended since moving to Indianapolis, right out of college. Jessica accompanied him occasionally, but not enough to feel like the member the church roll indicated she was.

Londa raised an eyebrow, but responded with a comment instead of a question.

"Yes, in some circles, the TV series is regarded as unseemly for Christians to watch because of the sins Kerry Washington's character commits; but I can name at least a dozen ministers I follow on Twitter who post details and share their thoughts about the show every time a new episode airs, so I guess it's more about personal preference, versus a blanket choice for all people of faith."

Londa leaned forward and peered into Jessica's eyes. "I am curious, though, how faith has played a role in your swift rise to success. You're still a young woman, with a lot of opportunities ahead of you and a lot of room to grow. Has faith been a pivotal part of that journey for you?"

Jessica now understood why *Essence* routinely gave this woman plum assignments: she would take you places you'd forgotten were part of your path.

"You know," Jessica said. "I grew up in a black Baptist church in the Deep South, which was firmly rooted in tradition and protocol. My father being the leader meant I grew up learning the rules for being right and righteous, which Scriptures the rules were based on, and how to carry myself in a manner that reflected well on the church, on my parents and on my family as a whole. One of the reasons I chose to attend college on the West Coast was to give myself the space I needed to figure out what those rules meant for me personally and how I wanted to incorporate them in my life, if at all."

Jessica squared her shoulders and peered into Londa's eyes.

"While I value and appreciate my spirituality, I've come to the conclusion that I don't have to be co-dependent with God. And by that, I mean that he has given each of us the free will to choose whether to serve him, and if so, how and when. Honoring God outside of the confines of church and its strict codes of formality and tradition work best for me. So do I pray? Yes, I do. But it's not always a kneel-on-your-knees prayer or even every day; just when I have something I want to say. Do I go to church? On occasion, and when I'm there, I really enjoy it or learn something helpful. But I don't have the desire to go every Sunday for worship service or every Wednesday night for Bible study."

Londa raised an eyebrow, then nodded.

"I went through a similar journey of examining my faith when I was in college," she said. "I've landed in a pretty solid place; and I'm grateful."

Jessica's interest was piqued, but it would be rude to probe, so she didn't.

The waiter arrived with their breakfast check, and Londa slid it from his hand and asked him to standby. She inserted her American Express card into the black bill folder and handed it back to him.

Jessica's palms began to sweat. They'd been sitting here just over two hours; everything was stiff. Would she be able to get up without a struggle? And if she could, would it be at a Frankenstein-like pace? She couldn't allow Londa to see her like that. Jessica retrieved her cell phone from her purse while Londa calculated the tip and signed the meal receipt.

"Hmmm," Jessica said, pretending to scroll through a list of calls. "Looks like I've had a few people trying to reach me while we chatted. I think I'll sit here and listen to their messages before I leave."

Londa began putting away her laptop. "No problem. I'm sure I've had a few come in, too. I'll go back to my room to get some work done. It has been wonderful getting to know you. I'll call you or email you if my editor has questions, and either way, I'll be in touch to confirm which issue of the magazine will feature the article. It's scheduled for September, but if anything changes with the TV pilot launch date or with the magazine's space needs, it could shift."

Jessica nodded.

"Thanks, Londa. It was great meeting you as well, and please thank your editors for me, too."

Jessica waited until she felt enough time had passed for Londa to board the elevator to her room, and then began easing herself out of the booth, at a snail's pace.

This is ridiculous, and I must look ridiculous.

Despite that worry, Jessica tried to appear confident by fixing a smile on her face when reached the edge of the cushioned seat and gripped the back to push herself to a standing position. Then she leaned toward the middle to grab her purse. Once upright again, she began strolling toward the exit and was relieved to realize that the pain in her knee hadn't worsened. She was able to maintain a steady pace through the hotel's parking garage. After sliding behind the wheel of her car and strapping on her seatbelt, she popped another Tylenol and followed it with a swig of the car-temperature bottled water she'd left in the cup holder of her Lexus.

Hopefully she'd be feeling better by the time she made it back to her suburb and stopped at Marsh Supermarket. If not, she'd need to figure out a Plan B for getting the grocery shopping done. Delaney, one of her colleagues on the speaking circuit, often raved about the concierge service she used for purchasing groceries, delivering dry cleaning and taking care of other incidental needs; maybe she needed to give the program a closer look.

That wouldn't help her today, though, and she refused to ride in one of those motorized carts her neighborhood grocery store provided for disabled guests. Jessica also nixed the idea of reaching out to her retired mother-in-law or to her work-from-home buddy and neighbor, Brigit. When she'd been diagnosed with gout in her left ankle in late January during a speaking trip to Virginia, Mom Carolyn and Brigit had joined Keith in worrying her silly.

So then no - no one needed to know that she was suffering again from swelling, pain or a few recent episodes of random stiffness. She simply had to manage this flare up, without making it worse, or embarrassing herself further. She might not have run track since graduating from Stanford more than a decade ago, but her discipline endured. She would push through this health challenge like any good athlete. Her body, and the people around her, just needed to move in the same direction.

# twenty-nine

Jessica eased her car onto the Interstate, pushed her knee pain from her mind and drove in silence, reflecting on the answers she'd given Londa this morning. She thought the interview went well, but one never knew until the finished story was in print. Her cell phone rang, and instead of picking it up, she answered through the speakerphone built into her car's audio system.

"How was the interview with the reporter? Was she nice?"

Tari always seemed to call at the right time. She knew Jessica's schedule so intimately that she could keep better track of Jessica than Keith could sometimes.

"How did you know I was rehashing that this very moment?" Jessica asked and chuckled.

She and Tari seemed to have an intuitive connection. In the three years Tari had worked for her, they'd formed a mutually respectful relationship that extended beyond professional ties, and enhanced their work, because Jessica knew Tari cared about the mission of her business as much as she did, and Tari would do what it took to deliver excellence on her behalf.

"It went well; I'm just anxious to see what kind of angle she's going to take," Jessica said about Londa. "The photographer for the story should be contacting you soon to set up a time for the shoot. Anything else going on?"

Tari shared a few tasks she had taken care of to close the loop on several of Jessica's recent speaking engagements. She also asked for permission to confirm two new ones with colleges in Nebraska and Michigan that wanted her to speak to students during the next school year and also participate in summer workshops.

"Don't forget that I'm going to Alabama for Mother's Day in May, and I'll be filming the episodes for Bravo the entire month of June. If we can plan around those dates, we're good to go, on all requests."

"Yes ma'am; got it," Tari said in a slow, southern drawl that Jessica considered charming. "You decided yet how long you're staying in Atchity when you go home?"

"Just through the weekend, as usual. Keith and I will fly back on Monday morning. Can you order a nice gift for my mother and tell me what you choose?"

Jessica was glad Tari would help her without judging her for not picking a gift herself, or at least offering suggestions. Her life was in overdrive; as much as she could hand off certain tasks to someone else, the more productive she could be in the areas that mattered most. This was the one strategy she reiterated in her speeches and presentations that she practiced often.

"Need me to do anything else today, or for this month?" Tari asked.

"Just make sure we're all set for the TV pilot planning meeting with Ron and Paula next week, and also for my engagement at the University of Indianapolis. I need to know who will meet me at IU when I arrive, and be sure to tell them that Keith will be accompanying me, so they'll need to reserve a seat for him. I'm sure other things will come up, but we're good to go for now. Call or text if you need me."

"Got it. Have a good rest of the day."

"You, too, Tari!"

Jessica turned into the grocery store lot and managed to slip into a parking space near one of the entrances. She planned to prepare a home-cooked meal this evening, which meant she'd have to stand on this knee for quite a while; so any shortcuts she could take in the meantime would be helpful. Hopefully the pain wouldn't ruin her mood, or the romantic evening she had in mind. Joint cream and Ibuprofen didn't go well with low lights and soft music. Knowing Keith, he probably wouldn't complain, but she wasn't going to give him any reason to think it was time to trade her in for a newer model.

She hadn't said anything to him, but she'd been paying attention. Over the past year, several of his colleagues at Kline-Carter Pharmaceutical had dived into what she privately called a second-wives club. Jessica had no plans to allow her husband to become a candidate for membership. So date night was mandatory, achy joints and all.

# thirty

Jessica's quick trip through the grocery store turned into a community relations hour, with shoppers who had seen her baby announcement on WNVX stopping to congratulate her, and even offer advice.

She graciously accepted their warm wishes, hugs and shared excitement, and forgot for a few minutes that she wasn't actually with child.

"You really look great," one woman gushed. "You're beautiful anyway, but even with a little baby weight, you look fabulous."

Bam. There it was. The commentary that had led her down this path in the first place. And yet, the comment hadn't been hurtful or derogatory. She didn't need to be a size 6 to be successful, or beautiful. Would the Bravo execs agree, though?

Jessica thanked the woman for her warm wishes and for viewing her segments.

By the time she finished her tour through the store and packed the groceries in the rear of her SUV, she saw that she'd missed two calls. The next one came through as she was backing out of her parking space at Marsh's, and she tapped the brakes long enough to grab the cell phone from her purse on the passenger seat. Brigit's smiling face graced her smartphone screen, and she picked up quickly so the call would transfer to her car speakers.

"Hey, lady! Whatcha up to?"

"Just checking in, darling," Brigit said, with her usual flair. "You're so big time now, I'm surprised you answered your own phone. How was the *Essence* interview?"

Jessica rolled her eyes and chuckled.

"Big time? Whatever. Guess you got lucky and caught me between errands."

"Well, how did your meeting with the reporter go – are they putting you on the cover?"

"Interview went great, but I doubt I'll make the cover just yet."

The women chitchatted for a while about their workday while Jessica navigated traffic, then the conversation turned to Autumn's baby news.

"Evan and I keep trying... I guess it's going to happen at some point," Brigit said. Her sadness and yearning were palpable, and Jessica was surprised; they hadn't discussed this before.

"I didn't know you were actively trying, B," she said. "Don't worry – it's going to happen when you least expect it. Just relax and enjoy all that practice."

Jessica hoped her friend wouldn't turn the lens on her, but of course she did.

"I hope you're right. I'm the only one in our friend circle still waiting for it to happen. How long did you and Keith try?"

Jessica's voice caught in her throat. She didn't want to lie, but she couldn't tell her friend the shameful truth, either.

Brigit split the silence a few seconds into Jessica's rumination. "You still there?"

"Oh, yeah, sorry about that; I was watching the car in front of me. How long? We weren't actively trying, it just happened."

Brigit was silent for a few minutes before rendering a response filled with sadness.

"Well, that's great. I saw his face the other night when Autumn and Damian shared their news. He's ready to be a dad. Where are you with this?"

Jessica realized she'd been so focused on how her actions would affect her husband that she hadn't considered the fallout from everyone else in their circle. Announcing a pregnancy might strain her ties to Brigit, who was trying, and bring her closer to Autumn. Yet when she faked a miscarriage, the relationships could likely shift in the reverse. What had she done, and what could she say that was noncommittal but wouldn't be revealed as a blatant fib down the road?

"I'm still getting used to the idea of being a mom," Jessica finally responded. "It will definitely slow me down, and that will make Keith happy."

Jessica giggled, and was surprised when Brigit seemed to bristle at her joke.

"And what would be wrong with that?" she asked. "Some women love staying home with their kids. That's what I'm going to do when Evan and I start our family. That's what my mom did."

Jessica sighed. She had put her foot in her mouth once again, sounding like an overzealous career woman instead of a thoughtful, independent wife.

"I was just teasing, B," Jessica said. "As I've mentioned in the past, my mom stayed home to raise my sisters and me, so I know that's a full-time job. What I meant was, having a baby and starting a family will be an adjustment, that's all."

Brigit was silent so long that Jessica thought the call had dropped. "You there?"

"I'm here," Brigit slowly responded. "Just thinking."

"About what?"

"Just that you don't always win at planning out your life to a T, or chasing big dreams, my friend," Brigit said with an uncharacteristic solemnness. "I know you've been an overachiever since kindergarten, but Keith loves you without all the accolades you've been wracking up lately. Maybe you won't decide to be a stay-at-home mom, and that's fine. Maybe all Keith wants is for you to slow down long enough to consider your options, and appreciate the blessings you already have. But I'm not judging you-this is all offered in love! As long as you'll let me babysit for you, and agree to babysit my little angels when the time comes, I'll be in your corner."

Brigit's unsolicited opinion left Jessica feeling queasy. Was her quest to be the best professionally costing her more than she realized? Was that a bigger issue for her husband than the annoying physical ailment she'd been struggling with lately?

If Keith had shared some frustrations with Evan that Brigit knew about, Jessica realized she had more to be worried about than just her elaborate pregnancy scheme. Was Keith less content with their lives than he appeared to be? If that was the case, she needed to do something fast, quick and in a hurry. The miscarriage was going to only make him unhappier; their marriage needed to be in tip-top shape before something like that rocked it.

# *thirty-one*

Jessica and Brigit wrapped up their call just as Jessica reached their subdivision, and she willed the anxiety mushrooming in her spirit to subside.

She knew Keith loved her, and that he appreciated her commitment to her work; he just didn't like that it required so much travel. The thought of scaling back, though, made her panic. If she gave up her work, she'd be giving up who she was. Being onstage, or preparing to be onstage, energized her like nothing else. She scheduled her life around those special moments. What would keep her going if she lost her place on the circuit?

*What will keep you going if you lose your man?*

A knot formed in her gut as that question filled her spirit. It was one she never wanted to have to answer.

Jessica pulled into the garage and made a couple of trips to the car with only a slight hitch to her gate, to retrieve everything she had purchased. She glanced at the digital clock on the microwave while she unpacked her purchases.

It was just one-thirty, and Keith's wouldn't arrive home for work until just after five. That gave her plenty of time to prepare the garlic mashed potatoes and grill the salmon, then take a nap. All she'd have to do right at five was roast the asparagus for a few minutes and warm the rolls she'd picked up from their favorite bakery, along with half a dozen cupcakes.

Jessica paused at the granite island and searching her purse for her bottle of Tylenol. One more dose wouldn't hurt since she was going to be moving about for a while. She headed to the fridge to grab a bottle of water, but did an about face before retrieving it when her cell phone rang. Keith's smiling face filled the screen, and Jessica answered on the second ring.

"Hey hon; what's up?"

"Hi, babe. Just left a meeting with Craig about our sales numbers for the quarter. My team helped increase revenue by twenty-five percent, so they gave me a gift card for Chef Joseph's at The Connoisseur Room. Wanna go out to dinner tonight, to celebrate?"

Jessica glanced at the salmon she'd just rinsed and placed on the broiling rack and the potatoes boiling on the stove.

"Well, I actually was going to surprise you with dinner tonight, since I haven't cooked in a while. I guess I could go ahead and finish my prep work and we could eat it tomorrow...."

Her voice trailed off because she didn't want to finish the sentence, which would have ended with *if* her body behaved and she wasn't in too much pain to move. Keith's long pause was her answer.

"You know what, babe? This is a big deal," Jessica said. "Tell me what time to be ready and I'll put this food aside until tomorrow. I'm proud of you, and you deserve a special night out."

"I won't argue with that," Keith said, and she could envision him leaning back in his leather office chair with a grin lighting up his face. "Can you be ready by 5:30? If so, I'll make our reservation for 6. And don't worry – if you aren't feeling up to cooking tomorrow, I'll prepare the meal for you."

Responses like this were among the reasons she loved him – and why she was willing to do whatever necessary to keep him loving her.

# *thirty-two*

Jessica and Keith agreed that the moment they entered Chef Joseph's, they felt swept into another era. The red-themed restaurant with wood panel walls seemed straight out of the 1920s or '30s, and the lounge area near the baby grand piano was... well, grand. A female singer with smoky eyes and a long, slinky black dress was leaving for a brief intermission as they were seated.

"Maybe we need to fix up the space around our piano like this?" Jessica said and winked at Keith. They didn't own a baby grand, and the black, upright piano they purchased a few years ago merely served as part of their living room décor. Keith had taken lessons during childhood and so had she; but when Shiloh had emerged as the family musician, Jessica had slacked off on practice, until Mama finally relented and allowed her to stop. Keith played every now and then, at Mom Carolyn's insistence, and he was decent, but nothing like the entertainer who was tickling the keyboard tonight. On the rare occasions that Mama or Shiloh visited, they also gave it a good play.

Jessica watched Keith take in the scene before them and could tell he was impressed. They had dressed for the occasion, making their late-week dinner outing a true date night of sorts. He looked dapper in his dark suit jacket and slacks, and she hoped she complimented him well in her sleeveless black sheath.

Despite having a reservation, there was a ten-minute wait to be seated, but Jessica didn't mind; it allowed her to snuggle close to her honey. He draped his arm across her shoulders while they sat on an indoor bench and listened for their last name.

"How was the *Essence* interview this morning?"

Jessica smiled and shrugged.

"I think it went well. The reporter was very personable, and I hope the photographer I'll be working with next week will be as easy to get along with."

Before he could reply with a follow-up question, the hostess ushered them to a table in a far corner of the restaurant. It was softly lit and romantic, and just as Keith pulled out her chair, the pianist and his accompanying singer launched into a mid-tempo, jazzy number that made Jessica want to move to the beat. Their waiter appeared and draped linen napkins across each of their laps before pouring them complimentary glasses of wine and taking their preferred drink orders.

They chatted as they perused the menus, then Jessica ordered grilled swordfish while Keith picked an herb-crusted lamb chop with a French name that he stumbled over, making Jessica giggle.

"What time do you speak to students at UIndy on Tuesday?" Keith asked, using the local nickname for the University of Indianapolis, not far from where they were dining tonight. "If it's between eleven and two, I should still be able to leave work to come and hear you."

Jessica finished chewing before responding.

"I have to be there at 10:30, but I won't speak for another hour. If you arrive by 11 they can seat you. Thanks for coming out, babe. You haven't heard me deliver one of my presentations in a while."

Keith polished off the last of his lamb chops and wiped his mouth with his napkin.

"Figured I'd better do it now before the paparazzi and groupies start following you around. You know you're about to blow up."

Jessica gave him a dismissive wave. "Whatever! I'm sure you'll still have me picking up your clothes from the cleaners, buying the groceries and all of the other 'fabulous' things I currently do."

"Nah, lady. You'll be able to hire help, in a minute," Keith said and they both laughed.

"I could hire help now; I just like to do some things myself, thank you."

He peered at her over the cup of coffee he was now sipping. Their waiter had deftly and without question placed a cup in front of each of them, anticipating their desire; but Jessica nudged hers toward the center of the table, before Keith had a chance to remind her she needed to avoid caffeine.

"Do you think you'll want help when the baby arrives? Maybe a part-time nanny?"

Jessica mustered a smile and a shrug as she gazed into Keith's kind eyes. She recognized a deep longing and hopefulness residing there, and questioned what was wrong with her. Her biggest desire was to make it through the pretense of the next few weeks so she could turn her attention fully to combating the RA and taping the pilots. Maybe the maternal yearning would kick in after the stress of those two big endeavors settled. For now, she and her hubby weren't on the same page, and she wasn't sure there was anything she could do about it.

She thought she had turned off her phone for their romantic evening, but she heard a ping indicating that she had a text, and when she look to Keith for guidance, he nodded. "Go ahead and check it. But if it's one of your girlfriends, get back to them later."

The message from Paula was a gift.

"Yes!"

Her excitement caused Keith to look up from the dessert menu.

"This is Ron Tennyson, my Bravo production guy. We've landed a slate of basketball wives who are also entrepreneurs for one of the first three pilot episodes," she told him. "And Kobe's wife, Vanessa, will come on the show to announce a series of fundraiser teas she's hosting throughout California to help girls who've been caught up in human trafficking."

Keith sat back and smiled. "Wow..."

Jessica winked at him. "Exactly. That's the reaction I'm aiming for with every episode."

She quickly texted Ron a thank you and the "thumbs up" emoji, but switching her phone to silent and tucking it away. In a matter of seconds, she felt rejuvenated, excited and ready for tomorrow. Was this how she was supposed to feel about pregnancy and the baby, too?

# thirty-three

Jessica opened her eyes to familiar aches and pains, but decided she had no reason to fret. Well, maybe just a little, seeing as today she would speak on stage to nearly two thousand students.

Keith would be by her side for the first time in a long time at one of her engagements, and that alone would make the day marvelous. It was nice to have him drive so she could review her speech on the way to UIndy, and she loved walking in on his arm.

The program opened just before noon and flowed as planned. Jessica was in her zone, and everything about her presence allowed her to own the stage. She stood behind a podium, but every now and then would grow expressive and step away just long enough for audience members to admire her burnished gold dress, flawless makeup, and elegant side bun.

The roomful of college juniors and sophomores seemed transfixed by both her beauty and the wisdom she shared about the value of authenticity and focusing on the finish line. She knew her presentation was striking a chord when she saw a row of students near the back of the auditorium furiously scribbling note, and texting or typing notes on their smartphones, while other pockets of students stood watching her, without budging.

"The best gifts you can give to the world are gifts you must first give to yourself: truth and clarity about who you are and what you stand for; a sense of purpose in everything you do, so that you become passionate about doing it well; the willingness to forgive others so you'll receive that same measure of grace, and the courage to say, 'I don't know; I'm sorry; I will do better next time; or give me another chance.' Mastering these four phrases will allow you to soar both personally and professionally, and will help you create a reputation of integrity that you'll want to uphold for yourself and see extend into the next generation of your family – to your children and to your children's children, and to their children. I know that's a lot to think about at this stage of the game - especially when you're trying to pass this semester's classes, or land a summer internship, or find a J-O-B; but if you start with the baby step of being consistent with good habits and positive actions today, you'll eventually see the lasting impact of your choices to be diligent, focused, and honest."

Thunderous applause enveloped the auditorium at those statements, as they had throughout her speech. However, just as the audience settled down again, a shot of pain radiated throughout her left knee, and it took all of her strength not to cry out. Terror crept up Jessica's spine, beneath the veneer of calm and poise she exuded

*Lord, help me.*

That arrow prayer must have worked, Jessica decided, as she managed to keep speaking and even move about a bit behind the podium, to guide the students through a series of PowerPoint slides on a big screen behind her. She delivered her final sentiments to the students, while her mind did double duty, racing to figure out if she could get off the stage without limping or crawling in front of the filled-to-capacity audience. If she didn't come up with a plan, they would be gaping at her in pity in a few minutes.

Jessica fixed her gaze on Keith, who was on her right, in a front row seat.

Please, God, please let him see me staring. Give him a sign that I need him.

"And so, I admonish you again, my young friends, as you complete this semester of your sophomore and junior years as

UIndy Greyhounds, don't just focus on fun during summer break, or on getting a summer 'job'; think strategically about how to use this down time to build a path to a long-term career, in a field that gets you excited, and work on strengthening your professional network. People help people they know and respect; you need to put yourself in positions that allow you to be known, respected, and elevated. I'm rooting for you!"

Jessica continued to lock eyes with Keith as the audience gave her a standing ovation, in which he participated, and when she saw him returning her gaze, she winked while gripping the podium. At first he frowned and appeared confused. Then, as the applause began to fade, he seemed to realize she hadn't moved. He left his seat and trotted up the stairs leading to the stage and strode toward her. The audience fell silent and Jessica leaned into the microphone and smiled.

"This is my handsome husband, Keith, everyone. An alum of your university who helped lead the basketball team to a Final Four matchup! He was able to join me today, and I guess he has decided to escort me off the stage!"

Her quip received cheers, whistles, and more applause. When Keith reached her, he waved at the crowd, then hugged her and whispered in her ear. "You okay?"

"Can't walk. It's my knee," she quickly responded.

He grasped her around the waist and led her offstage, toward the black velvet curtains. He positioned her on the inside of him, blocking her limp from the audience's view.

"Thank God you were here," she said when they were out of view.

He nodded, before squatting to take a look at her knee.

"It's pretty swollen, and it's hot to the touch. We need to get you to Dr. Raymond."

Before Jessica could respond, Dr. Hollins, Dean of the UIndy Honors College, approached them. Keith rose to his full height and shook the administrator's hand.

"Nice to meet you, Mr. Arnold. I've heard so much about you, and we appreciate your alumnus support of the university."

Keith nodded and smiled. Jessica could tell he was growing

impatient with the fact that this small talk was occurring when she didn't feel well.

"Your wife is a dynamic presenter, and we've enjoyed having her talk to our sophomores and juniors every spring. They really benefit from her wisdom."

Dr. Hollins turned toward Jessica.

"You alright, Jessica? You seemed to be limping when you left the stage."

Her heart sank. Some of them had noticed. Not to mention the fact that she'd never required an escort off stage before.

"Yes, I'm fine. My knee is swollen, though, so I must have sprained it at some point. That's why Keith came to my rescue."

Dr. Hollins nodded. "I see; well I'm sure the students were so wound up that they didn't see anything out of the ordinary. Hope you'll be okay. Do you need some help getting to your car?"

"We'll be fine," Keith said. "But thank you for the offer, and thank you for having us. Jessica loves your students."

Dr. Hollins handed Jessica an envelope containing the balance of her fee and shook her hand.

"My assistant saw me trotting back here and asked me to deliver this," he said. "See you next spring?"

"Definitely," Jessica said. "UIndy and these students are right here at home, and I want to keep encouraging them. Give my assistant Tari the dates for next spring when you'd like me to come out, and I'll be here."

Dr. Hollins shook Keith's hand a second time and grinned. "You're my witness – you heard her say it."

He turned toward Jessica and patted her shoulder. "You go on and get that knee checked. And take care of yourself. Again, great job, as usual."

Keith helped Jessica leave via a back hallway, so she could avoid any students who might be waiting to speak with her. She typically chatted with them after her presentation, but this knee pain was fierce; she just didn't feel up to it. Dr. Hollins promised to share her website and email addresses with any students who had hoped to meet her.

Keith wrapped his arm around Jessica's waist again and

boosted her to a standing position. When they reached a side door that led to the visitor parking lot in which Jessica's SUV was located, he paused and kissed her.

"I'm sorry you had all this trouble at the end, babe, but your presentation was excellent. I'm glad I had a chance to hear you; it's been a while, and I see why you're in such demand."

Jessica responded with a hint of a smile – all she could muster as her knee pain increased.

Keith pushed opened the door, and even though they exited the building at a snail's pace, Jessica flinched with each step. When they reached a stone bench on a sidewalk a few feet away, Keith eased her onto the seat.

"You wait here and I'll go get the car."

Jessica nodded. As he strode to a nearby parking lot, she lowered her head and closed her eyes – something she found herself doing more than usual these days, despite the anger at God she'd expressed a month ago.

*Lord, I don't know why you helped me get off that stage, but thank you. Please let this knee behave so I can keep going. While you're at it, can you please just grant a miracle and heal me completely?*

Keith zoomed up a few minutes later and helped her into the passenger seat of his Acura. Once she was buckled in and comfortably positioned, Jessica leaned her head back, closed her eyes, and exhaled.  She felt the car slowing down a few minutes later and opened her eyes just as Keith turned onto the main road outside of campus.

"Where are we going? I usually take the other direction home."

"We're not going home," he said, without looking her way. " I called Dr. Raymond's office, and she can see you in twenty minutes."

"Keith..." Jessica started to protest, but his visible anger silenced her.

"You can't put this off and push through like you always do, Jess. This issue with your knee could be more serious than you think. And you are carrying our baby. You can't play right now. Why do I have to keep reminding you?"

He stole a quick glance at her before returning his attention to the road. Jessica grew nauseous.

How was she going to fix this?

"Why are you afraid to go to the doctor?" Keith asked. "Aren't you more fearful of having something be seriously wrong and letting it linger?"

Jessica hadn't seen Keith this fired up in ages – if ever - and she realized that the frustration boiling over now had been simmering for a while. It didn't seem like a good time to make a confession.

"I think it's just another episode of gout, Keith. Really," Jessica said. "This shouldn't affect ...the baby."

"Oh really? We'll be at the doc's office in twenty minutes and then we'll know. Cause your mom-and-pop diagnoses are no longer sufficient."

Jessica leaned back onto the headrest and closed her eyes again. She was hurting and didn't have the strength to contradict him. Plus, it was clear she needed her doctor's help, since this pain was now interfering with her onstage work.

Jessica hoped that whatever Dr. Raymond said in Keith's presence wouldn't give away the fact that she had already been diagnosed with arthritis, and that she had been placed under the care of a specialist just recently. Plus, Jessica needed to somehow ask for tests to reveal there was no baby - and make it seem like a spontaneous miscarriage had occurred. Her mind raced through the potential scenarios about to unfold, and she felt like raising her hands in surrender.

Keith either could be furious to find out that she learned about the arthritis a month ago and hadn't told him; or he could be upset that she hadn't sought treatment earlier, if she somehow convinced him the diagnosis was being revealed for the first time today; or he could be so devastated by the news that the baby was gone that he blamed her refusal to get to the doctor sooner.

Whatever scenario played out in the next twenty minutes, her husband was not going to be happy with her. Plus, he'd be heartbroken about the miscarriage. Jessica's head began to pound, seemingly matching the rhythm of her throbbing knee.

*Why have I done this?*

She opened her eyes and turned toward Keith to say the one thing that mattered most to her, and that she hoped would continue to matter to her husband.

"I love you, Keith. We can get through anything together, right?"

# thirty-four

Neither Keith nor Jessica spoke as they sat side by side in Dr. Raymond's waiting room, listening for Jessica to be called back for examination.

He seemed lost in worry and frustration; she was lost in worry and desperation. What could she do to get a few minutes alone with Dr. Raymond, before Keith joined her in the back? Before she could brainstorm options, a nurse opened the door that led to the exam rooms and bellowed her name.

"Mrs. Arnold!"

Keith once again encircled her waist with his chiseled arm and helped her to designated area.

The nurse glanced at Jessica's knee and smiled at Keith.

"Good thing you have some help today, huh?"

If she weren't in so much pain and turmoil right now, Jessica would have taken the time to nip the young woman's flirting, with a few choice words. Right now, that was the least of her worries.

The nurse escorted them to a room and asked to see Jessica's knee after they explained what had brought them in today.

"Oh my," she said when she saw that it was swollen to the size of a grapefruit and was hot and tender to the touch. "This is extremely inflamed."

She jotted a few notes for Dr. Raymond and scanned Jessica's file.

"Did you take your medicine this morning?"

Jessica could see Keith's puzzled glance, but she kept her eyes on the nurse.

"I did not," she said. "Guess I was rushing and didn't take them on time. You think that's what caused this?"

Nurse Ella shrugged, but frowned, with disapproving eyes.

"We'll let Dr. Raymond determine all that, but I suspect your inflammation was primed to rage out of control and missing the dosage gave it the start it needed. We'll get you straight. Let me go get her now."

When the nurse was gone, Keith settled in the chair across from the elevated patient table he had helped Jessica climb onto, and peered at her.

"So forgetting to take your gout medicine caused this kind of reaction? That doesn't sound right. Plus, why aren't we in a room where we can see an ultrasound? Won't she check out the baby, too – especially if you have all of this inflammation?"

Jessica knew she had seconds to offer an explanation he would accept, before Dr. Raymond entered.

"Keith, she's not an OB/GYN; she's not specifically checking on the baby. We have to do that at Evangeline's office. Plus, this was an emergency sick visit, for my knee."

He sat back and folded his arms, his square jaw indicating he was still angry. Before Jessica could formulate more, Dr. Raymond lightly knocked on the door and stepped inside.

"Hi Jessica, I'm so sorry you're having trouble."

She approached the table to shake Jessica's hand, but lightly jumped when she saw Keith.

"Oh, hello, sir. You must be the hubby? Jessica talks about you whenever she comes. Dr. Raymond; nice to meet you."

Keith shifted in his seat and extended his hand toward the doctor.

"Hello, Dr. Raymond, Keith Arnold; nice to meet you as well, although not under these circumstances." He nodded toward Jessica.

Dr. Raymond turned back toward Jessica.

"Yes, yes, I agree."

She walked over and slightly lifted Jessica's dress, at the hem, so she could examine her knee. Her eyes grew wide.

"My goodness, young lady. You are in the middle of quite a flare up. We've got to get this under control. This isn't good for your joints. Anything else going on?"

Jessica's heart pounded in her ears, and she had to fight to unstick her tongue from the roof of her dry mouth. "Um...yeah... yes..." she stammered. "Can you just run some bloodwork to make sure everything else is okay?"

Dr. Raymond gave her a quizzical look.

"I haven't had my cycle in a while you know..."

Lord, please let Doc take the hint...

"Ah- " Dr. Raymond said. "Sure, we can run some tests to make sure all is well. In the meantime, we're going to get you a brace for that knee, to keep it stabilized, along with a shot of prednisone and something for the pain. And you have a follow-up scheduled with Dr. Kent, right? You need to be seeing him regularly, especially when your arthritis is flaring up. You can do some serious joint damage and cartilage damage if they go untreated, so you have to take your medicine on time and consistently."

Jessica glanced at Keith, who was leaning forward in his seat and frowning. Dr. Raymond helped Jessica down from the bed, so Jessica could go into the bathroom with a specimen cup. The walk was so quick that Jessica still didn't have time for a private word with the physician, but Dr. Raymond leaned in close to her ear while they walked and made a query: "You want a pregnancy test, right?"

Jessica nodded. This was the only way for Keith to be alerted there was no baby.

A nurse waited for her outside the bathroom, and five minutes later, helped her back into the patient room a few minutes later.

When she and Keith were alone he glared at her.

"What is going on, Jessica. What's all this talk about arthritis, when you've been telling me you have gout? And who is Dr. Kent? Have you been hiding something from me?"

Jessica stared at him and tears welled up in her eyes. She might as well get this part over with, before Dr. Raymond returned.

"Yes, Keith. I'm sorry."

Jessica spoke in hushed tones, her voice quivering.

"I have rheumatoid arthritis. I found out about a month ago, and it was confirmed by Dr. Kent - a rheumatologist at IU Health Center, three weeks ago. I didn't know how to tell you, and I've been so terrified about what this condition will do to me, and to my career... I just, I –"

The pain Keith's eyes reflected ripped her heart, and the pitch of his voice grew higher with each word in his question.

"You mean to tell me you've known this for a while, and even went and sought a second opinion without telling me? Jessica, who... what?"

Before he could say more, there was a light rap at the door and Dr. Raymond returned, looking perplexed.

"Well, where do I start?"

Jessica frowned and sat up straighter. Keith mirrored her actions.

"Is there something wrong?" he asked.

What more could go wrong?

Jessica couldn't fathom more. Dr. Raymond walked over to her medical station in the room and took a seat on the stool positioned there.

"Jessica, Keith, congratulations - you're four weeks pregnant."

Keith's frown deepened.

Jessica's world began to spin. She was...what? One word was missing from Dr. Raymond's declaration – the "not."

"Jessica? You with me?"

Before she could respond, Keith chimed in and spoke directly to Dr. Raymond.

"Dr. Raymond, don't you mean eight weeks? Or nine? How did you come up with four?"

Now it was the physician's turn to frown.

"Not sure what you're getting at, Mr. Arnold, but our tests are pretty accurate in accessing the age of a pregnancy, based on the level of hormone in the urine or blood. Is there some reason you're thinking the estimate is off? We can check again, if that would be helpful, but I believe..."

Dr. Raymond paused and flipped through her chart. Jessica couldn't move or think or speak.

Finally, the doctor found the page she was looking for.

"Yes, here it is. Jessica, is it okay if I share this in your husband's presence? I have to ask, because of the HIPAA privacy laws."

Still numb, Jessica nodded her consent. What good would it do to hide anything now?

Dr. Raymond perused the chart and offered the facts.

"When you were last here, Jessica, about five weeks ago, we ran a battery of tests to diagnose the arthritis and also ruled out pregnancy, so we'd know what kind of meds to prescribe."

She looked from Keith to Jessica, who sat on the patient table, weeping.

"So in answer to your question, yes – I'm sure, because Jessica was not pregnant and there were no pregnancy-related hormone spikes in her blood or urine when we ran those tests. That means our estimate is correct. She is about four weeks along."

Keith closed his eyes, and lowered his head to his chest. Dr. Raymond rose from her swivel stool and approached Jessica.

"Is everything okay? Do you need some water, Jessica?"

Jessica shook her head and tried to regain her composure so she could process Dr. Raymond's words.

"We still need to treat the primary reason you're here today – the inflamed knee. Prednisone is safe to take during pregnancy, but we'll lower the dosage to 30 mg instead of the 60 mg I was planning to give you, in lieu of the dosage you missed this morning, and we'll also change your regular prescription dosage to 30 mg for the time being, until you can get in touch with Dr. Kent for his assessment. That okay?"

Jessica's thoughts were racing and she didn't know how to respond. Pregnant *and* arthritic?

Keith cleared his throat.

"Since it doesn't seem she's going to ask, I will," he said. "There is a baby affected by this now – even if there wasn't one before. Will taking this medicine long-term harm him or her?? And how is this inflammation going to affect the baby?"

Keith's words were choked with emotion, and while Dr. Raymond clearly remained confused, she also sensed that both Jessica and Keith needed to be calmed.

"Okay, let's all take a deep breath," she said, as she stood between the two of them, in the tiny room, and looked from one to the other. She appeared to be waiting for a visible shift in their levels of hysteria, and peered at Jessica with a question in her eyes.

Jessica lowered her head into her hands and once again, began to weep. When she was able to form words, she explained what was happening to Dr. Raymond, without looking her way.

"I didn't tell him about the arthritis."

She heard the doctor stifle a gasp, but ever the professional, Dr. Raymond quickly pressed forward.

"I see," she said. "I'm sorry you've received the news this way, Mr. Arnold – both the news about Jessica's health challenges, and the baby. But this can work out. Plenty of women with arthritis get pregnant and manage to control their chronic ailment and deliver healthy babies. Sometimes, a pregnancy will throw the condition into remission and give the mom a break from the flare-ups and joint pain. I hope that will be the case for Jessica. In the meantime, we do need to treat today's severe flare-up and keep her on meds to maintain her health. The prednisone is safe for the baby in lower dosages, and so are some of the other medications."

She continued to talk to both of them, but paused to peer at Jessica, and Jessica knew she was checking to see if any of this information was sinking in. It was, but only in a fleeting way. Jessica knew she'd need to hear all of this again at some point, but she was still stunned by today's announcement.

She was going to have a baby. And she was nowhere near ready – emotionally, physically, or otherwise.

"I will make a few calls and see if I can score you some appointments this week with Dr. Kent at IU Health, and with your OB/GYN. You two are friends, right?"

Jessica's eyes grew wide. There was no way she could go back to Evangeline and really be pregnant, after Evangeline had scolded her. But Keith answered before she could protest.

"Yes, she and Dr. Atkins are friends, but you can go ahead and make the appointment through your formal channels," he said. "That way we'll be on the official appointment calendar and can have the time we need. I want to make sure my baby is okay."

Jessica flinched at how he said, my baby. Not "our baby."

Dr. Raymond nodded. "I understand. That okay with you, Jessica?"

Jessica nodded. "Yes, it is."

"Okay, while I make those calls to get you worked you in, Nurse Ella will be back to give you a prednisone shot for your knee. All of the other prescriptions you have at home are safe during pregnancy. Be sure to take them as directed and stay on schedule. Your staying healthy is going to be key for the baby to remain healthy."

She slipped out of the room and Jessica stared at the door, afraid to look Keith's way. She felt him glaring at her.

"I'm sorry, Keith. I'm so sorry."

"I'll wait for you in the lobby." And with that, he was gone.

That chilly response sent a shiver up her spine.

Ella entered with the syringe filled with prednisone and with some Tylenol for pain, and Jessica took both the shot and the pills without flinching. No pain could surpass how awful she felt seeing Keith so angry, and devastated, all because of her. If nothing else, what should have been one of the best days of her life would go down in history as the most life changing.

# thirty-five

The half hour ride home was awkward, and stiff with unsaid words.

Jessica was more worried about what would happen when they arrived, though, than she was about the thick silence that had settled between her and Keith. She knew the signs: when he was this angry, he stopped talking and he stopped listening. He maintained his composure and did what he had to do, but she knew he was fuming. What she wasn't sure of was whether Keith would stay or pack his bags. She wouldn't dare ask, for fear of giving him the idea to take off.

Once they were home, he helped her into the house and settled her into bed.

The next thing Jessica knew, he was removing clothes from the dresser drawers and from his section of their walk-in closet, and she felt her breathing go shallow.

"Keith, what are you doing? Where are you going? We have to talk about this!"

He emitted a bark that resembled a dry laugh and glared at her, while making repeated trips from the closet to the chaise lounge near the foot of their bed, to stack the clothes he was removing.

"What's there to talk about? The fact that you pulled off

the best performance of your life when you staged a fake baby announcement? Or the fact that you've been diagnosed with a chronic illness that affects the both of us, and you let me go on thinking for a month that you had gout, when you're popping all kinds of pills to manage arthritis?

"I guess it's a good thing that I wanted to hear you speak today, and that you forgot to take your precious medicine. I might have been left in the dark for who knows how long?"

His pain spewed from his lips, and he began pacing the floor.

"And how do you fake a pregnancy and not produce a baby? What were you going to do - steal one? That's what crazy people do. But you know what? That's what you're acting like – a crazy person. I don't know who you are anymore, Jessica."

Keith paused and glared at her. "The person I married would not do something so selfish and hateful and....devastating."

Jessica couldn't remember the last time she'd seen him this emotional, let alone crying, but tears coursed down his cheeks. She greeted his gaze with sobs. They shook her body all the way to core of her being; but she had no words, because no explanation could make sense of what she had done. The truth finally smacked her square in the gut as she watched Keith's outburst. What was worth all of this? Her career? One she might not have anyway, now that she had two major issues - arthritis *and* a baby on the way.

Was God poking fun at her? Was this the consequence of lying? Whatever the explanation, she could not lose her husband.

"Keith, I am a fool and I was stupid. But please stay and let me explain. Please don't leave me like this. We are going to have a … baby."

She felt horrible saying those words, knowing that she'd uttered them as a lie weeks ago, to this same man, when they were nowhere near true. In fact, if her calculations were correct, this baby had been conceived on the night she shared the news of the fake pregnancy, in a spontaneous moment of tender and gentle intimacy. She pushed aside the shame of that truth and used the only trump card she had left.

"Keith I love you. I need you. This baby needs you. . Please stay and give me a chance to make things right."

Keith sank onto the end of the chaise lounge near their bed and stared at the wall, his back to her. After what seemed like an eternity, he turned toward Jessica, but stared over her shoulder. When she shifted her gaze to see what had his attention, she flinched at the sight of the framed ultrasound on their dresser.

Keith strode over to the picture and chucked it forcefully into the small trashcan adjacent to the dresser.

"You may be the mother of my child, but you are not the same woman I married. I will stay until you're back on your feet and take you to your doctor's appointments so I can hear firsthand what I need to know about our baby's health and well-being. Beyond that, we're through."

He grabbed his clothes from the chaise and headed toward the bedroom door. Without looking back, he left her with instructions: "Text me if you need anything. I'm gone."

# thirty-six

Jessica was grateful for simple favors. At least, thank God, Keith hadn't left her completely.

Even though he didn't come home until 4 a.m., and had chosen to sleep in the guest room when he showed up, he was here, just down the hall if she really needed him.

Jessica had wept all night, until her pillow was too soaked to lay her head on, and this morning, it took her a moment to remember why he wasn't lying next to her. She reached for him soon after opening her eyes, only to find his side of the bed empty and cold. And then, she remembered how her plan to stage a miscarriage had failed - miserably.

Jessica peered down at her stomach and rubbed a sore hand across her belly. Was this really happening? Was a life actually growing inside of her?

It all seemed so surreal, especially after spending the past month faking a pregnancy. A new terror filled her heart: what if she had done something or consumed something that could be harmful to the baby? In keeping up her ruse, she'd been careful under Keith's watchful eye to eat healthier, eliminate caffeine and avoid anything toxic. But had she been that careful on her own? Was this baby really going to be okay if she still consumed the arthritis medications?

The stress of all that had unfolded was smothering. Jessica slowly pulled herself into a sitting position in the bed and instinctively rubbed her swollen knee. It was still hot to the touch, but somewhat less tender.

She looked at her nightstand, preparing to reach for the Tylenol, but hesitated. How could she take anything now without worrying? She was going to have a baby. And she was going to do it with a chronic illness.

*God, please help me. I am scared.*

That was the first prayer to escape, but she knew she needed to be pleading for forgiveness as well. It was the only way she could fix the mess of things she'd made with Keith.

Her stomach rumbled, and as if on cue, Keith pushed open the door and peeked inside. When he saw that she was awake and sitting up, he opened the door all the way with his shoulder, and approached the bed with a breakfast tray.

Any other time, he would have greeted her with a kiss and a flirty comment. But this morning, his eyes looked blood shot, and beneath them were dark half moons. His lips were melded together in a grim line, and he refused to look at her.

"Figured you might be hungry, and you probably need to take your medicine."

Jessica's heart melted. As furious and as hurt as he was, he knew how stiff and sore she was in the mornings, and how it important it was to take her medicine on a full stomach. She reached for one of his hands when he set the tray down beside her on the bed, in the spot that he usually claimed as his own. He flinched and pulled away.

"Don't, Jessica."

"Keith, let me explain."

He turned and walked toward the door, as if he needed to escape.

"I can't hear you right now, Jessica," he said, his back still facing her, on his way out. "I can't believe anything you say. You just need to take whichever medicines the doctor says won't harm our baby, and allow your knee to heal. I'll work from home today, in case you need anything. Just text my cell, since I'll be down in the basement. And…"

Terror seized Jessica's heart at what he might say next, but Keith didn't continue. He kept walking and closed the door slightly behind him.

When he was gone, she glanced at the tray of food and lost what little appetite she had. Her gaze swiveled from her knee, to her stomach to her aching hand. What had she done? And what was going to become of them? This must have been what her Granna went through, with Gramps. The complete wrecking of her life due to issues related to her health, and her resulting negative attitude and behavior.

Suddenly, her big chance to be on national television didn't matter squat, and she really didn't care all that much about local WNVX viewers, either. Neither did her looming photo shoot for *Essence*, her speaking clients nor her reputation matter, or anything beyond where she sat right now: in her beautiful home, with a life growing inside of her, created with the man she desperately loved and didn't want to lose. As she had that thought, Jessica moved to try and climb out of the bed and follow Keith downstairs. But the moment she shifted, the pain that shot through her knee like a bullet told her she wasn't capable. At least not yet.

Tears poured from her eyes as she did the only good thing she could, right now. Force herself to eat enough of the oatmeal and toast on the tray next to her so she could take her medication. She had to get well so she could get out of this bed and save her marriage.

# *thirty-seven*

The weekend was a blur of sleeping, eating, crying, praying and pleading with Keith to let her explain, all to no avail.

He did his husbandly duty by taking care of her needs, then made himself scarce. Jessica wondered if he had told his mother and sister what was going on, or their buddies. Autumn and Brigit had called her several times, but when she didn't pick up, they had resorted to texting her, and she'd sent them a chipper response.

Thanks for checking on me girls. Not feeling well right now, but I'm overall okay. Appreciate your love. Xoxo

That reply had calmed their frantic efforts to reach her, and allowed her to escape the scrutiny she would have endured if they had talked with her by phone and heard the anxiety and fear in her voice.

The weekend of rest paid off, and by Monday morning, Jessica's knee was back to its normal size. She slid on a brace, though, when she dressed for a mid-morning appointment at WNVX, to tape her Thursday motivational segment. Afterwards, Keith would be accompanying her to Dr. Kent's office, so the two could meet.

Keith helped her find something comfortable to wear and even brushed her hair into a sleek ponytail, but the words between them remained few. Once they were settled into his Acura and on the way to the TV station, Jessica lowered the volume on the radio and tried again.

"Keith, we have to talk about this. I need you to hear me out."

He kept his eyes on the road, and fixed his jaw into a firm line that indicated he'd rather just drive. Jessica knew better than to push him, especially while he was behind the wheel. She sucked in a dose of air to keep from releasing the sob nestled at the base of her throat and closed her eyes. The first thing that came to her was one of the same verses she had relied on when this crazy journey began - Psalm 23, which Mama recited out loud any time something was troubling her.

The fact that the words in the scripture were bubbling forth comforted Jessica. For the first time, she was grateful those years of special occasion recitations at church had served a purpose. These words were lodged in her memory bank.

The Lord is my Shepherd, I shall not want …. Yea though I walk through the valley of the shadow of death I will fear no evil; for thou art with me….

Keith stayed in the car while she spent an hour inside the news station, recording her segment. She wasn't as focused as usual and required a few retakes, but the producer who worked with her while Sage was out of the office today, was patient, and both he and Jessica were pleased with the final result – a five minute segment on the healing power of reading, and research proving that fiction and nonfiction reading can reduce stress by nearly 70 percent.

When she returned to the car and slid into the passenger seat, Keith kept his head down, reviewing his pharmaceutical notes. She decided not to interrupt him, and a few minutes later, he started the ignition.

"What's Dr. Kent's address?"

She shared it with him again, then returned to silently reciting the psalm, as he navigated the light traffic. She needed something powerful, something greater than herself to cling to in this despair, and the truths in these verses seemed to be helping right now.

Half an hour later, Keith turned into the parking lot that led to the medical complex they'd be visiting, and drove up to the entrance, so he could drop off Jessica. He put the car in park and strode around to help her out, and over to a nearby bench, where passengers routinely waited for pickup.

"Be right back," he muttered, before driving away to park.

He returned about five minutes later and escorted her into the building and onto the elevator that led to Dr. Kent's sixth floor office. Thankfully, she could maneuver a lot better today than last Thursday.

"Thanks for rescheduling your managerial team meeting today to help me," Jessica told him.

Keith responded without looking her way, and with little expression: "Wouldn't miss it. In fact, I couldn't miss it, in order to be sure I have the truth about what your condition will mean for the baby. That's why I asked Dr. Raymond to go ahead and get us on his schedule, and Evangeline's. By the way, her office called this morning. They can see us late this afternoon."

Jessica winced, both at his coldness toward her, and over the fact that she was going to have to face Evangeline, too.

*The Lord is my shepherd....*

They arrived at Dr. Kent's office, and even though Jessica had been worked into the schedule at the last minute, they didn't have a long wait.

When Dr. Kent entered the patient room, Keith stood and shook his hand. Then Dr. Kent turned toward Jessica with a slight smile.

"What brings you back so soon?"

Out of the corner of her eye, Jessica saw Keith tense up, at the mention of this being a return visit. She cleared her throat.

"Um, Doctor, not only did I have a major flare up in my knee last Thursday, I found out that day that I'm four weeks pregnant."

"Wow-congratulations!" Dr. Kent said and grinned. "This is your first baby, right?"

"Yes; it is." Jessica lowered her eyes, afraid to glance at her husband or the doctor.

"Don't you two worry," Dr. Kent said, seemingly oblivious to the thick-as-butter tension between her and Keith. "I'm going to take care of you, and your baby will be fine. Many women with arthritis get pregnant, and for many of them, the forty-week period of the baby's gestation throws a mother's arthritis into remission. The critical piece here will be for us to carefully decide which medications to give Jessica throughout the pregnancy, and to closely monitor both her reactions and the baby's. You have an OB/GYN already?"

Jessica nodded. "We're seeing her this afternoon."

"Good," Dr. Kent said. "She may also consider referring you to a perinatologist – an OB/GYN who specializes in high risk pregnancies, to make sure that we watch the baby closely. This doesn't mean that your pregnancy is high risk; this is just insuring extra care and attention for you and the baby."

Jessica nodded again, and he paused to check her file.

"I see here that Dr. Raymond gave you a low dose of prednisone last week, which is fine, as well as a low dose of pain medication. All of these are in keeping with what I would have done, knowing that you're pregnant. It will be important for you to schedule an appointment with me every three weeks during the pregnancy, so I can monitor the medication in conjunction with your OB/GYN monitoring the baby's growth and health. Who is your doctor?"

"Evangeline Atkins."

"Yes – I've had patients see her before. They speak very highly of her, so I know you'll be in good hands."

Any other time, Jessica would have grinned at Keith, as they shared the inside knowledge that Evangeline was also like a sister to her. But now, none of that was resonating, or even accurate.

"Any questions?" Dr. Kent asked.

"Yes," Keith said, speaking for the first time since the visit began. "What about the medicine she was taking before we found out she was pregnant? Will that be harmful, too?"

Dr. Kent opened Jessica's file and scanned his notes.

"Typically, we put women of child-bearing years on pregnancy-friendly meds anyway, because you never know what can happen, so we're okay. There are no lurking dangers. We just have to make sure she gets the proper rest and stays stress free and eats well."

Keith smirked and Dr. Kent raised an eyebrow.

"Is this a problem?"

"I haven't checked her calendar lately, but I doubt there's any room in it for rest," Keith said, still avoiding eye contact with Jessica.

Jessica's heart sank. He was right. She had two more Bravo TV episodes to prepare for and film, her weekly WNVX shows to research and record, magazine articles and blog posts to write, not to mention the cocktail party tomorrow tonight to kick off the unveiling of her first pilot episode for Bravo executives. What was she going to do with all of this...stuff? How was she going to fit a pregnancy, let alone a baby, into her hectic life? And was she going to have to do it alone?

Dr. Kent looked from Keith to Jessica and seemed to sense the tension between them. He laid his medical folders on a nearby table and perched himself on the edge of the patient table, on which Jessica sat.

"Look, I've been around the block a few times and I've seen everything. My best advice to you right now, Jessica, is to make your health, and this baby's health, your number one priority. Clear your schedule – completely- for the next two weeks and let your knee heal and any other simmering inflammation in your body settle down. Then ease back into a schedule that has you on the go maybe just once or twice a week."

Jessica's eyes grew wide.

"Again," Dr. Raymond said emphatically. "The baby is a priority, which means your health must take precedence over everything else."

He turned to Keith.

"The best thing you can do is just be there for her, help keep her stress low and remind her that you're in this together."

Keith hung his head, and when he lifted it again, sadness swam in his eyes.

"I used to think that too, Dr. Kent. I guess this will be our big test."

# thirty-eight

For Keith to reveal his doubts so openly to Dr. Kent today and give the rheumatologist an indication that they were having problems erased any lingering doubt she might have had about her marriage being in trouble. She knew there was nothing she could do at this point, but give it time, and keep putting one foot in front of the other. And, as Dr. Kent insisted, rest as much as possible between mandatory steps.

She and Keith had departed from Dr. Kent's office walking in tandem, but with enough space between them for a third person to fit, and Jessica's mind raced with ideas to ease the tension. How she wished she could turn back time to early March, right before the TV production company approached her, and before she learned she might have arthritis. If she had heeded Evangeline's advice after concocting her crazy pregnancy scheme, she wouldn't be living a nightmare right now.

Now here she was, heading to Evangeline's office with Keith, prepared to humbly ask for her help with an actual pregnancy - one that might have been a truly joyful experience had she not marred it with controlling lies. The reality of her actions fueled her tears, and as Keith drove, she began to cry uncontrollably, to the point that she grew embarrassed.

Keith remained aloof. Once he snagged a parking spot in the

complex where Evangeline's medical practice was located, he reached across Jessica to open the glove compartment and retrieve a pack of travel size tissues. He opened the pack and handed her one, which made her weep harder. In the past, he would have reminded her that he hated to see her cry, and he might have kissed her damp cheeks to soothe her. Not today. Jessica was beginning to wonder if this was the beginning of never again.

Ever the gentleman, Keith gave Jessica time to regain her composure, then climbed from behind the driver's seat so he could open her door and help her inside the doctor's office. As soon as she signed in, a nurse called them back, so Jessica could receive an ultrasound before seeing Evangeline.

Jessica lay on the table and tried not to squirm when the nurse squeezed a clear, cold solution onto the lower half of her belly. She had no idea how this woman would hear the baby's heart beating, when her own was so loud. Yet Jessica's biggest fear in this moment was that *she* wouldn't hear her baby's heartbeat, and for the first time since receiving news of her pregnancy four days ago, she realized she didn't want to lose her baby. She wanted to do everything she could and should to avoid a miscarriage.

She glanced at Keith, who sat in a chair near the elevated table on which she was reclining. His head was bowed again, but this time instead of crying, his hands were clasped and he was praying. Jessica doubted the prayers were for her, but just in case they were for the baby, she chimed in with her own silent requests.

*Please, God, let this baby be healthy in every way. And fix things between Keith and me. Please, Lord, fix it.*

Minutes later, the whooshing sounds of fluid moving through her abdomen and uterus greeted Jessica's ears. And then, there it was: the tiny sac, with the tiny shape inside it, with a moving, pulsing heartbeat.

This was real – not a picture she had pulled off of someone else's Facebook page. This was the child growing inside her body, with her DNA and her husband's. With a single glance at the amorphous figure, she fell in love.

"Everything looks good, Mom and Dad," the nurse said. "I'll get Dr. Atkins for you, so she can also take a look and chat with you."

A smile spread through Jessica's body and quickly reached her lips. She glanced at Keith and witnessed a similar reaction. Pure joy - greater than what she'd experienced when she had staged the baby announcement - canvassed his whole being. This man had waited long enough to become a father, and she could tell by gazing at him that he was ready. Jessica extended her hand to him, and hesitantly, he grasped it and held on, while still peering at the ultrasound screen. Her shoulders relaxed, and she finally exhaled, and allowed herself to hope that maybe they could make it through this storm.

"Meet your baby, Keith," she said softly. "For real this time."

He squeezed her hand, but didn't speak.

Evangeline poked her head in the room, looking perplexed.

"It *is* you," she said when she stepped inside. She paused by the door, taking in the scene before her, then locked eyes with Jessica, and Jessica knew exactly what she was thinking: When they had last seen each other, Jessica was in this office begging for a fake ultrasound, with plans to keep life moving so her dreams could do the same. Now here she was viewing a real one, with her husband in tow?

Jessica gifted Evangeline with a wry smile.

"Hey, E. Looks like God got the last laugh."

# thirty-nine

Jessica's attempt to lighten the awkward moment flat lined.

Evangeline didn't crack a smile, and the usual warmth between the two long-time friends was uncomfortably absent. She approached Keith and gave him a light hug, then looked into his eyes.

"Congrats, Keith; you doing okay?"

"I'm glad to see my baby's heartbeat, Evangeline, to know that it's real. Otherwise, under the circumstances, I'm doing okay. You gonna take care of the baby...and Jessica? Will the arthritis cause major complications?"

Jessica could tell that Evangeline seemed surprised Keith knew about the arthritis, but she remained professional. She nodded and patted his shoulder.

"You know I'll do my very best, Keith. And don't worry – I've had numerous patients with arthritis, and other autoimmune conditions, deliver healthy babies. You all should be fine."

Then she turned toward Jessica, who was sitting upright on the patient table, waiting to be acknowledged.

"Congrats, Jessica. I know this must be a surprise, but I hope it's a welcome one."

Her formal tone pierced Jessica's heart. She briefly lowered her eyes, before defiantly looking into Evangeline's. Even though

her friend had no idea of the extent of damage she had done –
going ahead and faking a pregnancy against Evangeline's advice –
she knew Evangeline could sense that all wasn't on the up and up,
and Evangeline didn't trust her motives.

"Yes, this is a surprise, Evangeline," Jessica said, dropping the
nickname she'd used for her friend since their college days. "But as
I said, God must have a sense of humor. He knows what He's doing
even if we think something different should be in the cards. I'm
glad to hear you can take care of us, and that the baby should be
okay."

Evangeline paused and peered at Jessica, then walked a little
closer.

"So…there are a few things you're going to have to do
differently now – at least until the baby is born."

Jessica's heart began to race. Dr. Kent and Dr. Raymond both
had mentioned an increase in her downtime; did Evangeline have
more in mind?

"What do you mean?"

"Well, at thirty-four, your age puts you on the cusp of being a
high-risk pregnancy anyway, when additional tests and monitoring
are required. Having a chronic health condition also lands you
in this category, so we'll be running a battery of tests today, and
occasionally throughout the pregnancy, and seeing you every
two weeks to make sure you and the baby are faring well. One of
those visits will be with me, and the other will likely be with Dr.
Dawes, a perinatologist in our practice who helps me insure the
health of moms and babies who need to be monitored closely. This
also means you are going to have to cut way back on your hectic
schedule."

Evangeline paused again, clearly waiting to see how Jessica
would handle this declaration.

Jessica shrugged at hearing what had become a physician-to-
Jessica refrain. She was so numb from all that had unfolded in the
past few days, that nothing fazed her right now. She'd deal with
whatever she had to deal with career-wise as it came up. For now,
the outside world wasn't on her radar. This was her family, and this
was her focus.

"I'm sure Dr. Kent explained that some pregnant women's arthritis goes into remission, and they have no pain or joint and bone issues during the pregnancy," Evangeline continued. "I hope you fall in that number. But even if you do, you'll need to maintain a low-impact exercise regimen, such as walking, and get a tremendous amount of rest, because your body is now working for two. You'll also have to reduce stress. So...some of those big projects you have mind... may just have to be put on hold. You with me?"

Evangeline stared at Jessica, and Jessica knew she was making a veiled reference to the talk show TV pilot for Bravo. She noticed Keith glaring at her, and she felt like she was being attacked by their laser-beamed judgment.

At one time both of them had been her biggest cheerleaders, nudging her on to excellence, and to great things. This afternoon, however, they both seemed fed up, and maybe even disappointed, at what she had become.

How had this happened?

"Any questions – from either of you?" Evangeline asked, turning back and forth between Jessica and Keith.

Keith piped up first.

"Does she need to cut out travel, as well? I think she has some out of town engagements in the next couple of months."

Jessica sat up straighter and frowned.

"Yes, I do have a few contractual obligations to speak outside of Indy – two next month and a couple the month after that. Will that be a problem?"

Evangeline raised her palms.

"Let's not get ahead of ourselves. I don't see any reason why you can't honor those commitments, as long as you don't have extremely lengthy flights planned, and as long as you get plenty of rest before you go and plenty when you get back. So whereas in the past you might have had a busy week of travel and speaking, for now you need to have a few days of downtime built around your speeches and training sessions, and even your segments for the local TV station. This will change the frequency of when and where you go, but hopefully it's just temporary. We'll just take this week by week, and day by day, if we need to."

Jessica was relieved that Evangeline didn't seem to be nixing the talk show, but she decided not to bring it up specifically.

"Thank you for fitting us in, E – Evangeline," she said, "And thanks for walking through this pregnancy with us. I admit it – this took me completely by surprise."

That revelation slipped from her lips before she thought about how Keith would react to hearing her confirm that her plan had gone awry. She glanced at him, and his eyes narrowed before he looked away from her.

"I didn't plan this, but it is a blessing," Jessica continued. "I'm going to embrace it."

Evangeline's eyes softened, and she rubbed Jessica's arm.

"Good to hear, Jess. Good to hear."

But Keith kept his back to her. His words of support were what she needed, but his silence spoke volumes.

# forty

Two hours later, an exhausted Jessica finally prepared to leave Evangeline's office, after enduring a battery of tests that ensured she and the baby were healthy and thriving so far.

Evangeline had warmed up during the course of the afternoon, and she gave Jessica a light hug as Jessica and Keith prepared to leave.

"Call me if you're up to doing dinner one evening, soon, Jess. We need to catch up. And take care of yourself, okay?"

Jessica's heart lifted.

"Okay, friend, and yes, Doctor."

Keith navigated the traffic to get to the lane he desired, then glanced at her.

"Want to get a bite to eat somewhere, or just grab some takeout?"

Usually she loved having dinner out with her husband and took every opportunity to enjoy a date night with him, even if it were just a weekday meal. But today she was emotionally spent; plus, if he were willing to sit across the table from her to share a meal, she wanted to use that time wisely, and take the opportunity to explain herself, and the stupid lies she'd told to get them in this predicament.

"Mind if we just do carryout? What do you have a taste for?"

He shrugged.

"Whatever is fine with me. Want to call it in?"

She reached into her purse to retrieve her cell phone, and her fingers grazed the ultrasound pictures she'd tucked there a few hours ago. The real ultrasounds. Of her baby.

This new reality was still settling in her spirit. She wanted to be excited, but there was so much to fear instead – from how her husband had discovered her deceit and pregnancy, to what this would mean for her career, to whether she had the chops to be a decent parent. Jessica just didn't know.

This is how single pregnant women, or pregnant teens must feel, she surmised.

But for her, it was a ridiculous predicament to find herself in. Here she was, a grown woman who had been married for years, feeling scared, ashamed, and inadequate.

It would have been different, if you had handled things differently. Lies yield consequences.

Jessica quieted the persistent whispers invading her spirit by dialing the number for Kountry Kitchen, a soul food restaurant that Keith loved. He'd had such a rough day that something even as simple as a meal needed to be focused on what he enjoyed.

"May I get an order of smothered pork chops and gravy, collard greens and yams?"

Keith kept his eyes on the road and didn't say anything, but his jaw relaxed, and she could tell he was surprised when he heard her ordering his favorite dishes. When he reached the exit he would need to take off the Interstate to reach the restaurant on College Avenue, he did so without a question.

"Be right back," he said when he pulled up to the curb alongside the restaurant.

Jessica knew from experience that would be about a ten or fifteen minute wait, even for carryout, because this place was always hopping. She turned the key in the ignition to shut off the engine so the car wouldn't be idling, then she pressed the button on the radio that would allow it to continue playing. Adjusting the volume filled the car with the melodious sounds of India Arie, singing the soothing lyrics to one of her tunes, *Get It Together.*

As the neo-soul artist sang about healing one's heart to heal one's body, and forgiving those who hurt you and accepting oneself, Jessica got the message loud and clear.  Humph. God was always speaking. However, and whenever he wanted.

# forty-one

Jessica looked across the dinner table at her handsome husband and wanted to weep.

Keith's wan expression and sad eyes crushed her, and she was ashamed for being the source of his unnecessary pain.

"Keith…I…I need to talk to you." She wondered if he could hear her heart beating; it rang in her own ears.

Keith's eyes remained fixed on his plate, and he took a few more bites before shrugging.

"Say what you gotta say. Don't know if I'll believe any of it, but go ahead."

Jessica wanted to bang the table and demand that he look at her. Instead, she slumped in her chair and sighed. After what she'd put him through, she had no right to make any demands.

*I. cannot. lose. you.*

Those words screamed through her mind, but she didn't utter them aloud, as much as she wanted to. After everything they'd endured the past few days, she doubted he would care, let alone believe her.

She peered at him while the food on her plate grew cold. Kountry Kitchen's macaroni and cheese, greens and cornbread usually beckoned her, but tonight she really didn't want to eat. She knew Keith would say something if she didn't, though. She was eating for two now, and having her do that right mattered to him, even if she didn't.

Keith took a few more bites, before pushing away his plate. He reared back in his chair and folded his arms.

"Have at it," he said and shrugged. "What you got to say?"

She wished she could simply say *I love you* and have everything go back to normal between them. But for this situation to get resolved – and soon – she had to try and explain.

Jessica laid down her fork and pressed the palms of her hands together in front of her, in a teepee formation. She leaned forward and peered into her husband's stone face.

"Keith, I have to start with I'm very, very sorry about all of this. I realize now that I was being selfish and just plain stupid – trying to fix everything to fit the way I wanted, and I was wrong. I was dead wrong."

She sat back and sighed.

"The week you went to Phoenix for your company conference turned out to be the week of my follow-up appointment with Dr. Raymond regarding all of the pain and aches I'd been having, and this time she finally felt like she could give me a diagnosis. I just knew she was going to confirm that it was gout and tell me to continue the current course of treatment. But she said the tests showed conclusively that it was early onset rheumatoid arthritis."

Keith frowned.

"They have a test that can diagnose arthritis?"

Now it was her turn to be exasperated. He worked in pharmaceutical sales and was in and out of doctor's offices and didn't know this? But she knew she had a lot of nerve. Plus, his job wasn't selling arthritis-related drugs; he could certainly and legitimately not know.

"Yes. It can identify spikes in certain markers in the bloodstream, or something technical like that. It can tell you how much inflammation is in the body and how aggressive an arthritic flare up is going to be. So Dr. Raymond went through a whole spiel, telling me I had arthritis and how it was going to affect me the rest of my life and all that, and I...I just wasn't ready to hear it, Keith. I couldn't bear that at my age I was going to be crippled like my

Granna. I don't want to be angry and unable to function like she was all those years."

A flicker of recognition filled Keith's eyes, and Jessica knew he remembered how difficult her grandmother had been, even though she loved her family.

"I didn't want to be like that, Keith.  Or lose you, like she lost my grandfather. So instead of telling you right away and getting you all upset I decided to get a second opinion as soon as possible, so I'd know if this were true or not."

Keith stared at her. "But you knew it was. This explains everything. Gout wouldn't have lasted this long. And your issues would have been more contained. Your pain floats around now, to different parts of your body."

Anger surged in Jessica's chest over his agreement with the diagnosis, but she quelled it. She couldn't pick a fight with him over something that was definitively true.

"Long story short, a day after the diagnosis, Tari gets a call out of the blue from a production company that has been watching my work and somehow learned about the show I had pitched to the OWN network. And, well...this is the part of the story I did share with you. As you know, since my pilot was never picked up by OWN, Ron and Paula Tennyson wanted work with me and pitch it to Bravo. I called you the day we got the green light to move forward, remember, while you were at the conference?

"You may remember that Sage went with me to the meeting, and over lunch afterward she mentioned that viewers on WNVX had begun to comment on my weight, and the extra pounds might be an issue for the Brave execs long term. I panicked, and the lie started there, with me telling her I was pregnant.

"Well, you know Sage. She took it to the next level and insisted that we do a news story about it, both to help with ratings for my weekly segment, and to explain my weight gain. I went along with it, because I feared that taking the RA medicine was only going to make me gain more, and I needed an explanation that wouldn't get me fired from both gigs."

She paused and saw that her explanation was resonating with Keith.

"So you staged the dining room for the TV station, not for me?"

Jessica nodded and exhaled. "Exactly. You weren't supposed to come home until the next day. I would have cleaned it up by then, and had your favorite meal ready for you instead."

She lowered her eyes and uttered a silent prayer that he would believe her, because this as the truth.

"But why didn't you tell me that night what was going on, Jessica? It's one thing to lie to the general public – which in and of itself was crazy; but it's another to lie to your husband. Why didn't you just come clean?"

That was the question she'd been asking herself, too. No excuse was worthwhile, so she continued with the truth.

"I was, drowning in great news and terrible news at the same time. I knew if I told you about the arthritis diagnosis you'd make me slow down and sit at home, when that was the last thing I needed to be doing for this show to launch successfully. And the show... Wow. This is my second chance, Keith, to prove myself *to* myself and to the world that I'm really about something."

Keith frowned again. "You're about something? What does that mean? You've been 'about' something for as long as I've known you. You're an extraordinary, internationally sought after speaker. You change the course of lives with the messages you deliver and with your trainings. Why wouldn't they want to produce a show with you? But I'm still waiting to hear why, in all of this, you decided to lie to me about being pregnant, Jessica. With our first child. Explain that one."

She raised her palms in surrender, knowing that nothing she was about to say would really make a difference.

"You may not be able to tell because you see me every day, but I feel like I'm ballooning by the day, Keith, taking these steroids. I knew I couldn't tell the production company I had been diagnosed with a chronic illness, but I still had to explain the weight gain and make it plausible enough to not lose the weight right away... This was all I could come up with."

"So you lied to me, too?"

Oh, the pain in Keith's voice. She had no worthwhile response.

"I'm talking to you, Jess. Why? And why so elaborately done? Were you purposely trying to hurt me?"

"No, Keith, no! You walked in on the staging and I didn't have the courage to tell you I was a liar."

"So you just...lied even more? So you could go on and do what you wanted. How were you going to explain the lack of a baby in a few months?"

Jessica lowered her head and whispered the truth. "A miscarriage."

Keith sat back with a thud. His eyes slowly stretched, and Jessica realized he was processing how the visit to Dr. Raymond's office had unfolded last week.

"What the... So you were truly shocked to find out you were having a baby. You thought Dr. Raymond was going to come back and say everything was normal. Then you were going to act upset and tell me about the so-called miscarriage, weren't you?"

Keith pushed his chair back from the table and stood up.

"You know what? You can take your trifling lies all the way to TV stardom, Jessica Arnold Wilson. Enjoy the ride. By yourself."

Keith turned the corner and disappeared.

Jessica leapt up to follow him, but was stopped by the words that trailed his footsteps.

"Get your mama or your sisters or your girlfriends on the phone," he called to her as she heard him pound the stairwell on his way up. "Somebody needs to come stay with you for a while, cause in a few days, I'm outta here."

# forty-two

Keith meant it.

Jessica had called Ron and Paula immediately to cancel the looming Bravo TV pilot cocktail party, because she knew her husband wouldn't come. It wasn't a lie, either, when the excuse she gave them was bed rest, per doctor's orders.

And three days later, after she and Keith sat awkwardly through church service with his mother and sister, he stood in front of the bedroom mirror, removed his tie and made the announcement she'd been dreading.

"Since you're so good at making up stories, I guess you can tell folks I'm gone on a business trip for the next few weeks. I'm actually going to be across town, a little closer to the office."

Jessica had just plopped on the edge of their bed to slide out of her low heels. Her breath caught in her throat.

"What are you talking about? Stay across town? A business trip? You don't have another one until the next quarter."

She knew his calendar better than he did. Keith paused with his fingers grasping the knot of the tie and turned toward her.

"You're right – I don't. But I can't stay here like this, Jessica. I need some time to myself. I don't know if I can trust you anymore after what you've done. I just don't know who you are anymore. I gotta take some time to clear my head. I know you can't be here alone, with your arthritis and being pregnant, so I'll make up the story about the conference, and you can invite whoever you want to stay here with you, without them being all up in our business."

Jessica's body went cold.

"You're leaving me?"

Her voice sounded pitiful to her own ears as she whispered the question, not believing those words were escaping her lips.

Keith didn't answer, but he strode to the walk-in closet closest to his side of the bed and retrieved a small black suitcase. He laid it on the bed and began packing his socks and underwear.

A wave of nausea hit Jessica like a tsunami. She placed her hand protectively over her plump belly and tried to steady her voice, so she could speak a little louder this time.

"You're leaving me, Keith? And our baby?"

He paused, with his back to her, then resumed packing, without responding. A few minutes later, he delivered an answer that felt like a slap across the face.

"I'll never desert my child, Jessica – no matter what happens to us."

# forty-three

He was gone by dinnertime, and Jessica was a weeping mess. He had texted her the name and number of the downtown hotel he was staying in for a few days, and other info she didn't want.

At the Hyatt Place through Friday, then moving to Jason's. Housesitting for 14 days while he's in Europe. Take care.

That was it? Take care?

Jessica crumpled into a ball on the floor. She had driven away her heart. Nothing was worth this. She lay there until the room grew dark and a full moon was glaring at her through the slats of the open blinds in her expansive bedroom.

Her phone chimed, and thinking it might be Keith, she struggled to stand.

By the time she reached it, voicemail would have kicked in. She started toward the phone and was surprised when it began ringing for a second time. She also was surprised to see the name that flashed across Caller ID.

Lena. Someone who would understand.

"Hello?" Her own voice sounded foreign to her ears.

"Jess? Are you okay?"

"Not really."

"Is Keith there with you? Are you sick?"

"It's nothing like that, Lena. I.... I just have a lot going on. Did you just call a minute ago?"

"Yep. I wasn't going to leave a message but I decided to call back and do so, just in case my name didn't show up on your Caller I.D. You okay, Jess? You don't sound like yourself."

"Guess I'm not."

Lena was silent for what felt to Jessica like an eternity. She thought the phone line had gone dead.

"Do I need to hop on a plane and come to Indianapolis? What is going on?"

Jessica's best college girlfriend knew her as well as she knew herself. There was no use trying to hide her anguish. Still, she wasn't ready to share it.

"I'm going through some things right now, Lena, and you, you just caught me in a bad moment. I'm okay. I'll fill you in soon."

Lena remained silent for a long stretch before finally uttering, "Guess that depends on how you define 'okay.' Is Keith there? Are you all alone?"

Jessica wasn't ready to tell her friend that Keith's leaving was the reason for this meltdown. Saying those words out loud would be too much; plus, it was too soon to be spreading news like this across the miles. Keith might change his mind and come home tonight, or in the morning.

Jessica inhaled a bucket of air to steady her voice and ease Lena worry. If she didn't get her bearings, Lena would be at the Chicago airport boarding a flight that put her on Jessica's doorstep first thing tomorrow. Plus, she didn't want Lena picking up the phone and calling Evangeline, who might fill her in on more than Jessica was ready to share. Doctor-patient privilege would keep E. from revealing certain pertinent details; but girlfriend to girlfriend, more would be shared between these college buddies than should, as far as Jessica was concerned.

"I promise I'm fine; just a little stressed and a lot tired about all that's going on with my work," Jessica finally said. "So, what is up with you, Ms. Lady? What prompted this call?"

Lena's hesitation was palpable.

"I'm doing fine. All is well with work and fam. I'm calling because... God put you on my spirit, Jess. I know that sounds crazy, but for the past hour every free thought I had was consumed with your face and name. So I decided to be obedient and at least check on you. Guess He knew you needed to talk to someone?"

Lena's gentle offer to lend a listening ear was touching, and Jess knew it was genuine. But for now, the most she could accept was the offer. She wasn't ready to take her friend up on it.

"I'll keep that in mind, Lena. You amaze me."

"Likewise, superstar! Whatever's troubling you, it's going to work itself out. It always does, when God is leading the charge."

Jessica shivered. Maybe that was the problem. She hadn't relied on God to lead her for a while. But Lena wouldn't know that about her, because Jessica had been a fabulous PK representative, adept at what she considered to be "preacher speak" and when to say it and what to say: "Praise the Lord; God is good, all the time!" and the like. Lena seemed to have adopted some of it herself, but then again, she was a preacher's kid, too. Sometimes you couldn't escape your parents' shadow, and honestly, unlike Jessica, Lena had never tried. Since their college days she had herself become one of God's front-line ambassadors, even though her work in Chicago took her nowhere near a pulpit.

Jessica was certain that where she found herself now, and how she had gotten in this predicament, was a place and space Lena would have ventured and wouldn't understand. Jessica wrestled with that truth and with the crossroad she faced at the moment. Either she was going to open up to her friend and accept some solid support, or she would have to figure out on her own how to get her husband back, deal with pregnancy and motherhood, and save her career.

A daunting task - which was why these multiple hats had never interested her in the first place. Some people were cut out to raise families, and others might be best suited serving as aunties. As much as she had dodged the former, however, it seemed life had other ideas. When she was ready to deal with that status quo and the truth of where she'd landed, Lena would be one of the first people she would call for support. Tonight, though, she would graciously accept her friend's prayers and leave it at that. If God knew the whole story, wasn't that enough?

# forty-four

By the time she crawled into bed for the night, Keith still hadn't come home, and Jessica grew sicker by the minute. She wanted to call his sister and ask Karis to talk some sense into him – to urge him to talk with her and work things out. Or maybe his mother, or their friends Damian and Evan, could get through to him. But none of those options seemed fitting. Deep down, she knew they'd all absolutely understand why he'd left, when they learned how deceitful she'd been.

So she resumed what she'd been doing since about 3 o'clock that afternoon when he walked out – sitting in the middle of their bed, alternately weeping, raging at herself and pleading with God to help her fix things. She kept returning to a recent conversation with Brigit, in which her friend urged her not to worry if she was going to pray, and if she was going to go ahead and worry, then there was no need for her prayers.

Jessica finally crawled under the covers and turned off the lamp on her nightstand. She hugged her pillow and tried to swipe her tears with her thumb before they soaked the pillowcase through. When her eyes adjusted to the blackness, illuminated only by a sliver of moon peeking through the window, Jessica peered at her husband's empty side of the bed. Her heart ached, and she felt tempted to pick up the phone and call him. Her internal argument seesawed between doing so, to prove how much she loved him, and letting him be, to respect his request for space. Before she could decide which step to take, her eyes landed on Keith's nightstand, where his Bible and a small book were perched in a spot that was usually empty. She sat up and scooted to his side of the bed and turned on his lamp, which revealed the book to be a male-centered devotional. Jessica frowned in surprise. When had he begun reading spiritual materials, other than what he used to prepare for his monthly Sunday School teaching stint? She didn't recall seeing the book there before, and realized he must have meant to take both items with him when he packed.

She turned over the book to read the back cover. It was penned by a male author she hadn't heard of, and offered tips on how to pray for one's wife, and be the husband a wife needed.

Jessica's heart melted and broke all over again. Keith wasn't trying to run; he had been trying to find a way to stay – and be happy in doing so. She flipped through the book and saw that he had dog-eared certain pages. One talked about being a protector in good times and bad. Another page focused on serving your wife even when you felt she didn't deserve it. And one broke down the meaning of Corinthians 13, verse by verse.

Verses 8-13 sucker-punched her. She read them again, and then for a third time.

*Love never fails. But where there are prophecies, they will cease; where there are tongues, they will be stilled; where there is knowledge, it will pass away. For we know in part and we prophesy in part, but when completeness comes, what is in part disappears. When I was a child, I talked like a child, I thought like a child, I reasoned like a child. When I became a man, I put the ways of childhood behind me. For now we see only a reflection as in a mirror; then we shall see face to face. Now I know in part; then I shall know fully, even as I am fully known. And now these three remain: faith, hope and love. But the greatest of these is love.*

The fourth time she read the passage, she began to see herself – her lingering childish ways, her arrogance in thinking she deserved answers about why health issues had afflicted her, her lack of faith, hope, and even love, in trusting that everything would work out for her good, without her having to manipulate the circumstances.

The truth caused her to shudder.

*Lord, have mercy on me?*

She silently rendered this plea in the form of a question, realizing that in her current state of wrongness she had no right to make any requests. Jessica sat in stillness, allowing the verses she had read, and the recent memories of how she hadn't lived up that standard, course through her spirit. She didn't know how to push through this sadness and the fear she was feeling over the fact that her life would never be the same – because of the arthritis and the baby for certain, and possibly because of troubles in her marriage. She had missed a powerful truth unfolding right before her: Keith didn't need her to be perfect, or to be superwoman, in order to love her. He had been here, steadfast in the middle of her mess, loving her as she was.

Jessica closed the devotional book and Bible and put them back where they had been.  She picked up her smartphone and almost tapped the code to speed dial Keith, but instead laid the device back on the nightstand. She had done enough of forcing her way with him. If he felt the need to leave, after all of the reading and prayer it was obvious he had been doing, she needed to give him this gift of space. She had to find the will to love him in the way he needed right now, even if it meant allowing him time away from her, and even if it killed her a little more each day. *This* was what all those Scriptures must mean about dying to self. Those Bible passages never talked about how painful the process would be, Jessica realized; but she decided that's what she needed to finally do – love Keith enough to let him go, and during the process, hopefully win back his love.

She felt another rush of tears threaten to erupt, but she inhaled deeply and slowly, and forced them down.  She swung her legs over the side of the bed and nearly cried out from the sharp stab of pain that spiked through her knee. Her intention had been to get down on her knees and pray, but that was going to be impossible right now. Instead, she perched on the side of the bed, sat up straight, bowed her head and closed her eyes, humbling herself before God for the first time in a long time, and silently pleaded for forgiveness, mercy, grace, and wisdom. Words wouldn't come, but for the first time she understood what Daddy meant when he repeated one of his favorite phrases: *God knows the heart.* She didn't have to use words for God to hear them flowing from her heart, and for this, she was thankful.

# forty-five

When the sun rose over Monday, Jessica awoke exhausted and emotionally drained.

Her tearstained pillow was proof that she had continued to cry throughout the night, even in her sleep. Her profession as a globetrotting speaker and Keith's corporate work commitments meant they regularly spent nights away from each other, but this felt different. A sense of doom enveloped Jessica as she remembered that Keith wouldn't be crossing the threshold in a few hours, lighting up their home with his calm spirit and mischievous smile. Would he ever come back, and if he did, would he ever look at her in that special way again?

She couldn't erase from her mind's eye the image of his defeated trek through the kitchen to the garage yesterday, or the mixture of sadness and anger clouding his face as he closed the door behind him, without saying goodbye. That moment kept looping through her memory like an annoying Snapchat video.

She shifted in bed and winced at the pain that followed. Like clockwork, the heat of inflammation climbing her limbs was her morning reminder that she was mired in a new way of life. She gingerly sat up and swung her legs over the side of the bed. The clock read 8:20 a.m. She checked her cell phone, and when she confirmed there was no morning text from Keith for the first time in forever, she felt like crawling back under the covers.

He is really gone.

She wanted to close her eyes and sleep away the nightmare her life had become. But it was game face time. Her clients awaited her motivation and her expertise. They had no idea that her world had turned upside down; she had to pull herself together and perform, without letting them know about the drama going unfolding in her life.

More lies, huh?

That forthright whisper to her spirit struck her like a jolt of lightning, and her usual ability to ignore uncomfortable musings evaded her. A heaviness settled in her bones as she realized she wasn't going to be able to shake this off as usual and plaster on a smile.

She shuffled to the bathroom, where she gazed at her reflection in the mirror for a few minutes, before turning away. Looking into her own eyes was painful. When and how had she become the deceitful, self-serving woman staring back at her? How had she turned into a person who allowed the stuff Daddy always called 'idols' to wreck her life? According to him, idols were anything that took your eyes off God and your heart away from God. In this moment, Jessica had to admit that her obsession with her career had lured her down this path. Now, the consequence of that temptation was a tenuous relationship with Keith.

She brushed her teeth and washed her face before gingerly stepping inside the shower, hopeful that she could wash away the unsettling feelings that lingered. As the soothing, warm water roll down her back she closed her eyes and willed herself to get it together. Her strength hadn't failed her in the past; now was not a good time to start.

By the time she stepped out of the shower, however, Jessica was ready to face the truth. With her life crumbling around her, she couldn't be superwoman today. Plus, she needed to follow the doctor's orders and listen to her body. With great reluctance but equal resolve, she texted Tari and informed her that she would be staying home in bed. Then she drew the blinds to darken the room and climbed back under the covers, willing peace to envelope her, however it wanted to come.

# forty-six

Paying the bills that Keith usually handled and picking up his dry cleaning from a month ago was how Jessica entered the second week of life without him.

Just as she was hanging up his suit, the phone rang. Although he hadn't done so yet, she scrambled to pick up the cell as fast as her body would allow and peeked at the screen. Disappointment engulfed her when Lena's name and face greeted her. She decided she would let the call go to voicemail, but instead of leaving a message, Lena followed up with a text.

Call me. Got an opportunity I don't want you to miss. xoxo

Lena ran a women's health organization in Chicago and always had something interesting going on. The old Jessica would have been dialing her back within seconds, eager to find out what was up and how she could get involved. This Jessica didn't know if she wanted to get involved or if she could even manage to take on anything new in the near future.

Instead of responding, Jessica sat up in bed and honed her attention on her closet, which with the door ajar gave her a perfect view of the designer dresses, pantsuits and fabulous shoes she usually wore onstage to give her audiences visual candy, or what she considered a tangible example of what it meant to live one or more steps above ordinary. Jessica felt disconnected from that belief process now, as if it belonged to another person, in another lifetime; one that would be out of her reach going forward.

She laid her head in her open palm and turned toward the window. The blinds were closed, as she'd kept them since climbing into bed a week ago, and she wondered what was going on beyond them.

Life, that's what. Without her. She needed to get it together.

Jessica threw her covers back and left her king-sized comfort zone. She strolled over to the cranberry sofa in the sitting area of her bedroom and tried to ignore the fatigue that plagued her, wondering if it were caused by the medicine she was taking or by the arthritis itself, or by the pregnancy. At this point, it didn't matter; she was weary, in body and spirit. She relaxed into the sofa and fixed her gaze on the ceiling, running through memories instead of seeing the light fixture in her view. What were those phrases and platitudes she always shared with young people? *Push through. Stay strong. Choose joy.*

In that moment, she realized that she was exactly what Londa, the *Essence* reporter, had indicated – just like her daddy. The only difference was her directives didn't have religious overtones. But if you were going through something difficult or needed someone to stand with you or to offer you tangible help, the soft words she often uttered could only soothe you momentarily. Jessica didn't know what actions or deeds might be of better solace for herself right now, but the surface-level encouragement she'd been routinely sharing with the masses for years wasn't enough. What she was feeling right now made her wonder if she had been speaking truth to her listeners without telling them how to obtain it. In the midst of a personal desert, she now questioned whether she'd really been helpful to them, since she had given them little more than some hyped-up cheerleading sessions.

Jessica allowed these epiphanies and their accompanying questions, to wash over her, and for the first time, she entertained the possibility that she might never get the answers she craved. But even this felt better than lying in bed and sleeping away the present. The haunting of these unanswerable queries might at least help her sort out for herself what she was supposed to be learning in this moment in time, and how she was supposed to use these lessons in her life. If nothing else, she still believed there had to be meaning for experiences like this, even when one played some role in causing them, or didn't understand them.

Jessica awoke about an hour later, with a sore neck from having dozed off at an odd angle. She wondered if she had missed another call from Keith and strolled over to her bed to find her cell phone. It was tucked beneath her pillow, and when she retrieved it, saw that she actually had missed three calls – from Tari, Lena and Mama.

Lena had followed up with a second text:

Listen to your voicemail, busy lady! Then call me! Hope you're okay.

Tari had left a voicemail, and so had Mama, but Jessica didn't feel like speaking with any of them, especially her assistant. Work was the last thing she wanted to deal with right now, a realization that was so out of character it made her squirm. When had she not cared about her career, or her life's mission, which she considered her professional speaking to be? When had she dared fall behind on a deadline for anything?

She had an urge to stand in front of her massive bathroom mirror and make sure she was still Jessica. Then her sister-in-law Karis' voice came to her, as clear and authoritative as if Karis were in this room, prepping Jessica to testify in one of the court cases she handled as a city prosecutor: "You need to practice what you preach, sis. Push through this challenge. Get up and get back to it – back to your life!"

Karis had left that voicemail sometime yesterday, when Jessica was sleeping. Jessica had been angry for two reasons when she heard it – first that Karis dared "preach" to her when Karis didn't know what she was going through, and second, that Keith had taken it upon himself to share her diagnosis with his sister and his mother in the first place. It was her news to spread, not his, yet Karis indicated in one of her messages that Keith had told her and her mom about the arthritis, so they could check on her while he was away on business. Apparently he had alerted their neighborhood buddies, as well, because Autumn and Brigit had been blowing up her phone, and when she wouldn't respond, they had resorted to leaving meals on her back porch in the evenings and ringing her doorbell to alert her that the daily care package had arrived.

It was obvious he had chosen not to tell his mother the full truth. Had he done so, by now Mom Carolyn would have packed her bags and moved in to care for Jessica, or she would have insisted that Jessica pack hers and move on. That one favor from Keith gave Jessica hope. Keith knew she cared for his mother but couldn't always tolerate her. He was still thinking about her needs and desires, even at a time like this.

The longer she languished in bed, in her dark room, the more grateful she grew that she didn't have to explain herself or her sudden disappearance to Autumn and Brigit, or even to Karis and her mother-in-law. Since Keith had given them a plausible reason for her drastic shut down, that gave her permission to stay gone as long as she wanted. And truthfully, her friends' kindness was a blessing. It allowed her to eat healthy for the baby without thinking about it, or trying to maneuver in the kitchen with a sore knee and body. When she mustered her strength, she would give both of her girlfriends big hugs. They had no way of knowing that she was also mourning the state of her marriage, or officially carrying her first child; but without their love and attention, she would be in much worse shape.

Jessica listened to Karis' voicemail again and decided that maybe her sister-in-law was right. She needed to push past the despair and pity entombing her spirit and live up to what she coached others to do. She didn't have the right to say one thing on stage and do another behind closed blinds, and still be considered authentic. She had to stare down this challenge and get herself together.

Jessica didn't know what that would require; but today she could at least acknowledge her desire to reclaim her life, so she could someday tell her student audiences and the young people she would help on her TV show that she tried.

# forty-seven

Jessica's baby step that afternoon had been to sit in her office and review the numerous emails that accumulated during her mini-sabbatical.

Tari had probably already responded to them, but she wanted to stay in the know, so she browsed through the updates, requests, thank yous and more. About an hour before Tari's workday was scheduled to end, Jessica reached out to apologize for her seven-day absence.

"Finally – a return call!" Tari declared. "I was about to contact the National Guard and have them put out an All Points Bulletin for you! Now that I know you're alive and well, I'll try not to be offended that you've been dissing me."

Jessica chuckled. Leave it to Tari to lift her mood.

"I should have called you back," Jessica said, "but I've been going through some things. I'm sorry. I'm going to have to pull back on work – doctor's orders, so maybe tomorrow we can walk through what that might look like."

Tari remained quiet for what felt like an eternity. When she broke her silence, her voice was quivering, but she sounded resolute.

"This is probably TMI and I hope it won't offend you; but ever since you've been avoiding my calls, I've been praying for you. I know you've been dealing with health challenges, and with being super busy as you try to juggle all your clients and business opportunities; but whatever's going on, I've asked God to cover you."

Jessica sat up straighter. This was a side of Tari she'd never met – virtually or otherwise. She was grateful for the Too Much Information revelation.

"Wow, thanks, Tari. That was sweet of you. I didn't know you went to church or any of that, but I appreciate your prayers."

"You got 'em," Tari said. "And yes – church girl I am, born and bred. Preacher's kid, just like you."

"What... How..... Why are you just now telling me?"

"It never came up," Tari said. "And I never want to offend my clients by mixing religion and business, so I tread carefully. My daddy was a great man, rest his soul. He loved me dearly, he loved Mama dearly, he loved everybody. And he taught me to never give up on God. There've been times I wanted to give up on myself, but never the Lord."

Jessica heard the tenderness with which Tari talked about her dad and understood why Tari had never mentioned him: she knew how Jessica felt about her own father, and Tari didn't want to hurt her. All of these revelations caused Jessica to respect Tari all the more, because Tari had never judged her for her snide comments about her parents, or for her lack of attention to her own father; nor had she seemed to question Jessica's lack of faith or participation in church.

Perhaps someday Jessica would muster the courage to probe further. For now, she was grateful to hear that some "PKs" bucked the stereotype. Tari's childhood obviously had been blessed and had shaped her into the loving person she was today. Would Tari be this understanding if she knew the truth about who she was working for, though? That was one more thing Jessica needed to make sure never happened.

# forty-eight

Jessica's new normal at least meant she made it to her desk most mornings. She might not make it through all of her emails or through all of the requests awaiting her, but Tari had been a godsend.

She managed by informing regular and potential clients that Jessica's schedule was booked solid, and adeptly steered them online for trainings, speeches and ebooks they could buy and use immediately. The past two weeks of feeling unable to work left Jessica deeply grateful that she had followed the advice of a business coach she hired five years ago and developed products to provide multiple streams of income for her company. At least some money was coming in while she was partially incapacitated. Getting dressed each day was a big deal, and getting back in the swing of things was going to take time and energy she just didn't have right now. She missed her husband. Nothing else really mattered.

Jessica opened another email this morning from Brigit checking on her, with Autumn copied.

How are you? We miss you!! Call us and let us hear your voice. Or open the door and let us see your face. We can stay for dinner one evening, just the three of us. Or we can bring you lunch. Please reply, Jess!!

That email was four days old, and Brigit had sent a second one just yesterday, but this time it didn't include Autumn:

Hey Jess, this is an awkward question, so forgive me if I'm out of line. But I'm asking in case you think this will help you feel better and take your mind off things. Do you still feel up to helping me plan a baby shower for Autumn? I know you've been under the weather and have a lot going on, so just let me know, and I'm sorry again if asking you isn't appropriate right now. Didn't want to leave you out; I know how much Autumn means to both of us.

Jessica sighed and reared back in her black leather chair. How could she help plan someone else's baby shower when she wondered if she'd be raising her own child alone?

The split second she had that thought, however, she knew it was selfish. What was going on with her was not Autumn's fault. She had to get over herself and get on with life. She leaned forward and wrote a brief response to Brigit.

Count me in. I'm not at 100 percent right now, but I'll help however I can. Talk soon.

She closed the Internet browser and turned away from the computer screen, just as her cell phone rang. Tari's smiling face flashed across her screen.

"Sorry I forgot to call you half an hour ago, as planned," Jessica said as her greeting. "I started catching up on emails and forgot."

Tari's customary patience reigned.

"I know this is hard, Jessica," she said, reminding Jessica that her assistant still thought she had gout. "And this may sound so trite, but you are alive, able to freely move about on your own, and still have flexibility in work and life; you have a lot of positive things to focus your energy on."

"You're right." Jessica agreed for the umpteenth time, as she had during their talks over the past week. She wasn't sure how Tari had turned into a confidante and worthy advisor, when she was still the boss, but with the absence of her local friends, and others not even aware of what she was going through, Tari's encouragement was welcomed.

She hadn't mentioned her faith again since their chat about it a week ago, but Jessica had no doubt that her assistant, turned friend, was lifting her up to God. She felt that reassurance and peace each time they talked, especially when Jessica found the courage late last week to follow Dr. Kent's advice and cancel two appearances scheduled for June on the West Coast. Rather than leaving her hosts without a speaker, she had passed along the names of two of her colleagues, who were thrilled to be recommended to speak before audiences of 5,000 or more.

Losing the fee hadn't hurt Jessica as much as the opportunity to spread her mission and message, one that could help these students thrive, and Tari must have heard her spiraling into pity-party mode as they finalized the changes. She had dutifully listened to Jessica's whining, and minutes after wrapping up their call had texted Jessica a reassuring message, along with a Scripture, Ecclesiastes 3:11.

You're in a valley right now, for whatever reason; but take heart - although everyone hasn't ventured there with you, you are not alone.

God's seasons for your life and God's timing are perfect.

He will open the doors he wants to open for you.

Tari's ministering had been helpful, and oddly, it made her long to talk to Shiloh. As she contemplated calling her sister to fill her in on some of her recent challenges, her phone pinged with another text from Lena. Jessica knew she needed to return Lena's call; she just hadn't summoned the strength to respond to her friend's questioning concern.

Am I going to have to come to Indiana to get your attention? CALL ME. I'm not resting until you do.

Jessica chuckled at Lena's text. Some people, and some things, never changed. Lena would always be dramatic, but she would also always be sincere. Jessica decided to call her sister-friend before she talked herself out of it.

Lena was so happy to hear from Jessica that she launched into her purpose for texting multiple times before asking any questions. She poured out details about an opportunity to join her and eight other girlfriends for a weekend retreat at Martha's Vineyard.

"One of the board members at the women's health organization is a gazillionaire," Lena joked. "She's offered to let all of the staff use her home there for free, as long as we reserve it a month in advance," Lena said. "I've booked it for July, and would love for you to come to this ladies' getaway. Since I'm planning it, you know it's going to be fabulous!"

Jessica's response was blocked by the lump in her throat. Should she tell Lena about the arthritis, the high-risk pregnancy, her crumbling marriage, or none of the above? Her heart pounded. Then she took the safest route, blaming her inability to go on the fact that she would be just wrapping up the pilot for *Boundless* in July and wasn't sure she could get away. Technically, all of the filming was scheduled to take place in June, but anything could happen.

"You know I love you, Lena; if anything, and I mean anything, changes that would allow me to come and spend this special time with you and your girlfriends, I'd love to do that."

As soon as that PR perfect answer left her lips, Jessica felt sick to her stomach. At some point, she was going to have to stop faking the funk. Lena's long silence told her now was the time, but she couldn't. Dealing with Keith's absence was hard enough. Talking about it to another person would be too much. The best she could do right now was reveal the arthritis diagnosis, and so she did.

"Oh, Jess, I'm so, so sorry. How are you feeling?"

"That's always the big question, and I'm learning to frame it as, 'How am I feeling right now,'" Jessica answered. "I've gained some weight because of the meds I'm on, and I'm having to give away plum speaking engagements. I'd say my life is crumbling down around me; but I'm hanging in there."

Even the verbose Lena was speechless for a few minutes, but when she finally responded, her answer wasn't surprising.

"I'm not going anywhere, Jessica, and if you need me to fly to Indianapolis to be there with you for an appointment or physical therapy, let me know."

Lena's words of support meant a lot, and what was even more beautiful was the fact that Jessica knew they were sincere. Lena would hop a plane or train in a minute and be where she needed or wanted to be, at a moment's notice.

"You can handle this. Fight, Jessica; just keep standing."

With a response meant as encouragement, Jessica's spirit deflated even further. This is why you didn't tell half-truths. By not revealing everything that was going on with her, Lena had no idea that Jess was already flat on her back.

# forty-nine

Jessica stepped out of the shower and couldn't believe God had answered her prayer that quickly. Keith was calling.

She was so stunned to see his name and picture surface on her cell phone after eleven days of no word from him, that she was motionless, and almost didn't pick up. She reached for the phone and tapped "accept" before the fourth ring.

"Keith?"

"Hi. Today is the follow up appointment with Evangeline, right? Just wanted to confirm that you hadn't canceled or changed the time. I'd like to be there."

That was it. No 'How are you?' 'I miss you' or anything in between. Jessica's heart fell.

"Yes, Keith. It's today, at 10 a.m. I'm getting ready now."

"Great," he said. "I'll meet you there. See you soon."

And with that, he was gone. Jessica held the phone away from her ear and stared at it for a second. Had that just happened? As quickly as she felt a natural high, she sank lower than she had been when he first walked out.

She laid the phone on the edge of the sink and stumbled to her bed, where she sat, staring off into nothingness for a few minutes. When she refocused, she saw that it was 9 a.m. sharp. She could not be late for this appointment, no matter what. That realization compelled her to get dressed and make it out of the door and into the car by nine-twenty. She drove to Evangeline's office with the radio off, silently tossing around in her mind how she would handle seeing her husband and what she should say to convince him that she was deeply sorry for her transgressions.

As timing would have it, they pulled into the parking lot of E.'s OB/GYN practice at the same time, and as luck would have it, the only two open parking spots were next to each other. Jessica's heart started flip-flopping, and her mouth went dry. She inhaled and exhaled deeply several times to calm herself, then unbuckled and opened the door of the SUV to climb out.

Keith was standing there when she looked up, and she almost screamed.

"Didn't mean to startle you," he said, with as little emotion as he had a short while earlier, on the phone. "Just came over to help you out of the truck."

She put her hand in his and gripped his palm while climbing down.

Jessica wanted to reach up and wrap her arms around his neck, but she restrained herself, and instead matched her gait to his as they approached the medical office building. She wanted to ask him how he was doing, and tell him he looked as tired and as weary as she felt; but she held her tongue. The fact that he had come this morning was a blessing; she wasn't going to run him away by making it all about her and what she wanted or needed to say.

Once she had checked in at the nurse's station and they were waiting to be seen, she settled in the chair next to him and expressed her gratitude.

"Thanks for coming, Keith. It's good to see you."

He glared at her before responding, and for those few seconds, her heart soared. In his eyes roared the anger and resentment she had coming; but Jessica also saw a hint of the pain she felt, the anguish of being apart. It gave her hope that today's visit wasn't the start of what would become a long-term co-parenting practice for two separate households.

"I came for the baby," Keith said.

Evangeline's nurse saved her the trouble of replying by stepping into the lobby and calling her name. Keith helped her to her feet and together they followed the nurse back to a patient room with an ultrasound machine. When the nurse placed the device on her belly and she saw the tiny image that was her child and heard the swooshing heartbeat, suddenly all felt right with the world. There was a person growing inside of her, and she loved him or her. Just like that.

Jessica looked up at Keith and saw his eyes glistening with tears. She wondered what he was thinking and feeling, and wished she felt comfortable grasping his hand and asking him. Before she could formulate a response, Evangeline stepped into the room. When she saw the baby on the monitor a broad smile spread across her face. She leaned down to hug Jessica's shoulders.

"Look at my little niece or nephew! All healthy and growing at the perfect rate!"

The new information caused Jessica's tears of relief to slide down the sides of her cheeks, but a sweet peace spread through her spirit, too. E. hadn't called her since her last doctor's visit and she knew her friend was still upset with her. Today's comments indicated that she was willing to forgive and move forward.

As the official visit wound to a close, Evangeline asked her nurse to give her a few minutes alone with Jessica and Keith. Once it was just the three of them, she pulled two business cards from the pocket of her white coat and held them in the air.

"I've been thinking of you two and praying for you every day since you were last here. I haven't talked with either of you since then, but I know you both well enough to know that despite the exciting news about the baby, there's some tension between you two."

Keith and Jessica glanced at each other, but neither responded.

"I love you both, and I want this baby to be born healthy and to go home to a happy household," Evangeline continued. "In order for that to happen, you can't be stressed out during this pregnancy, Jessica. Even with the arthritis diagnosis you have to maintain a healthy emotional state and sense of calm. The baby will be negatively impacted otherwise. And when the baby comes home, the household needs to be welcoming and nurturing and focused on creating an oasis of love. That's something you both have to work at to make happen."

Keith looked away and then at his feet. Jessica hoped he didn't think she had put Evangeline up to giving them this lecture.

"I shared all of that to say that I'd like you to get some help. On one of these cards is the name of a marital therapist I highly recommend. He's great with couples and doesn't pull any punches. Please call him asap to get on his calendar, and tell him I recommended you."

She extended the first business card to Keith, and after a moment of hesitation he took it. Evangeline rested her hand on his forearm and peered into his eyes.

"Please don't be too manly to do the right thing, Keith. Talking things out can be medicine for the heart and soul, just like going to a doctor for your physical issues is. I hope you guys will think about it."

Keith tucked the card in his pocket, but remained mute. Evangeline handed the second card to Jessica.

"This is the contact information for a dynamic wellness consultant that I met at a health expo about three years ago. Catherine has a small studio in Fishers, but she also does in-home sessions with groups of neighbors or with individuals who need her services. She offers everything from nutritional counseling to Tai chi and yoga lessons to mindfulness training. I think she can be very helpful in terms of you crafting a plan that helps you cope with the arthritis and also with pregnancy. Please look her up."

Evangeline stepped back and tucked her hands in her pockets. "That's it, fam, until the next two weeks, when I see you again. You'll be about eight weeks along then, so I'll make sure our perinatologist joins us."

Keith stepped around the patient table on which Jessica lay and leaned down to hug Evangeline. "Thanks, I'll give this some thought."

Evangeline accepted his hug then poked his chest.

"Don't waste time overthinking this, Keith, and don't let your pride get the best of you. Put your family first and make the call. Today."

She peeked around him and smiled at Jessica. Jessica returned the gesture.

"Lena called you, didn't she?"

Evangeline shrugged.

"At least I convinced her not to show up on your doorstep. I didn't share any information, or even tell her you're expecting; you know I can't do that. I just told her I'd take care of you. Call her back and let her know you're going to be fine, okay?"

Jessica nodded. "I can do that."

She waved the business card she'd been given in the air. "And I can do this, too."

Then she glanced at Keith, who watched their exchange with a noncommittal expression.

He helped her down from the patient table and they departed together, but didn't hold hands or touch. Jessica stopped by the nurse's station to make her next appointment and they boarded the elevator together.

When they reached their cars, Keith opened her door and helped her climb up and settle behind the wheel. Then he stood there and dropped a bombshell.

"I'm going away for a week or so, for work."

"What?!"

Jessica couldn't believe what she was hearing. Why had he waited until now to make this grand pronouncement?

"When? And why?" She recalled again that his company's next quarterly conference wasn't until fall.

Keith released a slow, heavy sigh and rubbed his hand across his head.

"I need to get away, Jessica. And it just so happens that one of the managers in the Philadelphia office had a family emergency in the middle of a department audit. They issued a company-wide request for two volunteers to oversee their territorial managers for two weeks so all of their onsite staff can focus on the audit and its looming deadline. I'll go one week – I'm leaving on Sunday - and then a guy from the Phoenix office will come the week after me, when I return home."

Jessica was numb. Was he trying to run away for good? Transfer to Philadelphia or something? Was this a farce?

"Are you coming home before you leave?"

Keith frowned. "No, Jessica. I wasn't planning to. I still need some space right now."

She didn't know what to think. But Evangeline's words rang through her mind. She needed to do all she could to save her marriage, even if it sounded like begging. Today was Wednesday. Getting in to see the therapist before he left town was a long shot, but she had to try.

"Will you do one thing before you go, Keith – for our baby?"

He stuffed his hands into the pockets of his slacks and stared at her.

"Will you call the therapist and see if by any chance he can fit us in tomorrow or Friday? I know it's a very, very long shot. But maybe if you tell him E. referred us, and tell him it's an emergency, he may be able to fit us in. Evangeline is right; we have to try. I don't deserve it; but our marriage does, and so does our child."

Keith frowned again and turned away. He lowered his head for a few minutes and Jessica wondered if he were praying. When he raised his head, he briefly turned toward her before stalking to his car.

"Sit tight. I'll try to call now."

As she watched him slide into the driver's seat and glare at the card before dialing the number, Jessica found herself calling on God, like she never had before.

"I mean it, Lord," she whispered softly. "You save my marriage and I'll give you all the glory and the praise."

# *fifty*

The answer had been disappointing. Dr. Carlin was booked solid for the next month and had no openings this week. Keith told Jessica he had taken an appointment for mid-June, but had also requested that their names be put on a call list, in case there was a cancellation before he left town.

"I'll call you if I hear back from his office," he said through his car window. "And I hope you'll check out this Catherine lady, to see if she can give you some helpful strategies for your health."

It took all her strength not to break out in sobs, but Jessica held fast. She nodded at Keith.

"I'll call her today. Will I hear.... will you call before you leave town?"

Keith shrugged. "If I don't call, I'll text you and let you know when I've arrived in Philly and when I'm headed back. You know if anything comes up – if there's an emergency you can reach out to me. I'll be accessible by phone. And you know Autumn and Brigit are a phone call away. That's why I told them about the arthritis."

Jessica couldn't have an attitude with him for sharing her personal business. She knew he'd done it out of love, and responsibility.

"So you told your sister, too, huh? She's an hour away."

"But she's still family," he said. "And I'm sure you didn't want me calling your mom in Alabama."

What she really wanted was for him to be calling her. But how could she tell him that when she had broken his heart and didn't deserve him at all? She wondered if when he looked in her eyes he could tell how miserable she was. She hoped he could.

"I love you, Keith."

He bit his bottom lip and started the engine, and Jessica knew he was restraining a smart retort.

"I'll let you know when I get to Philadelphia, okay? Take care of yourself, and try to take it easy."

He didn't know she'd done nothing but lie in bed for the past week and a half, or that everything within her wanted to return there, now. He didn't know that a part of her would die if he left her. She simply nodded and watched as he pulled away and turned out of the parking lot, without looking back.

And then, she bowed her head again and asked God one more time for grace, mercy and a miracle.

She sat there for another ten minutes and let the tears flow, oblivious to who was coming or going around her. The last time she'd called on God so fervently it seemed he hadn't heard her. Now, almost twenty years later, she had to believe that something had changed in her favor. And since she was desperate, she would call in one of her reinforcements.

# fifty-one

Jessica hadn't meant to tell Shiloh everything, but when she started explaining her immediate need, all of the ugly truth came spewing forth.

The medical diagnosis. The talk show opportunity. The lies. Keith's untimely discovery of them. And now, her desperate attempt to save her marriage and her sanity.

Jessica called her sister as soon as she pulled into her garage, and started pouring out her troubles before she climbed out of the car and entered the house through the kitchen. Forty minutes later, she sat on her family room sofa, wrapping up her uninterrupted spiel. Sobs wracked her body, and all she could decipher was Shiloh whispering, "Shhh," interspersed with brief words of prayer.

Jessica knew her sister was stunned; they'd never been close enough to share this kind of intimate information, especially about their marriages. But Shiloh had come to mind in her moment of desperation, and she took that leading to mean that for the first time, she should trust Shiloh with her stuff, and not worry about it winding up on the church prayer list as a juicy piece of holy gossip.

"Oh, baby sis," Shiloh said, her own voice thick with tears and emotion. "I'm so sorry you're going through this. I'm so sorry you've been dealing with all of this. Alone and pregnant."

Jessica was finally calm enough to respond.

"I'm alone because of my own stupid choices," she said and wiped her swollen eyes with the back of her hand. She slowly eased off the sofa and padded toward the nearby bathroom to grab a few tissues to blow her nose, grateful that Shiloh didn't dismiss her response or try to sugarcoat it.

"We'll deal with that later. Right now, I need to know if you are physically well enough to stay by yourself, while Keith is out of town."

Jessica explained that she was fine so far, and that her friends had been kind enough to share meals with her in the evenings.

"They know Keith has moved out?"

"They think he's been on a long-standing business trip. Guess the lie he told them led to an actual one, since he's flying to Philadelphia this weekend."

Shiloh was quiet for a few minutes.

"Do you want Randy to talk to him, Jess?"

Jessica sat up straighter and shook her head, as if Shiloh could see her. She loved her brother-in-law, but she wasn't ready for anyone else in the family to know all of this drama was unfolding in her seemingly perfect life. Plus, if Randy knew, there was a good chance he'd tell Daddy since they were so close, and that was the last thing she needed to deal with.

"Please don't say anything, Shiloh. Please."

Her stress sounded palpable to her own ears; she hoped her sister picked up on it as well.

Shiloh's voice was soothing when she replied.

"Your life and business are your life and business. I only made that suggestion because I know Keith respects Randy, and Randy would never break his confidence. As a pastor, he has more than enough knowledge about people's personal pain and private issues to take to the grave with him someday. But I am here for you; I will follow your lead. What do you need me to do? I can come and stay for a while..."

Jessica frowned.

"All the way from Alabama? What about the boys, and your other responsibilities? Aren't you teaching?"

"Didn't I tell you those teenagers don't need me? Maybe if they go without my home-cooked meals for a while they'll appreciate me more. And I'm pretty much done with my classes and students, since I teach an elective. They're taking final exams the next two weeks."

Jessica glanced at a framed picture on her wall-length bookshelf, taken almost three years ago, when the family had gathered in Alabama for Thanksgiving. She and her sisters sat smiling, while Mama and Daddy stood behind them, portraying the tight-knit couple they always had been. Because they all felt so grateful that Daddy had survived a sudden health crisis, the image didn't seem forced, and it hadn't been.

That holiday season actually had been the catalyst for a warmer relationship between Jessica, Shiloh and Dayna; but the three sisters were still finding their way. Jessica didn't know how much more open she could or should be with Shiloh just yet. She felt exposed and self-conscious from all she shared today; but she couldn't take it back. She'd have to live with the fact that her sister knew her halo was tarnished, and that her sins might cause the death of her marriage.

"I really am fine, Shiloh. And I really appreciate you letting me get this off my chest, and praying for me. I haven't turned to prayer in a long, long time, but these days it seems to be my first course of action."

Shiloh chuckled.

"You were raised by a minister; why do you seem so surprised by that?"

Jessica wished she could join in on the slight teasing, but she just wasn't up to it.

"I guess, because I've spent so many years not trusting that prayer makes a difference."

If she was being honest about everything else, she mused, she might as well tell the truth about this, too. "I'm in a fix that's so bad now, calling on God seems to be the only thing that might work. I don't have any other choices."

Shiloh didn't respond, and Jessica knew she was calculating what to say.

"You've always had a choice, Jess," Shiloh finally said. "And you didn't have to wait until you got into a fix. God has always been there for you, even when it didn't feel like it, and He will continue to be, as long as you let him in.

"But hear me when I say that regardless of whether you pray every day or go to church every Sunday, God's ears and heart are open to you. Mine are too, little sis. An illness can throw you for a loop, but it doesn't have to be the end of the world. You are the same person now that you were before your troubles sent you spiraling. Love yourself, and know that I love you, too. I'm a preacher's wife, but I'm still a sinner saved by grace. Believe me - I have my baggage just like you and everyone else, Jess."

Jessica was speechless. She'd never taken the time to have this kind of conversation with her own sister before and hadn't known what she was missing. Shiloh had a beautiful spirit, and tons of wisdom that she'd been missing out on.

"Best advice I've received in a long time, Shiloh. Thank you. I will do as you said."

Jessica had questioned that church cliché "God is there" for years, but suddenly, everything within her wanted to believe it to be true, and to also embrace her sister's offering of unconditional love. For the first time in a long time, if ever, Jessica realized she wanted to trust God the way Shiloh did, and the way Dayna seemed to be learning to do. Living by platitudes and possibilities was fine when all was going well, but today had taken her to a new place of fear and a new level of emptiness. She was ready to be filled with the peace and pure love that Daddy and Randy, and even Lena, regularly described. How on earth could she get there from rock bottom?

# fifty-two

The persistent ringing of the doorbell startled Jessica awake. She glanced at the clock on her nightstand and felt confused. It was just three o'clock. Autumn or Brigit usually brought her a hot meal closer to dinnertime, and each of them always texted to let her know it was waiting. This early-bird ringing had to be a postal employee or some other unusual interruption. Since it hadn't stopped, she climbed out of bed and peeked from a second-floor window that overlooked her beautifully landscaped front yard.

There was no car parked near the sidewalk that ran alongside the front of the house, and there was no vehicle in the driveway. Who could this be?

Stiff from lying in bed all day, she slowly descended the staircase, gripping the rail. The bell rang about three more times before she reached her foyer.

A muffled voice came from the porch. "Come to the door please! It's hot out here!"

Jessica moved as quickly as she could and peeked outside the window closest to the door. When she saw two women standing there – Shiloh *and* Dayna – she lost it.

Caught up in her tears, she jumped when the bell rang again, and this time strode as fast as she could to open the massive front door. The second she saw their smiling faces hers morphed into an ugly cry. Out poured grief over years of longing for their unconditional support and never feeling like she had it. The overflowing tears were also a release of the pain she had stuffed down, by pretending their reciprocated aloofness didn't matter.

When Dayna grabbed her and pulled her into a hug, she clung to her eldest sister and let the sobs she'd held at bay one too many times course through her body. Shiloh stood next to them, rubbing her back, and even in her own tumble of emotions, Jessica heard Shiloh's sniffles. When had they ever cried with her?

Jessica wasn't sure how long they stood in the doorway, but eventually Dayna released her from the embrace and led her inside by the hand. Dayna guided her past the dining room where she'd told the devastating lie that had created her current reality, to the kitchen, where Dayna helped her find a seat at the kitchen table. Shiloh retrieved a glass from one of the cabinets and poured her a glass of water.

The tears began to abate, and for a split second, the sniffling and red-eyed Jessica was embarrassed. Then she looked into her sisters' eyes, and realized what really mattered in this moment. She had finally allowed herself to feel what she was really feeling, without trying to sugarcoat or pretty up the deep emotions roiling inside of her. She realized that their gesture of dropping everything going on in their hectic lives to be here for her when desperately needed some family support was something she had convinced herself she'd never experience.  No wonder the dam finally broke.

Looking at them, with their compassion and empathy emanating toward her, for the first time ever she felt their love. She also took note for the first time how much the three of them resembled each other. Because their personalities were so distinct and they were known in Daddy's church and in their Alabama community for their individual merits, few people had remarked on their similarities when they were kids and young adults. But as Jessica gazed at them now, it was obvious that she and Dayna shared the same sharp jawline and tawny complexion, while she and Shiloh shared almond-shaped eyes and wide smile.  Their eyebrows reflected the same width and arch, and even the way they sat in their chairs spoke of the mutual training they had received in social graces from Mama.

It dawned on Jessica that she'd been so busy being annoyed by their differences and by how Dayna and Shiloh excluded her or treated her as an afterthought that she'd never paid much attention to their natural connections. She wasn't really sure why any of that had grabbed her attention now; other than the fact she was struck with gratitude by their showing up to be here with her, when her world had crumbled.

Over the years, she'd sought solace, counsel and encouragement from her closest friends, thinking they understood and knew her better than her own family; and truthfully, most of them probably did. But it occurred to her now that maybe that had been the case because she'd never had the courage to push through the anger and resentment and frustration that would have been required to make those same heart connections with her sisters. She could self-select likeminded friends; she couldn't tinker with the family God had given her, even when she felt like they'd failed her.

This morning, though, none of that mattered. What counted most was that they were here, and in this moment, she had a choice to make. She could wipe her tears and crawl back into the shell that allowed her to mask her pain and imperfections; or she could stay raw and real and give her sisters the chance to know the real Jessica. With all that had happened in her life the past few weeks, the answer was clear. The mask was cracked and dusty; it was time to live without it, blemishes and all.

# fifty-three

An hour later, after Dayna and Shiloh had settled into guest bedrooms and slipped into more comfortable clothing, the sisters regrouped in the kitchen.

Jessica strolled in and found Shiloh rummaging through the fridge and the pantry.

"I'm not a gourmet cook like you, so you won't find much to work with," Jessica told her and slid onto the seat next to Dayna's at the round table. "You don't have to cook anything. We can go somewhere or order out."

Shiloh paused and turned toward Jessica.

"I was gonna whip up something so we could stay in and catch up and not worry about having to get fixed up to go out, but if you want to order in and give this Mama of always-eating teenage boys a break, I won't complain."

Dayna and Jessica chuckled simultaneously, and Dayna waved her hand in the air in testimonial agreement.

"Amen to that! My two menfolk are headed off to college in the fall, but right now? They are the proverbial human garbage disposals! Warren or I stop by the grocery store at least four times a week to restock something."

Jessica tucked in her chin, rubbed her stomach and sighed. An hour ago she was in this house all by herself, curled up in bed. She still couldn't believe they had booked expensive last-minute flights and taken Uber to her front door in a matter of hours; that they dropped everything in their lives to be here for her, or how much it meant to her. They hadn't come because she was standing on top of the world and they could brag that she was their hotshot little sister; they were here as part of her village, standing with her in the valley, and while it didn't make up for the last time they hadn't managed to be there when she needed them, it mattered more than ever right now. She peered at Dayna and ventured a smile.

"Can you believe there's going to be a baby in my arms soon? Question is..."

Her throat constricted before the words could come out, and Dayna grasped her hand.

"Question is..." Jessica continued in a tone that didn't really pose a question, "will the baby's daddy be here."

Dayna passed Jessica a napkin from the holder in the center of the table, so she could dab the fresh waterfall of tears.

"What do you mean by that, Jessica?" Dayna said, and looked from Jessica to Shiloh. "The only thing Shiloh told me was that you recently learned that you have arthritis, you're pregnant and scared, and you need our support. We agreed that you trumped everything else on our plates, and that's why I'm here. She didn't mention anything about Keith. Is everything okay?"

Jessica was stunned. Shiloh truly had honored her word. She looked at her with a newfound respect and saw that Shiloh noted her gratitude, without her having to utter a word.

"Your life and business are your life and business to share," Shiloh said.

Jessica turned back to Dayna and nudged the glass of water sitting in front of Dayna closer to her. "You may want to take a few sips of that. What I'm about to tell you may leave you woozy."

*Lord, please give me the words...*

Then another idea struck her.

"You know what? I've got to eat because I'm pregnant, and what I have to tell you isn't pretty. So let's at least enjoy each other's company over a good meal, first. Besides, you might want to pack up and go home after I fill you in on everything."

Dayna leaned across the table and laid her hand on top of Jessica's, and when Jessica returned her sister's gaze, she was surprised to see a tinge of sadness in Dayna's eyes.

"I guess that's what our family has always done before, huh?" Dayna asked. "Run for the hills when things got tough or ugly. No more of that, Jess. I guess it's time to be a better sister. I've had to learn some things the hard way in the past few years about finding the courage to stand in the ugly truths you help create, so I won't be casting any stones. I'm here for you, whatever you have to say."

Dayna scooted her chair closer to Jessica's, and Shiloh, who was standing at the kitchen island watching and listening, chimed in.

"Ditto what Dayna said. If you're willing to forgive us for not being there for you the last time you really needed us, we can get through this – together."

Jessica looked from one to the other. "Thank you. Thank you both. But this is nothing like last time, when I was an innocent victim. This time I was the perpetrator, and the person I hurt most is the man who has always loved me most. I don't know if my marriage is going to survive."

Jessica saw her sisters cringe, and before she lost her resolve to wait until after she fed them before saying more, she scooted her chair away from the table and picked up her cell, to order greens, baked chicken and sweet cornbread from a local Liberian restaurant that delivered. It wasn't the best food for watching one's diet, but it was delicious, and comfort food was what she was craving right now – even though her sisters' show of support continued to fill her. She wasn't sure what had turned the tide and she didn't plan to question it. If they were serious about wading through this muck with her, she was going to hold onto them, tight.

# fifty-four

Sometimes time standing still could be a good thing.

Tari had always been an assistant who could read through the lines, and after her last conversation with Jessica, she had taken the initiative to clear Jessica's calendar for the next six weeks and refer all speaking and training requests to the two colleagues with whom Jessica often partnered. So Jessica felt free and unencumbered, for the first time in a long time.

She hadn't particularly appreciated the expanse of unscheduled hours that lay before her in the past few weeks; but with her sisters' arrival in town today, she had been given a purpose for leaving her bed and exhaling. Their midday lunch had morphed into a need to hop into the car and visit one of Indianapolis' best locally owned dessert shops. Jessica got her usual combo of double fudge and raspberry ice cream, Shiloh ordered a gourmet cupcake, and Dayna got a slice of deep-dish peach cobbler.

"Lawd," Dayna said after about three bites. "This is so good! If Daddy were here right now, he'd be trying to douse us with holy water for coveting this food. But hey, we gotta eat; might as well eat something enjoyable."

Jessica slid a spoonful of homemade ice cream onto her tongue and rolled her eyes in delight. She was enjoying her sweet treat, but even more, her company. If she could bottle this moment, and this feeling, she would.

 Just as suddenly as she had that thought, however, a small still voice centered her.

*Don't worry about what comes next; stay in the moment as it is. Appreciate it for what it is.*

What a lovely thought, and a powerful truth, Jessica mused. If only she had been open to hearing and receiving that wisdom eight weeks ago, when she started down an inevitable path to wreckage, leaving broken trust and disappointment in her wake. She thought about what she always told the students she mentored and spoke to, and realized that despite being a grown woman with everything going for her, she had made choices and decisions that matched their college-aged level of maturity. What had she been thinking?

Even though she had bared her soul to Shiloh, she dreaded repeating her transgressions to Dayna and felt like a child confessing a wrong to parents that she knew would forever change their view of her. At this point, however, there was no turning back. Keith knew the truth. Shiloh knew the truth, and with each new step and word shattering her perfect image, she felt closer to an authentic version of Jessica than ever before, despite her anguish and fear. She was going to wear her big girl pants today and do the right thing. That was all that was left to do.

# fifty-five

It was late afternoon by the time Jessica and her sisters made it home from their dessert outing, and all three of them were more relaxed and sleepy than they had anticipated.

"You two have had long flights, and I'm just always tired these days. How about we regroup in the family room in an hour?"

Dayna touched Jessica's shoulder. "You sure our talk can wait?"

Jessica nodded. "Three naps on the way."

Jessica strolled into the family room ninety minutes later and found Dayna and Shiloh parked on the sofa, one of them at each end with their feet tucked beneath them, watching an old *Law & Order* episode.

The image reminded Jessica of the positions they always took on the sofa when they were growing up, and it looked like not much had changed. She sat across the room from them as she'd always done, on the love seat.

Shiloh lowered the volume on the TV as Jessica made herself comfortable.

"You sleep well? We didn't want to wake you, even though we passed the designated hour. Your body needs more rest than ever, now."

Jessica nodded. "That's what I'm learning."'

"Okay, we forgot to ask some pretty important questions over lunch and I need to know these things before we get to any of the Keith drama," Shiloh said. "When is the baby due? And how are you feeling about becoming a mother?  How are you feeling, period - not counting the drama?"

Jessica's tense shoulders dropped about two inches and she melded into the love seat.  Shiloh's questions were a reminder that this wasn't an inquisition; they had shown her today that they really were here for her.

"I'm about six weeks along," she answered, then cringed inwardly because this accurate gestation period reminded her that Keith had been expecting her to be in the second trimester – the safe zone – at this point. "So I'm due in late December - or early January, since I hear some first babies like to do their own thing and come late. And I guess I'm feeling okay. No morning sickness or anything. I've been more focused on my health issues."

She subconsciously shifted positions as she prepared to shift the conversation.

"Which brings me to what I want to share, Dayna. I know Shiloh filled you in on most things before you flew in, including the fact that I don't have gout; I have rheumatoid arthritis."

Dayna left Shiloh's side and crossed the small space between them and bent down to give Jessica a hug before squeezing onto the seat next to her.  When Dayna and Shiloh exchanged knowing glances, Jessica knew they were thinking about the first thing that had come to her mind.

"I know – Granna. My first thought after getting over the shock was that I was going to turn into her –God rest her soul.  The possibility of that happening made me even crazier."

Jessica described how she had suddenly begun experiencing joint pain and swelling and unusual and untimely aching, and how the various medicines her doctor tried had caused her always-petite athletic frame to fill out.

"You guys were being kind at Chloe's wedding, but I know Mama wasn't the only one to notice. Then a few days after I got the diagnosis, came the best news of my life."

Like the rest of the world, her sisters knew her deal with the

OWN network had fallen apart at the last minute. What they might not have realized from afar was how hard she took it, Jessica told them.

"It was a huge blow to my self-esteem and to my business, because people questioned whether Oprah's team had learned something about me that caused them to pull out, when it was really just a business decision to go in a new direction, and my show was cost-friendly collateral damage, because it hadn't yet aired. So you can imagine when a production company reached out with an offer from Bravo TV, I was on cloud nine."
Shiloh's eyes were wide with wonder.

"God is always blessing you, Jess. Is this really going to happen?"

Tears filled Jessica's eyes and she shrugged.

"Don't know, and right now, it's not a priority. The stupid stuff I did behind trying to make sure it happened is what has given Keith legitimate reasons for wanting to divorce me."

Dayna's eyes grew wide.

"Has he indicated that's what he wants?!"

"Not yet, but hear me out. When you find out what I've done, you'll see why that's what I'm afraid of."

# fifty-six

The silence that followed Jessica's confession left the room as still as the aftermath of a devastating tornado. That was indeed what her choices had created, she realized. Describing to Dayna for the first time, and to Shiloh for a second go round, what she had done was forcing her to be real with herself.

"Why?"

Dayna's simple question seemed to come from an honest stance of curiosity, rather than judgment. Jessica both felt and saw that, and she wasn't offended. It was a question she should have been asking herself all along, especially after Evangeline tried to talk her out of her scheme.

But as with so many things in her life, Jessica had barreled forward, focused on what she wanted and needed, without looking at the full possibility of consequences or results, believing everything would work out. Maybe this time it would, but maybe not.

"I don't have any answer that would make sense or add up to much," she finally told Dayna. "I really don't. Looking back, it was stupid and selfish and just downright dumb. I made choices that were simply idiotic. Maybe I can plead temporary insanity?"

Dayna leaned toward Jessica, her eyes filled of compassion.

"Yeah, little sister, it was."

Jessica was surprised by Dayna's candor, and ashamed that Dayna spoke the truth. Yet she appreciated her doing so, because for too long, she'd felt the absence of both of her older sisters' wisdom and opinions. She hated that it had taken this crisis to turn the tide, but she was unspeakably grateful that a shift had taken place.

Jessica felt like a boulder had been removed from her chest; but at the same time, she wondered if she'd ever walk through life happy again, or if her sisters would retreat to their previous ways of interacting with her, just as their relationship was warming up to a new level of closeness. She wondered if Dayna or Shiloh would tell Mama and Daddy about her mistakes, and cement her place in their parents' minds as the black sheep of the family.

Those things raced through her mind as she sat and watched her sisters' expressionless faces, but Jessica was surprised at the peace that resided in her spirit anyway. Telling the truth had a way of soothing one's spirit, of serving as a balm, she noted. She cared about what her family thought; but not in the same way she had in the past.

This time her caring had more to do with wanting an authentic relationship with them, with wanting them to know and accept her flaws and all, rather than for being the perfect little Jessica they could be proud of and brag about. Her audiences and clients could prop her up that way; she needed her family to love her simply because she existed, and it was time she did her part to deepen that connection.

Shiloh shifted from the edge of the sofa and strolled across the room, to stand in front of a picture window facing out onto the backyard that Jessica rarely frequented. She gazed out of the window for so long, not saying anything that Jessica wondered if her sister had fallen into a trance.

But finally, Shiloh turned back toward Jessica, who was still sitting on the loveseat. She pressed the palms of her hands together, as if she were positioning herself for prayer. The words that followed were deliberate and slowly rendered, with a love that Jessica could feel.

"You are the sum total of your experiences, Jessica – we all are," Shiloh began. "Yet we are also all responsible for our actions and the consequences that follow them. So I'll start by telling you how disappointed I am with how you handled all that you were confronted with. Mama and Daddy didn't necessarily do a good job of helping us bond as sisters, but they always talked about the importance of family. I would have hoped that would have kept you from creating the lie you did and carrying it out.

"On the other hand..." Shiloh shifted her weight and folded her arms. "You are a product of your environment. God bless Mama and Daddy, but they did more preaching and praying than modeling for us what it meant to put family first. I'm trying to break that mold with my sons, even as Randy's role as head pastor of our church keeps him busy. We are intentional about making sure the boys know and feel that they are a priority. You, Dayna and I didn't always get that when we were growing up. We were always put on hold or told to wait because something at the church was pressing. We always had to look the part of the perfect preachers' daughters – never mind how we really felt or what we needed or wanted. I can see how that could have affected you."

Shiloh turned back toward the window and visibly inhaled, as if summoning the strength to continue. Then she approached Jessica, and perched on the love seat next to her, on the other side of Dayna. She looked into Jessica's eyes and continued.

"And then....when you experienced the darkest night of your soul, you were told to pretend it didn't happen. And your family, which should have protected you and fought for you, kept up the façade and went through the motions required by church protocol – giving more trust and benefit of the doubt to the good church members and their child rather than trusting your word and taking care of you. You were taught in that moment that what you really felt and thought and needed didn't matter, weren't you?"

Jessica's eyes swam with tears and the lump in her throat kept her from speaking, but it was okay; Shiloh continued speaking, as if she already knew the answer.

"We told you to forgive and forget and not ruffle any feathers. We questioned whether you had done something to provoke the incident. We insinuated that you could be exaggerating to get attention. What we didn't do was ask if you needed to talk about it – to us or to a professional. We didn't rally around you and stand together with you, no matter what. None of that is an excuse for what you've done to your life and your marriage today, but it certainly serves as a foundation for where you are now."

Dayna grabbed one of Jessica's hands.

"Shiloh is right, Jessica, and I'm sorry. I never thought about any of that after Daddy told us to put it out of our minds. We treated you like a china doll who was cute and convenient, but without substance or relevance. In some ways, we made you into who you are, and being ten years your elder, I take responsibility for my part in all of that. Shiloh and I were teenagers when you were in elementary school and eager to get out from under Mama and Daddy's thumbs; and by the time you got to high school, we were immersed in our adult lives - checking on you when it was convenient, but otherwise oblivious to you and your world. We thought you were spoiled and got away with murder. But maybe we were the spoiled ones, getting away with murder. We certainly didn't do right by you as big sisters.  I'm sorry for my part in that."

Jessica wiped away a tear before it traveled to her chin.  Were they really speaking the words she'd wanted to hear from them all these years? And had it really required all this drama to achieve this level of honesty? The questions might be fair, she decided, but taking time to ruminate over them or answer them wouldn't make any difference at this point.

"Thank you both for everything you've said," Jessica told Dayna and Shiloh. "It means a lot. And yes, what happened in high school changed me, and changed the way I looked at our family, and the world. I felt like you two turned your heads and hearts away from me at a time when I didn't have anyone else to rely on. So I ran away from everything and everyone, all the way to Stanford, where I even outran my demons for a while. But I guess they've shown up almost twenty years later, after my mountain of lies and half-truths got too tall to climb, especially with arthritis.

"It's no excuse for what I've done. But thank you for letting me know you understand how difficult what happened with Xavier on junior prom night was. It changed me, and I guess not for the better, despite the front I presented to the world. Date rape is still rape. It's traumatizing no matter what you call it, and devastating when your family chooses to side with the boy's family and his version of what went down."

Shiloh leaned forward and once again locked eyes with Jessica.

"No more fronting, Jessica. It's time to be real. I told you when we talked by phone yesterday that I've been where you are, and you and Dayna don't know all of my dirty laundry. Just know that I own some, too, and when I stopped trying to pretend it was all white and pure, and 'wear' it, my life changed for the better. You don't have to hang yours all out to dry, either. Just stand in your truths and own who you are and where you are, and let God handle the rest. If you lose the talk show opportunity, it wasn't meant to be. As hard as it may be for you to hear that, it's the truth."

Jessica let those last words sink in, and she could tell Shiloh had paused to allow her to digest them.

"If you lose some mobility, God will give you other ways of getting around," Shiloh continued. "What you can't and shouldn't throw to the wolves or walk away from without a fight is your marriage, or your hope for your life. When either of those head south because you've given up, you can lose everything that matters most to you, Jess. I've seen it happen over and over with people Randy and I have counseled in church. And we all saw it up close with Granna. Nothing is worth sacrificing your sense of self or the relationships that are most important."

Jessica nodded. "What if it's too late, at least with Keith?"

Shiloh scooted closer to Jessica on the love seat, putting Jessica in the middle of her and Dayna.

"All these hips!" she quipped before extending her palms upward toward Jessica as an invitation for Jessica to place her hands inside. Once Jessica had done so, Dayna covered both sisters' hands with both of hers, and Shiloh invited them all to bow their heads.

"We don't have any answers, but God does. Let's pray and give this over to him. He can fix it."

# fifty-seven

A new day was dawning in Jessica's spirit, and despite the turmoil that remained, her sense of calm was growing.

Jessica couldn't remember the last time she'd attended church without Keith nudging her to go, or without him being by her side; but Dayna and Shiloh had insisted on going. She wondered if they'd heard her weeping in her bed this morning, when she awoke and realized that Keith was flying to Philadelphia for work and hadn't texted her. Their rooms were at the end of the hallway, and she'd tried to muffle the sound, but if one of them had been in the hallway for some reason, they could have heard her. All she knew was that thirty minutes later Dayna rapped on the door and told her to get dressed so they could go to her church or find a nearby one, and she better not argue.

So two days into Dayna and Shiloh's visit, the three sisters climbed into Jessica's Lexus and she steered them a few blocks from her home, to a small nondenominational church she had visited on occasion when her pastor served as the guest preacher. Jessica had decided against taking them to the church she and Keith attended, to avoid questions about why she had been away for a few weeks and queries about Keith's absence today. By visiting this church, they would all be newcomers and could simply enjoy the service.

Since Friday, they'd been enjoying each other's company - eating too much and laughing and catching up and being real with each other. Their presence had taken Jessica's mind off of her woes, and off of how much she missed Keith. Even a temporary distraction from the heartache had been helpful.

They slid into a pew in the middle section of the large sanctuary this morning just as the young adult choir launched into an opening song - a hymn that Jessica and her sisters had sung often in the youth choir at their childhood church in Atchity: *We've come this far by faith.*

Jessica leaned over to Dayna, who was sitting to her left, and whispered in her ear.

"I haven't heard that ancient song in years! Can't believe these young people even know it."

Dayna chuckled and whispered back: "They must have an old-school grandmother lurking somewhere around. They didn't find this classic on their own."

Then the choir soared into a contemporary rendition of *Amazing Grace* that brought Dayna and Shiloh to their feet. When everyone else around them stood as well, Jessica grew self-conscious and left her seat, too.

The pastor approached the podium and read the scripture that would be used as the theme of today's sermon, then teed up the next song, which would be a solo by a special guest recording artist, Jonathan McReynolds. Jessica had never heard of him, but at the mention of his name, Shiloh grew so excited, she snuck her cell phone from her purse to snap a picture of the young man as he entered the pulpit and strapped his guitar around his shoulders.

"I love his music! We need to get him to come to our church in Atchity," she leaned over and whispered to Jessica.

When he launched into song and belted out the lyrics in a range higher than many female sopranos could muster, a gasp of delight rippled through the congregation. Simultaneously, his initial lyrics ripped through Jessica's spirit, like a piercing arrow.

*Tryna make up for where I fell short, I let sense slip away...*

"Exactly, Lord. Exactly," Jessica said softly.

This singer had captured her heart's cry in a few words, and that was where she stayed in her spirit, meditating and asking God to do a new thing in her – not just because she had so much to lose; simply because she couldn't go on without him leading the way. All that she knew about God being merciful reassured her that he would give her another chance. Question was, would Keith?

Jessica wasn't expecting an answer right away; she knew she didn't deserve one. What mattered most right now was to be extended God's grace and covered by it. Mama and Daddy had been right all along; they'd been trying to tell her that for years, in regard to herself and to their missteps as parents. Finally, she was ready to hear, and to heal.

# fifty-eight

Their first-ever sister retreat was ending too quickly, as far as Jessica was concerned.

So much important clarity had been gained and so much fun had occurred, even in the pit that Jessica's life had become. She couldn't remember the last time she'd laughed just for the heck of it. She certainly had as recent as three or four months ago, before she fell ill, but that seemed like a lifetime ago. And she'd never opened up to her sisters this way or vice versa. Something good had been borne out of this difficult season, and she was grateful.

It was now Monday afternoon, and Dayna and Shiloh were preparing to fly home in the morning. They sat at the kitchen table enjoying light beverages and plates of the chicken alfredo and broccoli Shiloh had prepared for dinner.

Jessica wolfed down her final few bites, then reared back in the chair with a satisfied smile.

"Baby Arnold is satisfied and so am I," she said and feigned a frown. "But I don't know what I'm going to do when you leave."

Dayna took a bite of her food and raised an eyebrow. Shiloh mirrored the expression.

"I can see that you two have been talking," Jessica said.

"All in love, little sis," Dayna said. "We want the best for you, and we want you to be okay when we leave, regardless of what

Keith decides. I can tell you that he loves you. He texted Shiloh and me late last night and asked us to check on you because he was out of town. He had no idea we're already here, so that shows he's thinking of you.'"

That little tidbit of news made her heart leap with joy. There was still hope that he loved her.

"So we will be praying – for both of you," Shiloh said. "We love you both and we know you love each other. You did something really stupid, Jessica; that's the God-honest truth, and you know it. But God gives grace and second chances. We will be praying that all will work out with you and Keith and our new addition to the family. And because we are praying we're believing it *will* work out, deal?"

Jessica lowered her head and nodded. Phrases from Scriptures she'd heard her entire life came floating back to her: *prayers of the righteous availeth much; all things work together for the good of those who love God…*

"Now, about you…" Dayna continued. "I'm so sorry about this arthritis diagnosis. It breaks my heart. But you don't have to be like Granna, Jess. She lived in a different time, in a small Alabama town, with certain stigmas and cultural habits surrounding marriage and chronic illnesses and the like. She wound up being a victim of not only the condition, but also the environment. You don't have those same challenges.  There are so many technological advances in treatment, and you live in a metropolitan area with excellent health care options. You are going to be fine. Take some time to do some research on the condition to find out if there are any support groups in the area, so you can connect with other young mothers dealing with this. We have groups like this at the hospital system I work for in Florida. And I know you can go online and find some groups like this – in a hot second."

Jessica sat up straighter, her hope rising with each suggestion Dayna offered. Why hadn't she thought of any of this before? She didn't have to do this alone.

"And Jess?" Shiloh leaned across the table and reached for her hand. "Don't shy away from seeking the help of a professional counselor. You can talk to someone about all of these transitions taking place in your life, and you can go with Keith, if he's open to it, because these issues affect him as much as you. Being diagnosed with a chronic illness can take a toll on the patient, and on the entire family; it's okay to reach out for help. And for prayer. Go meet with your pastor and get the support of your church leaders so they can support you and Keith. And just keep praying. Constantly."

Jessica leveled her eyes at Shiloh.

"Now let's be honest. You know I'm not as saintly as you. I don't know that my prayers get through as clearly as yours."

Shiloh chuckled.

"There's no competition or rating chart; if you take the time to send them up, I guarantee you they're received. You might be rusty at talking to him, but God still knows who you are. "

Jessica shook her head.

"Your intervention 'pow wow' about me yielded all of this? I think we need to have a sister retreat every year, so I can return the favor. Thanks, you two."

Dayna sat forward.

"Let's get one thing straight. This isn't about being tit for tat. We should have been doing what we needed to do for each other and standing together way sooner than this. I'm sorry it took a crisis to bring us together. But I'm thankful that we're finally here. And thank you for being open to hosting us and hearing us. I agree with Shiloh about the counseling, Jess. And when you go, deal with what happened in high school, too. You've got to have some scars from that. I'm sorry I wasn't a better person back then, and able to stand with you."

"I'm sorry, too, Jessica," Shiloh said. "It was an uncomfortable situation so I did what was easiest to make myself comfortable: follow Mama and Daddy's lead in pretending it didn't happen and going on with life as usual. Everyone *was* able to go on, except you. And we were wrong for that. Please forgive me."

Jessica tucked her chin and she closed her eyes. How long had she waited for someone in her family to acknowledge that they had abandoned her when she needed them most? That she had been forced to fake a smile on the Sunday after the rape to keep the peace between Daddy and the chief church trustee, whose son was the perpetrator? As relief washed over Jessica, she realized that she'd actually been living a lie for half her life, since she was seventeen - the lie that everything was right and perfect with her family, with her heart, and with her spirit, when the truth was she had been violated, then told to tuck away what had happened for a greater good, as if she weren't worthy of justice.

It saddened her that this closure wasn't coming from Mama and Daddy, but in this moment, she realized she had to accept that it probably never would. She had to find a way to forgive everyone and love anyway. For her sake, for Keith's, and for their baby. The time needed to be now.

# fifty-nine

When Jessica returned home from dropping off Shiloh and Dayna at the airport, her house now seemed eerily quiet.

For the first time in a while, however, she no longer felt like climbing into bed. She wasn't ready to refocus on work, but a baby step would be to follow Evangeline's advice, and her sisters.

Her initial task was to text Sage at WNVX and ask for a phone meeting, followed by a call to Ron and Paula Tennyson to see if they could join her for lunch. This would be a full day, but she wanted to strike while she felt up to it. Maybe Autumn and Brigit could join her for dinner tonight, instead of simply delivering it. Then she called Catherine, the yoga and meditation instructor, to schedule a private consultation. Keith had taken the business card with the therapist's name on it with him, so she summoned the courage to text and ask him for that information, not sure if he'd respond, and if he did, if it would be serious or sarcastic.

After issuing her missives, she grabbed her laptop and plopped on the sofa that her sisters had graced the past five days, and turned on the TV, simply as background chatter. She typed in the words "living with rheumatoid arthritis" and was stunned to see a vast array of patient-authored blogs, organizational websites and social media posts populate the page. Her next search was for "pregnancy" and "arthritis," which yielded not only blogs and Tweets, but also pregnancy and baby-related websites, with expectant and new moms sharing their challenges and how they lived with their illness and delivered healthy babies.

Jessica found herself sucked into the Internet community of caring and sharing she had never thought to turn to, despite a career built on conducting research and making connections. Women were sharing tips on the best exercises to undertake while pregnant, and medicines that were deemed safest, or simply venting and sharing their stories. Some talked about their arthritis going into remission while they were pregnant, giving them a respite from the ailments everyone on the boards and blogs could relate to. What Jessica loved most was how they cheered each other on, and how even without someone posting a full explanation or overview of their situation, others could easily grasp and understand the concerns, because they had in some way experienced similar challenges.

Jessica was simply blown away, but also grateful. Her sisters were right; she was not alone by any means, even if the community was virtual. These women were expressing many of the fears and frustrations and the anger and pain she dealt with on a regular basis. They were going to be her lifeline.

Before she knew it, two hours had passed. Her rumbling stomach was her cue to get up and take a break. When she slowly unfurled her body, it felt lighter, and so did her mind and heart. The facts of her situation hadn't changed; but her sisters were right, it was time to change her mind about how she was going to manage life.

# sixty

The timing couldn't have been better. Sage called minutes before she stepped into the garage to drive downtown for her lunch meeting with Ron and Paula.

"I've been praying for you, you know?" Sage said after she and Jessica traded routine pleasantries. "You can't help that you needed bedrest. The baby comes first.  How is everything?"

Because Jessica had taken a medical leave of absence from taping her WNVX show, she and Sage hadn't seen each other regularly, and Sage didn't know that Jessica's due date was an entire month later than she had been told. After much prayer and rumination, Jessica didn't find it necessary to revisit all of that just now. If Sage was open to her suggestions, they could resolve it all when Jessica resumed her segments. If WNVX would still have her.

"It's a long, long story, Sage; but briefly, the baby is not due until late December. And in addition to managing pregnancy, I'm managing rheumatoid arthritis."

"Excuse me?"

Realizing this would take longer than a few minutes, Jessica sat pulled out a chair at her breakfast nook table, and gazed at the chirping blue jays while she filled Sage in on as much as she publicly wanted to share.

"I don't know yet when I'll be able to come back; I definitely want to get used to motherhood. But if WNVX is still interested in working with me at some point, I'd like to weave in segments on living with and successfully managing a chronic condition, whatever it may be and also a regular piece of encouragement for caregivers. That's so important."

Sage seemed stunned by it all, but also intrigued by the idea Jessica was pitching. "Well, what about your Bravo show? Is that on hold? How will you have time to do both?"

Jessica sighed. "I'll be meeting with Ron and Paula shortly, but I'm guessing it will be shelved, at this point. If it's meant to happen, God will orchestrate it in a beautiful, stress free way."

***

Forty-five minutes later, when Jessica shared that exact sentiment with Ron and Paula, they agreed more readily than she had anticipated.

"Life happens, Jessica, and you just have to move and flow with it, and find contentment in the softest and most loving place you can land."

With those word of wisdom, Ron rose from the meeting table and came around to hug Jessica. "You've become like a little sister to us through this process, you know? We know you've been going through a lot, and we don't regret the time we invested in trying to work this Bravo deal. But family comes first. Especially your new baby, and a new baby needs a healthy Mama."

He squeezed her gently one last time, before departing for a previously scheduled meeting a few blocks away, leaving Jessica and Paula to wrap up.

Paula gazed at her for a long while, without speaking. Because the stare oozed with affection and concern, Jessica wasn't uncomfortable. But finally, she had to ask, "What? What is it?? I know I look like a big bear."

Jessica chuckled at her own joke, and Paula couldn't help but laugh, too.

"You don't look anything like a bear, silly lady. I was gazing at you and praying over you, and giving thanks that you found the courage to come here today and have this conversation," Paula said. She leaned forward across the table, to make eye contact with

Jessica, and the intensity of the caring made Jessica want to cry.

"Ever since we abruptly canceled the pilot show cocktail party, I knew God wasn't going to give you the Bravo show, at least right now."

Jessica raised an eyebrow, and Paula nodded.

"Everything that glitters isn't gold, especially if the shine wears off after a little wear and tear, Jessica. Whatever was going on in your life at that time, and has been going on, was wearing and tearing, and you needed to live through that, instead of heaping a spotlight on a soul that wasn't centered."

Jessica sat back in her chair and hung her head. How did this woman know what had been going on in her life, when they weren't even that close? Had someone been talking? And then, the answer came in the form of a gift: Paula's own story.

"I too once wanted to host a national talk show, Jessica. I was an up-and-coming celebrity news anchor in New York, and I was going somewhere. But you know what I did? I decided that even though I was married, it wouldn't hurt to step outside my marriage just one time. Because if I landed the show, the fame, the influence, the money and all the other opportunities that came with the gig would make life better for me and Ron."

Jessica's eyes and mouth simultaneously flew open.

"You cheated? On Ron?"

Paula took a deep breath and nodded.

"I did. Twenty years ago. For nothing."

The two women sat in silence while Paula's raw truths resonated.

"But how...why..."

"He loved me enough to forgive me, Jessica, and I prayed for God to forgive me, too. We left New York and moved back here, to Ron's hometown and decided that whatever work God had for us to do, we would do it as a unit, walking in integrity, and surrounded by friends, family, and spiritual leaders who would hold us accountable. It was a bold choice. And I think I can accurately say that neither of us have regretted it. We will have been married thirty-one years in September, and each of our two sons have given us daughters-in-law and two granddaughters."

Jessica was openly weeping, and Paula reached for her hand.

"I don't know what you're going through or why, other than the medical diagnosis you've shared today. But I want you to know that I'm pulling for you, Jessica, and praying for you. I see a lot of myself in you: energy and ambition, but also loyalty and a big heart. Even though all of it's important, try not to lose sight of what matters most. And know that you've at least gotten two new friends out of the deal. When you're feeling up to it, Ron and I want to take you and Keith to dinner, okay? And we're coming to the baby dedication down the road, whenever that happens."

Jessica smiled through her tears, believing that if she held onto her hope and trusted her heart, God might make a way for her and Keith to one day fellowship in harmony again, and break bread with this couple. And having them at her baby's dedication would be a blessing.

She stole Paula's signature move and gave her a thumbs up. "Done deal."

# sixty-one

An unexpected joy coursed through Jessica that evening when she opened the front door and saw her two beautiful neighbors standing before her.

"It's been weeks since I laid eyes on you, and you're still picture-perfect. Heifers!"

Autumn and Brigit looked at each other and giggled.

"Praise God – she's back!" Autumn yelled. Then she leaned in and grabbed Jessica, holding her close for a heartfelt hug that radiated all the love and concern she didn't verbally convey. Jessica held her tightly, praying that her own message was getting through to her friend.

Brigit balanced a bag of food over the threshold. "I'm hungry and don't want to spill all of this good stuff. Let's go inside so I can put it on the table and get my hug."

Jessica led them to the kitchen, then stopped in the doorway and did an about-face.

"You know what? The fact that we're getting together for the first time in a while, and that I feel up to it, is cause for celebration. Let's sit in the fancy dining room."

Brigit grinned. "Alright with me, girl."

She turned around and led Jessica and Autumn there, and set the food on table. Jessica squealed when she saw the P.F. Chang's logo on the bags.

"When you texted I realized that this was going to be a special evening, so I ran out and got some of your favorite Chinese, to make it extra special," Brigit said.

"Thank you, B." Jessica finally held her in a hug. "I've missed you. I've missed you both, and I'm sorry."

Brigit pulled away and looked at her.

"No need to apologize, Jess. We all go through tough times. I'm so sorry about the arthritis. But you are going to be okay, cause we aren't going anywhere."

Autumn approached and put an arm around each of them. "She's right. Whatever and whenever, we're here for you. I know you've got to deal with the emotional stuff about the diagnosis, and that's why we let you breathe. But when it comes to the physical stuff you can't do, just call. Any time."

Autumn was glowing, and with it being her second pregnancy, her stomach was already protruding in a manner that made it clear she was expecting.

"It's those weak abdomen muscles," she said, when she noticed Jessica looking. "First baby ruined 'em!"

Jessica dismissed the comment with a wave of her hand. "You look great, as always."

"You do too, Jess," Brigit said. "I'm actually surprised."

Jessica motioned for them to take a seat at the table.

"I have to admit that I'm surprised, too; but I just wrapped up a great visit with my sisters, and it was such a blessing. I'm ready to try and get my life back."

Jessica realized they were only partially prepared for their meal and headed toward the kitchen.

"Sit tight while I go grab some plates and silverware. And do you want something to drink?"

Brigit stood up to follow her.

"I'll grab the water. That's all Autumn is drinking these days, and so I'm using her as my role model for healthy eating and drinking. What about you?"

"I'll have the same," Jessica said.

She and Brigit returned to the dining room with everything they needed for a proper dinner of takeout, and the three of them eagerly dug into the saucy dishes.

"Thank you, B," Jessica said. "You and Autumn have been wonderful to me. I can't thank you enough. Really."

"Again...no thanks needed," Brigit said. "We love you, Jessica."

Tears filled her eyes, and she distracted herself by enjoying the food.

They took time over the meal to catch up on each other's lives, and at some point, the conversation turned to Keith.

"Where is he again?" Autumn asked. "I know he's been working hard, so our hubbies haven't seen him either. Is he okay with the diagnosis? And how are you dealing with him needing to be away while you grapple with this?"

Here was another moment of truth. Jessica's thoughts raced as she questioned how to handle the questions being lobbed at her without betraying Keith or the confidences sacred to her marriage, and without making herself look like an innocent saint, without spilling her guts about her transgressions. She took a bite of spring roll and chewed it slowly, to buy some time before responding.

After a few seconds, Jessica took a deep breath and decided to be as frank as possible.

"What you should be asking is how am I dealing with the diagnosis, with Keith being away, and with the baby...

Jessica uttered a quick, silent prayer for this conversation not to cause Brigit personal pain, given that she had been trying for a while to conceive. "I'm due later than I originally told you guys. Surprise, surprise. I really do have a lot going on, don't I?"

The smile on Brigit's lips finally reached her eyes, which were filled with tears, and Jessica grew worried again. But Brigit's actions assured her it was okay to share this update. She hugged Jessica's neck and whispered in her ear, "Good for you, Jess. Good for you. Keith is very happy, I'm sure, and don't worry – you're going to be a great mom."

Those reassuring words made Jessica cry. She wiped her eyes with the back of a hand, and Brigit leaned toward the center of the table to grab one of the unused napkins Jessica had placed there for their meal.

"Guess I'll be hosting two showers, huh?" Brigit said and chuckled.

"I'll help you with Jess's." Autumn grinned.

"And I'm still helping you with Autumn's," Jessica told Brigit. Brigit frowned.

"Don't bite off more than you can chew, Jess. Taking care of yourself is your priority."

Autumn nodded. "I agree. This is baby number two for me. If for some reason you two decided you couldn't host a shower, I would completely understand."

Jessica smiled at them. "I am taking care of myself and I promise not to overdue it. The shower will be fun."

She waved at the plates, utensils and empty cartons on the table. "Let's leave all of this for cleanup later. Come with me."

When they were settled in the family room, with Autumn and Brigit sitting on the love seat like two mischievous school-age beauties in trouble in the principal's office, Jessica sat adjacent to them and tucked her feet beneath her on the sofa.

"I may need you two to help me get out of this position in a few minutes, but I'm comfortable for now." Jessica tried to chuckle at herself, but an unexpected wave of sadness hit her. Was this the kind of thing she would be saying forever?

She pushed that thought away and noticed that Autumn and Brigit seemed unsure of whether to laugh along with her or take her seriously. Jessica sighed.

"You know what, friends? None of this is going to be easy. I'm going to lapse into pity parties in the middle of a fun time; you might say something that sounds insensitive without meaning; we might all just get cranky and tired of each other on a particular day and need our space. Can we agree that we're going to muddle through it together, no matter what? That's what I need most right now. To know that I can be myself, and you'll be yourselves, and we'll still be okay. Okay?"

"Done." Autumn and Brigit uttered the declaration simultaneously, as if rehearsed.

Jessica belted out a laugh, and she was glad that she had trusted them with the truth, at least all she could bear to share at the moment. Between her sisters' support, her loyal friends and her growing relationship with God, she was going to be okay. And she wasn't giving up on her husband, either. Keith had a right to work through this in his own way, just as she had. She decided she was going to love him enough to give him all the time he needed.

# sixty-two

Life was expanding, in more ways than one.

The next few weeks are a blur of doctor's appointments, local speaking engagements that were already on the books and easy to fulfill, and strained dinners at home with Keith. Along with bloating from her steroid medication, her waistline had expanded due to pregnancy, and at thirteen weeks, she was finally beginning to develop a noticeable tummy bump. She loved looking at it, and when she caught Keith sneaking glances at her on more than one occasion, knew he did, too.

Since his return from Philadelphia two weeks ago, he informed her he was willing to go to counseling, as she requested, but he wasn't ready to move home yet. After the first therapy session, that same week of his return, Dr. Savage had recommended that they at least share a meal several times a week, so he could stay in the loop on the progress of her pregnancy, and they could begin to get to know each other again, as individuals and as friends. The effort was awkward, but at least they were trying.

Jessica was much more centered, now that she had a support system in place. Her first private consultation with Catherine had been last week, and she was already eliminating some foods from her diet and adding more of others that had anti-inflammatory properties or mood boosting properties, or other helpful, natural qualities. Catherine had suggested that she began researching websites and blogs that offered guidance on healthy eating for people with autoimmune illnesses.

"You'll notice a difference over time – in your energy level and in how you feel overall," Catherine had promised. "Plus, your skin will be more beautiful than it already is, and your post-pregnancy weight will naturally stabilize."

Catherine's guidance, plus the scriptures on healing that Shiloh texted her every morning, were so helpful. Dayna had gotten in the habit of texting her articles about the latest trends in arthritis treatment, and also pregnancy/mom-to-be websites, and Brigit and Autumn continued to keep her in their dinner prep plans a few times a week, so she wouldn't wear herself out trying to cook. Jessica knew she was blessed.

Yet the unknown future of her marriage still left her anxious. Keith no longer seemed angry; it was his indifference that now frightened her. She knew he loved her; but the question was, did he love her enough to fight for their life together. She wasn't so sure, and as the therapist had reiterated in their first two sessions with him, she needed to give Keith space and time to decide that for himself, and just remain consistent in showing how much she loved him and wanted to make their union work.

This afternoon, however, Dr. Savage took time in their hour-long session to push both of them to another level of honesty and commitment.

Jessica had met with him privately a few times, to discuss the teenage trauma that had occurred after being date raped at prom, and how that may have impacted the decisions she made all these years later, in her marriage. Today, he challenged her to talk to Keith about it.

Jessica turned her chair to face her husband and took a long, deep breath before looking him the eyes and revealing this traumatic chapter of her life that she had never shared. She decided to blurt it out before she chickened out.

"Keith, when I was seventeen, I went to prom with one of the best-looking guys at my dad's church. All the girls in my class were drooling over him that night, and jealous that I showed up on his arm. But when we left, I guess he decided I owed him something for making me the bell of the ball. I kissed him and all that, but I never said yes to more. And..." she gulped, fiddling with a corner of the table cloth. "He, uh." Oh gosh, she hated remembering. "He went all the way anyway, despite anything I did to stop him. He held his hand over my mouth, in the backseat of his car and raped me."

Jessica inhaled to center herself and to give Keith a few seconds to digest her words.

"I never told you before because honestly, it's something that I tried to put out of my mind," she said.

Keith clearly was stunned. He didn't speak for a few minutes, and finally, Dr. Savage prompted him.

"Do you want to tell Jessica what's on your mind?"

The pained expression on his face let her know how much he loved her. She could tell that he was angry on her behalf.

"I'm wondering why you kept quiet all these years. Did you tell anyone?"

Jessica lowered her eyes and took a deep breath, before looking up into her husband's perplexed eyes.

"I went home that night and stepped inside my house, where my mother was up waiting for me to return, and I fell into her arms and told her what had happened. At first she thought I had been kidnapped somehow and a stranger had harmed me, but when I explained that it had been Xavier her demeanor changed. She wanted to know how we would tell my father that the head of his deacon board's son had hurt me. She worried about the church gossip and about me being called fast. She asked me what had I done to lead him on."

The tears slid down each of Jessica's cheeks as she spoke.

"Then she urged me to go take a shower and get clean and not tell anyone what had happened. I did as I was told and cried myself to sleep – that night and for many nights afterward."

"What did Dayna and Shiloh say? Or do?"

Jessica lowered her eyes and shook her head.

"They're much older than me, remember? Dayna was twenty-seven and busy with her career as a nurse and the man who was her husband at the time, and Shiloh was already married with a child. I tried to tell them one day that something bad happened on prom night, but Mama had already put in their heads that I had been acting inappropriate and she believed I was trying to cover up something. They believed her and told me to stop being dramatic, or overreacting, or trying to cause trouble – the stuff they heard Mama say. Daddy did eventually ask me what happened that night, and I was so embarrassed, I couldn't tell him everything. I just told him that Xavier wouldn't stop when I said no. He didn't ask me anything else about it, and life went on as normal. I realized then what mattered most to them, and that next month, I applied to Stanford, and I stayed in my books to make sure I'd have the grades to get in and get as far away from Atchity and that church as I could."

Dr. Savage sat forward in his chair and raised an eyebrow.

"But you still go back to that church, to this day, and home to visit your parents, and your siblings. You did that on every college break, right? So you ran, but not far."

Jessica shrugged. "I went along with the game plan, that's what I did. I kept the peace. That's what made Mama and Daddy happy. As long as we looked like the perfect family, we had to be, right?"

Keith leaned over and reached for Jessica's hand.

"I'm so sorry that happened to you, Jess. We've known each other for more than a dozen years and been married almost ten years. That's a heavy secret to keep."

"Maybe," Dr. Savage told Keith, "it kept her locked in a pattern of trying to be perfect and create the perfect life at all costs. This doesn't excuse her from the lies she told or the choices she made; but do you see how they could have been driven by the devastation that ripped her soul apart that night, and going forward? Her parents compelled her to live a lie to protect the status quo, and it sent her a message that the church, the teenage boy and his family, and their reputation were more important than her truth and her well-being."

Keith closed his eyes and took in Dr. Savage's message. When he opened them, his eyes glistened with tears.

"I vow to never do that to our baby," he told Jessica, "I never want anyone I love to feel that way."

Jessica sat forward and longed to hug him. He looked miserable, and she wasn't sure why.

"You never have, Keith. I'm the one who hurt you, for no reason at all. I never thought that something that happened so long ago, that I had basically pushed out of my mind, could affect us, but I should have known better. It has affected my relationship with my family all these years. I'm still not as close to my parents as I could be, because there's still some resentment there for the choices they made in handling this. And I certainly pushed away God, because on that horrible night, I prayed for Him to intervene, but no one came. And on top of that, my parents didn't believe me. What kind of God answers prayer that way?"

A glimmer of understanding filled Keith's eyes.

"Is that why you've always been so nonchalant about attending church and all that?"

Jessica nodded.

"I guess so - yeah. Shiloh and Dayna and I finally cleared the air about this when they visited a few weeks ago. They admitted to turning a blind eye, and that was helpful. It showed me that I'm not crazy. They apologized, and you know what, even all these years later, hearing 'I'm sorry' was healing."

She extended her hand toward Keith and was grateful when he placed his palm inside hers. Touching him made her want to weep, but she contained her emotions.

"I'm sorry for hurting you so deeply with a selfish, foolish lie, Keith Arnold. I love you with everything in me, and I'm grateful to be your wife and the mother of your child. If you can find it in your heart to forgive me, I'm willing to do whatever work is necessary to for us to find our way back to each other.

"I can't promise that I'm going to be all smiles and act like everything is okay when it's not, but I will do as my Granna used to demand when I was whiny as a kid and put my 'big girl pants' on. Whatever I have to do, I'll do it to get better, stay healthy and make our lives work."

As Keith stared at her, she saw a mixture of longing and hope and fear in his deep brown eyes, and it made her desire even more to make everything okay. She knew he was wondering if he could trust her again, and finally, he admitted it.

"I don't know what to say or do, Jessica. I just don't know."

Jessica wanted to hear him declare what he'd been telling her for the past few months before he found out about her lies, and truthfully, for their entire marriage: That he would be there for her, help her get through challenges, make her laugh, and insure that she was loved.

She longed to hear him say those words, although she didn't deserve to hear them right now. And in the same moment she had that deep craving, another reality struck her. Maybe, just maybe, Keith needed to hear those words from her for a change.

"Keith? I am with you, no matter what, and no matter how long it takes. You work your way through this however you need. I'm not going anywhere, and I'm not telling any more lies to fix what's beyond my control."

# sixty-three

Jessica drove away from the appointment with Dr. Savage more hopeful than she had been since she could remember.

Keith had walked her to her car and leaned over to give her a light hug.

"You shared a lot today. Thank you," he said.

She didn't know what that meant, but she would take it as his form of an olive branch.

"I meant what I said, Keith. You mean the world to me. I'm willing to do whatever work I need to, to get our relationship back on track."

He nodded, but remained noncommittal.

"I'll see you at the next doctor's appointment," he finally responded. "Thursday at 10 a.m. right?"

"You got it," Jessica said.

She climbed into her SUV and watched him saunter to his car across the parking lot. When he had driven away and was finally out of her view, she picked up her cell and dialed her hair stylist, Shanice.

"It's time," Jessica told her, after they exchanged pleasantries.

"I still have your appointment for this afternoon on the books," Shanice said. "Come on now and I can have you out of here by 7 p.m."

When Jessica eased into the stylish young woman's chair half an hour later, she watched through a mirror as Shanice ran a comb, then a brush through her shoulder length bob, to show her how it had grown, in just a few weeks.

"Pregnancy suits you, girl. Your hair is growing like a weed," Shanice teased.

Jessica chuckled. The old version of herself would have loved it and longed to keep it. But these days, she wanted to shed anything that hid her face or seemed to cloak her spirit. She didn't want to hide behind masks any more, whether literal or figurative. Her face was full from both the pregnancy and the steroids she continued to take for her arthritis, but she didn't care right now. Her beauty was going to have to emanate from within.

"It's cute, but let's cut it. I want a short bob."

This time Shanice paused.

"Are you sure?

"Let's go really short. Like Halle Berry, Jennifer Hudson short. Just make me slay."

Shanice sighed and then curved her lips into a smile.

"God is really working on you, isn't He? Let's do it, beautiful."

# sixty-four

After living in her roomy house alone for eight weeks, Jessica had grown accustomed to the late afternoon silence.

For the first few weeks after emerging from the cocoon of her bed, she had used the television both as background noise and her steady companion. Since she had begun working with Catherine, however, she appreciated long stretches of silence to think, and just be, and she found when she allowed her mind and her body to relax into simply breathing and existing, she wasn't as stiff or as achy in the late evenings and mornings. Catherine kept asserting that the mind-body connection was real, and Jessica was turning into a true believer.

After a productive day, Jessica shut off her computer and prepared to make herself some tuna salad for dinner. Thursdays were one of the few nights during the week that she prepared meals for herself; otherwise, Brigit and Autumn continued to take care of her. By now, they had figured out that Keith wasn't coming home any time soon, but they had said very little and had continued to love on her through visits, calls, texts and regular meal drop offs. Their silent support had meant the world to Jessica, and if anyone needed a tangible example of God's love in action, she had decided this was it.

Her doorbell rang about four p.m. and she surmised that one

of the sister-friends was dropping by on the way home. The more her belly grew, the more she felt like she was toddling, instead of walking. She loped through the foyer and opened her door to a surprise – one she wouldn't have predicted in a million years.

"Tari?"

Her virtual assistant was shorter and thinner in person, but her face and her bright smile were the same. In fact, the pictures didn't do her justice. She was downright lovely. Jessica opened her arms and leaned down to envelope Tari in a hug.

"What on earth are you doing here – in the flesh?"

"Coming to see you – in the flesh!" Tari quipped.

There was a teenage girl standing next to her, and Tari gestured to introduce her.

"Okay, the truth is, I came to visit the area with my niece, Braelyn, and her family. She'll be a freshman at Butler University in the fall. So this was just perfect for seeing you as well. I got here early this morning and got some work done by computer, and after today I'll spend the weekend with her and her parents, checking out the campus and city. She came along to meet you, in case you need a reliable mother's helper, or even a babysitter, in the coming months."

Jessica's eyes lit up, and she extended her hand to Braelyn.

"That just might work out perfectly. Nice to meet you, young lady."

Jessica led them inside and offered to give them a mini-tour. "This is my office," she said, and allowed them to peek inside the study on the first floor, just off the foyer. "This is where I'm sitting most of the time when we talk, Tari."

Then she ushered them into the family room, where they got comfortable while she went to retrieve water and soda for them.

"You have a lovely home," Tari said. "But I wouldn't have expected anything less from you. And I absolutely love your new haircut. It's so becoming on you!"

Jessica blushed. "Even with my fat, mama-to-be face and body?"

Tari waved dismissively. "You are glowing and you look amazing."

They exchanged a few more pleasantries, then Tari grew serious. "I do have some business I need to chat with you about, since I'm here. It's better to discuss this in person, any way." Tari turned toward her niece. "Can you sit in the car for a few minutes?"

Jessica frowned. There was more to this visit than she thought. "She doesn't have to do that." She leaned over to the end table next to the sofa and grabbed her iPad. Want to surf online or maybe go into the kitchen and watch TV?

Braelyn smiled.

"Sure, I can go sit in the kitchen, but I have my cell phone and I have a hotspot; I can just get on that while you two talk."

Jessica smiled and directed her to the kitchen, before turning back to Tari.

"She's a sweet girl. Thank you for introducing us; I may indeed need to call her to babysit, and one of my neighborhood friends who is expecting a baby might need her, too."

Tari grinned. "That would make her day. She's the oldest of four, so she knows her way around kids, and she's good with them."

She shifted slightly on the sofa and adopted a formal posture.

"So... here's what I wanted to talk with you about, and it's just God's divine timing that I get to do this in person, because this isn't easy news to share."

Jessica was itching to interrupt and ask if she were pregnant, getting married, quitting or something else, but she sat tight.

"There's no easy way to say this, so I'll just say it. You received a formal email notice from Bravo TV, indicating that their funding for your project had to be diverted to another project with a more timely reach. I don't think they stated the name of the new project, but ...."

Tari's voice trailed off from there, at least in Jessica's mind, because she didn't hear the rest of anything her assistant/friend said. Paula had hinted that this would happen, but hearing the words – for a second time on this particular project – sent her reeling.

When she forced her attention back into real time, Tari was still talking.

".... So what they are wanting to do is cut you a check for a portion of the production fee and the episodes that you filmed, then have you sign a document saying you release them from all responsibility otherwise."

"Why are they doing this again?"

Tari shrugged. "The letter said something about a more timely and pressing project was taking precedence right now. They are not saying it's over forever, but there's no reason to shoot a pilot right now, and there's no timetable for getting this back on track. I'm sorry, Jessica."

Jessica sat back and stared at the ceiling. She rubbed the small lump of stomach protruding from her shirt and told herself it was okay. Everything worked out for the good of those who love God, and this would, too. She looked at Tari, who seemed worried and anxious.

"You remember when I first shared my diagnosis with you, and you told me about your faith?" Jessica asked her.

Tari nodded.

"Well, mine has been growing ever since then, and little by little, inch by inch, I'm trying to transform into the woman God wants me to be, Tari. If he means for me to host this show, it will happen – without my pushing or pulling or fretting."

Jessica silently mused whether the cancellation was punishment for coveting the show so much that she jeopardized her marriage to secure it. If that were the case, she had no reason to balk. Or, could it be that the producers saw her recently at a pre-shoot planning meeting and had a change of heart when they realized how thick pregnancy already had made her. They didn't know that arthritis medication was playing a role, too, but they may have been put off by her swollen hands and feet, and her extra puffy face. Her friends kept reminding her how beautiful she looked, but these producers were all about business.

Jessica surprised herself by how calmly she was receiving this news.

"Don't worry, Tari, something else will fall into place, and it will be what God intended. I'm not going to fret over this or worry about their decision. They can send me my cancellation check and we can call it a day, okay?"

Tari's eyes widened.

"This is a Jessica I don't know...."

Jessica laughed.

"I'm trying to figure out who she is, too, friend. I'd like her to stay around a while."

# sixty-five

Just like that, one dream was deferred and another was born. Tari and Jessica embraced after their meeting and strolled toward the kitchen, where Braelyn waited.

"Whatcha doing?" Tari asked.

Braelyn shrugged. "Looking at some videos on YouTube. "

She looked from her aunt to Jessica. "I have to confess, I'm a nerd, and like to watch Ted Talks. See?"

Jessica chuckled. "No worries here; I'm a professional speaker, so I watch them all the time to borrow ideas and get pointers.'"

Braelyn's eyes grew wide. "You get on stage and do what they do? All the time?"

Jessica shrugged. "Pretty much."

It felt refreshing to talk about what she did, for a change, with someone eager to learn more. By the time Jessica explained her job of speaking on the college circuit and the dream "deferred" TV show, Braelyn was enthralled.

"Looks like I'll be keeping my day gig for a while. The TV talk show I was planning to film a pilot for has decided to 'move in a new direction.'"

Jessica sighed and rubbed her belly. This child growing inside her was her greater joy; she would be okay.

Braelyn shrugged, too. "Sorry about that, but why don't you do your own thing?"

Jessica frowned. "What do you mean?"

Braelyn pointed at the screen.

"Buy you a small digital camera you can set on a table, and film yourself sharing the messages you would have shared on the local TV stations. Then set up your own YouTube and Periscope channels, pursue followers and go from there. It's easy, and if you can get at least half a million solid followers, some TV shows will come looking for you, to have as a guest. New talent gets discovered this way all the time."

Jessica sat up straighter. This young lady was on to something.... She didn't necessarily need half a million followers, but why couldn't she spread her message however and whenever she wanted? She'd need to create a polished intro and exit for her videos to look professional, but she could do this after the baby came, to see where it took her and whether it made a difference. Something told her it would. This meeting, and this conversation, hadn't been a coincidence.

"What's your major, Braelyn?"

"Sociology."

"Cool," Jessica said. "If you need internship this time next year, remember this conversation. You just created an associate producer position for yourself."

Later that evening, after they were gone, Jessica sat in her bed, doing what she had done for the past few weeks since beginning the sessions with the therapist. First, she texted Keith good night and told him she loved him, with no expectation that he would return the gesture. So far, he hadn't.

Then, she grabbed her iPad and researched Periscope, learning all she could about this Twitter-related video app, which was skyrocketing in popularity. She downloaded the app to her iPad, then surfed over to YouTube, to see what the highest viewed channels and segments were, beyond the music videos. In her searching, she stumbled across a video with just thirty-five thousand viewers, but the title of the piece, "Mastering the Power of Surrender," caught her eye.

An older, Caucasian woman with strawberry blonde short hair had produced it, and Jessica clicked on the link to see what this woman had to share. Within minutes, Jessica found herself uttering the prayer the woman on the video insisted had changed her life.

"I surrender all to you God, for it's all yours anyway. I give thanks for being the steward you chose for my child, for my life partner, for my opportunities, and for my purpose at this moment in time. I treat them all with reverence and respect, yet I also surrender the paths and outcomes to you, and thank you for choosing me for these blessed roles. I let go, and surrender and trust that you will divinely work out everything for my highest and best good and for the highest and best good of those I love. Amen."

Jessica paused the video and replayed certain passages of the prayer over and over. She repeated them aloud, in a breathy whisper, trusting and believing for the first time in a long, long time that God had indeed heard her, and that he would indeed answer, in his own timing.

# *sixty-six*

Jessica sat by the window watching Keith sit in the driveway. It had taken a few weeks, but the sight of his car let her know that God was listening to her prayers. She didn't know how this would all turn out, but if nothing else, God was bringing Keith closer, for some particular reason.

Keith had been parked there for more than an hour, which let her know the balance could tip either way. He could finish wrestling with himself and drive off, or he could summon the strength to forgive her and come inside.

Jessica clung to the memories of the readings and scriptures she'd found at his bedside a couple of months ago, and prayed fervently that he would remember them, too. If he did, he would recall his will to fight for his marriage and for his wife, even if all he felt right now was numbness.

She finally pulled herself away from the window and opened her iPad. Just as a watched pot never boiled, neither would Keith. She had to let go. Her mind remained on him, though, as she clicked through various YouTube offerings presented on the main page, still trying to learn and grow from all that was there, in order to someday soon begin offering her online messages via her own channel.

After spending a few minutes doing the same with Periscope,

however, her restless spirit won. She clicked off the Internet and laid the iPad aside, so she could sneak over to the window and peer out again. This time, her heart fell. Keith's car was gone. Decision made.

She wandered from the family room to the kitchen, feeling numb and unsure of what to do next. She sat at the kitchen table and stared at her puffy hands, including the wedding ring wedged onto her ring finger, where she always thought it would remain.

And then, she heard a soft creak that made her heart leap. The door behind her was opening.

Brigit had a key to the house so she could enter in case of an emergency, and so did her mother-in-law, but they would have called or texted first, so she wouldn't be startled. Jessica shifted in her seat slowly, attempting to stifle the hope threatening to overtake her.

But there stood Keith, and suddenly, relief merged with joy.

"I got tired of sitting in the driveway for all the neighbors to see and decided to pull into the garage."

Jessica carefully pushed herself to a standing position and thought about waddling over to greet him, but she stayed put. *Let go...*

She lowered her eyes, fearful of the truth and consequences she might find in his.

He spoke first.

"I give up, too."

"Excuse me?" Jessica frowned and raised her eyes.

"I give up holding a grudge and nursing my mistrust of you," Keith said, his voice thick with tears. "I give up running from the beautiful life we created before your stupid lies. I give up trying to be so strong and avoiding telling you how scared I am about your health issues. What I can't give up is loving you, Jessica. Even though I'm still wrestling with how to live out all of that other stuff and get over my anger and mistrust, I still love you and I don't want to give up on us."

Jessica ignored the stiffness that cloaked her like a too-snug coat, and slowly approached her husband. When she reached Keith, she took his hands in hers and looked up into his eyes.

"I'm sorry for lying and for devastating you, and I'll keep uttering that apology for as long as you need to hear it, Keith. I'm sorry for being selfish, and fake. I'm sorry I let you – and us - down. The truth is, I love you with everything in me, and if I can't be your wife, I don't want to be anything else. No TV show or fame could make up for that. I'm grateful to be carrying our baby and I'm sorry that God had to teach me a lesson to get us here, in this parents-to-be stage. I'm still scared as heck about whether I can do this mommy thing; but I know now that I'm not doing it alone – we're not doing it alone. We've got a whole village behind us.

"Thank you for loving me – for loving us together- enough to come back, Keith. I'm not going to give up on us, either."

She wanted to ask if he was coming home, but she decided to be still, and wait. After what she'd put him through, she had no right to push with impatient questions. She had to follow the advice God had clearly led her to, via the YouTube video prayer she had watched and recited a few weeks ago - simply surrendering. If Keith said he was going to get his bags from the car and come home now, she would praise God and welcome him. If he indicated he needed more time to work up to coming home, so be it. Either way, she wasn't going anywhere. She finally was ready to commit to something bigger than herself and for a cause greater than herself: Her marriage and the love of her life. Their baby deserved to be raised by two *loving* parents, and she and Keith both seemed ready to keep that verb alive.

# Epilogue

It was unbearably cold outside on this eve of Christmas Eve, and after two days of snowfall, the fluffy precipitation had finally stopped.

Because Jessica was so large now, and still suffered from occasional minor joint stiffness, Keith had encouraged her to stay inside, off the slippery sidewalks, and she willingly had complied. But this evening, as she lay on the sofa in their family room, enjoying his after-dinner foot rub, she knew she'd be navigating the wintry mix sooner rather than later. She felt her baby boy kick for what felt like the hundredth time today, and surmised that if her body was on target, he would grace the world sometime tomorrow, or on Christmas Day.

Before she shared this prediction with Keith, whom she knew would fit the frantic, first-time dad stereotype to a tee, Jessica mentally ran down her checklist of necessary items: Her bag for the hospital was packed and resting in the foyer, at the base of the stairs; she had outfits ready to wear home for both her and the baby; and Brigit and Autumn had her list of family and friends to text or call when there was news to share.

Thankfully, she had followed the advice of her childbirth class instructors and placed a couple of towels beneath her any time she was in a seated position or lying down. So when her water broke just now, it didn't ruin the sofa. Jessica waited until Keith took a break from massaging her feet to grasp one of his hands and kiss it.

"Babe. It's time."

Keith bolted upright, almost knocking her to the floor. He lunged toward her and broke her fall with a hug, before his eyes stretched into full moons.

"Sorry about that, baby. But what did you say? It is? How do you know?"

"My water just broke, so I'm pretty sure," Jessica said and stroked his head. "Time to get to the hospital, Daddy."

***

Fourteen hours later, with her parents and Shiloh en route from Alabama; Dayna driving in from Florida, and Keith's mother and sister sitting in the patient waiting area with their neighborhood friend and a few colleagues, Jessica and Keith welcomed their son into the world.

Seconds after Jory Keith Arnold filled her arms for the first time, Jessica fell in love, at a depth she'd never known was possible. She kissed his soft, light brown cheek, and nuzzled his tiny hand with her nose. If God loved her half as much as the rush of adoration that swallowed as she cradled this baby boy, she now understood the measure of grace and mercy, and why he was the everlasting giver of hope, life, and second chances.

Jessica felt a fresh wave of gratitude for being able to enjoy this special moment without pain or stress. With her arthritis temporarily in remission, she wouldn't have to worry right away about dropping her son or being unable to change diapers because of inflamed hands. She would get to play mom, and enjoy this unexpected gift that God had recognized she needed.

"Hello, Jory. What a beautiful and unique name you have," Evangeline said, beaming as she stood by Jessica's side after delivering him.

The nurse who was recording his name for the birth certificate turned to Keith, and asked, "Does it mean anything in particular?"

"Oh yeah," Keith said and smiled at Jessica through his tears.

She wanted to get up and wipe her husband's eyes; yet knowing they were tears of joy was a welcomed sight, given all they'd been through. Keith motioned for her to respond to the nurse.

Jessica returned his smile and complied.

"Jory means 'God will uplift' in Hebrew. And guess what? God truly has."

# Acknowledgments

My intent in writing this novel was not to cast the spotlight on one particular illness or chronic life struggle, but to use the various issues faced by the characters in *Finding Home* to reinforce the reality that at some point in life, nearly everyone deals with challenges that are beyond their control. Yet when we choose, we can craft a journey filled with contentment and inner joy, despite the proverbial thorn in our side.

With that in mind, I sincerely thank every reader, friend, relative, and acquaintance who has shared some facet of your life's thorns with me and with others; for it is in the sharing of triumphs over trials that healing and hope to take root, and joy finds space to blossom. I also humbly thank my Heavenly Father for allowing me to serve as a steward of the written word. I am eternally grateful.

Those who know me best also know that birthing a book requires solitude, sacrifice, patience, and focus. I thank my family and friends who have journeyed with me through the process of birthing ten books and breathing life into my childhood dream of becoming an author. I still get excited with the publication of each book, and your love and encouragement have been my wind and wings on more days than I can count. My deepest love and gratitude go to the gifts God gave me to raise - my children, Sydney and Donald J. I'm honored to be your mom, to share your life's experiences and miracles, and to help guide you toward your purpose. I sincerely thank my siblings, Dr. Barbara Grayson, Henry Haney, and Sandra Williams, for your steadfast love and support, day in and day out. I honor the memory of my loving mother, Dorothy A. Hawkins, who always nurtured the writer in me, and my beloved sister, Patsy Scott, who now resides in heaven after her valiant fight with a chronic illness. To my spiritual mother and fellow writer Muriel Miller Branch, and dear friend Carol Jackson, you are irreplaceable gifts that I treasure; to my beta readers and sister friends Sharon Shahid, Maya P. Smart, Jacqueline Jones, and Christy Gill, thanks for your willingness to be the first to "meet" my characters and candidly share your thoughts. To my extended family, and treasured friends, including Gwendolyn Richard, Bobbie Walker Trussell, Robin Farmer, Otesa Middleton Miles, Wilbur Athey, Cheryle Rodriguez, Cassandra Savage, and so many others that I cherish, thank you for being among my cheerleaders; to Joanne Bischof – thank you for your insightful editing; to my beloved pastors, Rev. Drs. Micah and Jacqueline Madison-McCreary, my fellow worshippers at Spring Creek Baptist Church, and to my colleagues at Collegiate School, your kind wishes, prayers and other support are continuously appreciated; to my literary industry friends, including M.M. Finck, Ella Curry, LaShaunda Hoffman, Linda Evans Shepherd, Jeanette Hill, Linda Beed, Chandra Sparks Splond, Angela Breidenbach, and Mona Hodgson, thanks for continually championing the power of the written word; special thanks to my many, many author friends and colleagues, and last but absolutely not least, a huge thank you and virtual hug to my loyal readers and to book clubs, bloggers, booksellers and others who purchase my books and encourage other booklovers to do the same. Your support matters, and I appreciate you! And to you – the person reading this now - thank you for spending this time in my fictional world, with these fictional characters. I hope the reading of their make-believe trials and triumphs has graced you with gems that will bless your reality beyond measure.

Warmest Regards,
Stacy

# Parting Request ...

This is my first full-length independently published project, and your feedback matters more than ever. If you enjoyed this book, will you please recommend it to a friend and take time to write a brief review on the website of your favorite online bookseller? I'd love to hear from you as well, via my website or social media pages:

www.StacyHawkinsAdams.com
www.Facebook.com/StacyInspires
www.Twitter.com/SHAdams

Please also consider picking up the first two novels in the *Winds of Change* series, which are available in both print and ebook formats:
**Coming Home** (Book 1)
**Lead Me Home** (Book 2)

I've also reprinted in ebook and print format my third novel, **Watercolored Pearls,** which continues to be a reader favorite. Check it out!

Thank you again for reading and spreading the word about my work. I hope my writing will continue to bless and inspire you.

# Finding Home
# Discussion Questions

- Do you believe Jessica was an authentically positive person before she faced a personal challenge, or was she simply going through the motions?

- What benefits, if any, resulted from Jessica's diagnosis?

- Were Jessica's physical ailments her version of the "thorn in the side" that Peter referenced in 2 Corinthians?

- Do you believe everyone has a "thorn" (aka a challenge) with which she or he will always struggle?

- Is it possible for those who face a significant challenge at some point in life to live in contentment, no matter what? If so, what steps does this require?

- Was Keith's reaction to learning Jessica's truths understandable? How would you have handled such a revelation from your spouse or significant other?

- Did the eventual reconnection between Jessica and her sisters feel genuine?

- Do you believe Jessica made the right decision when she chose to trust her sisters again?

- By the end of the book, did you like Jessica more or less, and why?

- What, if anything, did experiencing Jessica's journey teach you about yourself?

- What did experiencing Jessica's journey help you understand about people living with a lasting challenge of some sort, whether a chronic illness or another issue?

- What are the most important lessons you'll take away from this story and these characters' lives?

CPSIA information can be obtained at www.ICGtesting.com
Printed in the USA
LVOW11s1622141016

508816LV00002B/533/P